The Outer Country

The Outer Country

A NOVEL

Davin Malasarn

ONE WORLD
NEW YORK

One World
An imprint of Random House
A division of Penguin Random House LLC
1745 Broadway, New York, NY 10019
oneworldlit.com
penguinrandomhouse.com

Hardcover ISBN 978-0-593-73165-9
Ebook ISBN 978-0-593-73166-6

Printed in the United States of America on acid-free paper

1st Printing

First Edition

BOOK TEAM: Production editor: Andy Lefkowitz • Managing editor: Rebecca Berlant • Production manager: Samuel Wetzler • Copy editor: Marinda J. Valenti • Proofreaders: Rebecca Maines, Taylor McGowan, and David Goehring

Book design by Susan Turner

The authorized representative in the EU for product safety and compliance is Penguin Random House Ireland, Morrison Chambers, 32 Nassau Street, Dublin D02 YH68, Ireland. https://eu-contact.penguin.ie

For Vanida

The Outer Country

Newborns

1

The son died. The daughter lived. The second daughter lived. The second son died. The mother's skin turned to clay, hardened by mourning and the heat of Phet Buri. The father had been hardened by war and spent each dawn meditating in Khao Na Khwang Cave as he searched for enlightenment. The third daughter lived. The third son lived, but he shattered the mother's pelvis during delivery. This was the latest incarnation of the Thrakoontong family.

2

Manda Thrakoontong arrived in the Outer Country on the same day her sister's contractions began. She rushed with her brother-in-law through the maternity ward of White Memorial Medical Center, her senses overwhelmed by the foreign land, her clothes burdened with seeds she smuggled over from Phet Buri. She longed to see her sister even more than she longed to return home.

Manda's arrival and the baby's delivery—their timing was a coincidence, but she didn't believe in coincidences. Life was an infinite karmic equation. If she landed in America on the same day her nephew was to be born, then their past must have brought them together. Maybe they had been coupled for multiple reincarnations. Maybe they had been friends or siblings or lovers or termites from the same colony. Maybe something between them was left unfinished and they had been offered another opportunity to resolve it.

In the dim, buzzing hospital room, she found her sister folding in pain. Siripon's contractions had begun at sunrise, while Manda was still in the air. The sisters clasped nervous hands. They were the eldest children in their family, the living daughters who had replaced the dead sons.

"I'm here now. You have nothing to worry about," Manda whispered, though she hesitated as she spoke. She didn't know how much relief she could offer. The two hadn't parted on friendly terms, and neither one was used to letting go of grudges. No one in their family was.

"Did you have a safe journey?" Siripon asked, huffing and straining.

"That's not important, Noi," Manda said. "Worry about yourself for once."

Siripon's face had matured since the last time the sisters saw each other. Her cheekbones were fuller, helping her large, watery eyes seem less frightened. Their neighbors in Phet Buri agreed she was the prettiest of the Thrakoontong daughters, unlike Manda, whose eyes were dark and wooden, whose nose was upturned, and whose body resembled a yam. A contraction came, and Siripon's body tensed. Manda rose from the bed and turned away. She reminded herself that her nephew was not arriving for the first time. He had been born successfully more than once. After this life, whenever it came to an end, he would be born again. "It will be over quickly, Noi," she said.

Siripon huffed. "Pi Neung, if anything goes wrong, you will help Kamron raise the baby, na?"

"Don't think like that, Sister. Believe that you will both be all right. Pray that you will both be all right." Manda turned to her brother-in-law, hoping he would do more to comfort his wife. Kamron only stood by the window, rigid.

Nurses rushed in. They ordered Manda out to the dull purgatory of the waiting room. She found a seat away from the crowd and rested her head against the wall. Her body still lurched from the undulations of flight, that unexpected weightlessness that accompanied her first time on a plane. Three years had passed since Manda and Siripon were last together. The night in 1975 when Siripon departed, Manda hadn't gone to see her off. Her annoyance at not being chosen first to go to America had still pulsed at her temples. For weeks, she had been forced to hear about the preparations: their mother hunting throughout the city for winter clothes, their father pedaling to the local temples to acquire amulets blessed by the monks. The family hoarded containers of Tiger Balm and Takabb Anti-Cough Pills, stuffing them into the pockets of Siripon's suitcases. They filled her shoes with doughy sweets, giving her strict instructions not to eat them all at once but to ration them out so that she would have something to comfort her when she missed home.

Now the sisters were together again. Manda had given up her job and her colleagues and her friends. Her only new acquaintance was someone she met on the plane, a religious older woman who had introduced herself only as "Aunt Seamstress." If she was correct, the two would be living less than an hour apart from each other, almost a straight shot on one of the main roads, though Manda couldn't remember which one. She shook her head, wondering why she had come. Across from her, the second hand of a clock lurched. She prepared to pray again, but Kamron entered the waiting room with a startled expression on his face. Manda hadn't yet inspected him properly, the news of the delivery too pressing when he found her at the airport. She had been frightened to be alone with him during their ride to the hospital, not certain of who he was or where he was taking her. But there had been no choice but to trust him—trust him or turn around. She glanced up. He was a brutish man. His face looked like it had been carved out of stone. The muscles of his shoulders stretched his denim shirt, and thick veins branched over his forearms.

"I have no place in there," he said, pressing his palms to his eyes. His hands were covered with hundreds of tiny hardened blisters. They looked like powerful hands. They looked like hands that could wring out the world. "I regret ever touching her."

"You can't return a mango to its tree," Manda replied. She considered trying to comfort him, but she held back, unsure if she approved of him. She was disappointed he came out to the waiting room instead of staying with Siripon. The sisters' father had been present for the births of all his children. Manda herself was delivered by him in the home of an aunt, as there hadn't been time to get to the hospital. Her mother, Gimjaa, had been sick with a fever, and Pradit took it as a point of pride that he was the one who sealed his mouth over Manda's nose and mouth to remove the mucus that plugged her airways. He sometimes recounted the story between lashes of a switch, as if he regretted allowing her to take her first breath. Manda's siblings were all born in the hospital, but her father was there, emerging after the delivery with a smile each time except for the last. After their brother Kiet's birth, when their mother was so badly injured, Pradit simply told the girls to be grateful everyone survived.

Kamron pulled out a rolled magazine from the pocket of his jeans before sitting. He wrote around the advertisement on the back cover, printing Siripon's name and, beside it, feminine variations: Sarai, Sroy, Ampon.

"You think the baby's going to be a girl," Manda said, looking down at his tentative scrawl. He didn't seem like a man who was used to handling a pen.

"And why are you so sure it won't be?" he asked, his voice darkening with a tinge of irritation.

Manda didn't answer. She closed her eyes and prayed.

3

Siripon was grateful she had gotten some sleep before her contractions began. She adjusted herself in the bed, already spent, knowing several more hours might pass before the delivery was over. The nurses stepped in and out, checking her vital signs, lifting the sheets to examine her. She surrendered to the idea that a crowd would see her vulnerable and exposed. Sometimes the wildness of the body was unavoidable. Everyone eventually became an animal again.

Earlier that morning, when the labor pains twisted Siripon out of sleep, she had known Kamron wouldn't be able to help her. He fumbled with the lamp, and she reached out to stop him, thinking that if she could remain undisturbed, if she could be alone with her pain, her body could tolerate it, even accept it. But he had turned the light on; the terrain of twisted sheets had emerged around her.

"Is it time?" Alcohol fumes puffed out with Kamron's soft words. His voice was always more tender after a night of heavy drinking. He attempted to stand but fell back onto the mattress, his legs jutting comically into the air.

"It's nothing, ja. Go back to sleep." Siripon pushed aside her uniforms and found a loose dress. She hurried out into the hallway, aware that Kamron was approaching behind her. He spilled out of the bedroom and bumped against the wall. Her body moved automatically, propelled by adrenaline and instinct. Coat, shoes, bag, keys. She had prepared weeks ahead of time for this. A part of her had always been prepared for this.

Outside, the darkness was washing away. A band of pale sky was visible above the roofs of the other houses. Siripon climbed into her car and locked the door behind her. Kamron had reached her by then. He pulled on the door handle. He knocked on the window.

"I'm sorry, but we have to think of the baby," Siripon said, knowing he could not hear her through the glass. She started the engine, stepped on the accelerator. Kamron stumbled forward and fell to his knees, but she couldn't go back to help him.

She drove through stop signs and red lights, honking her horn to announce herself. "My baby coming!" she shouted in English to the other drivers, trying to counteract their anger. It was a phrase she hadn't learned from her language books. How unprepared they had left her after torturing her for so long. They had been filled with words and phrases, but so few of them were relevant to her real American life. The hospital appeared, and her grip on the steering wheel relaxed. She had been lucky to work here as a nurse ever since her arrival. Straightening her fingers, she let the color flow back under her skin. The emergency room was closest, but she drove past it to her usual row of spaces near the southern entrance. The extra distance let her be alone as the next contraction came. The pain was becoming familiar. It was a new communication from her unborn child. Soon Siripon would be holding her baby. It would be a boy. She had known this as soon as she saw the positive pregnancy test. But she never told anyone in case she was wrong. Her daughter—if it was a daughter—would never doubt her place in the family. She would never feel insignificant.

Four more hours passed before the delivery was over. Siripon refused the epidurals, grateful the doctor listened to her. She trusted that her body would tolerate the process, and somehow, painfully, it had. She had given birth to a new human who would forever hold a part of her. Kamron and Manda came back to the room looking relieved but cautious. Siripon handed the baby to her husband; she would not indulge his trepidation. He looked at her apologetically, and she responded with a nod.

Whatever happened earlier would have to be forgotten. She wouldn't recount how Kamron had finally made his way to the hospital, navigating the public bus system for the first time and begging for her forgiveness.

"Boy or girl?" he asked, gently adjusting the baby's swaddling.

"We have a beautiful son," she said.

Beside her, Manda's face brightened, a look of triumph she had made often as a child. "I knew it. You wasted your time coming up with girls' names."

"Don't bother me," Kamron replied dreamily.

The baby's face had the softness of a peeled plum. He moved his limbs in that aimless way babies do, wriggling with emotion but no understanding. Occasionally, his eyes opened just enough for the family to see the pale rings of his irises, the remnants of his ghost self. Siripon took him back, pulling away the wrappings so that his skin could touch hers again. "I want to bring him home," she said. "Look at us. We left as two, but we'll return as four." She closed her eyes, letting herself slip away into sleep.

4

Kamron and Siripon chose the house on Caroline Street because it was two houses. The main structure stood stoically in front, visible from the quiet street, flat and yellow, offering a well-used but clean kitchen and three square, low-ceilinged bedrooms. The lot also had a guesthouse that hid on the other end of a concrete patio like a secret, visible only to people who had been invited beyond the gate.

Alone, each of the newlyweds would have been too timid to ignore the American customs, but together they were courageous. They would use the place the way they wanted to. They would cook and serve meals in the guesthouse and keep the main house free from the odors of hot canola oil, fish sauce, and fermented shrimp paste. The main dining room would remain empty of table and chairs. Instead, it would belong to the shrine Kamron mounted to face a northern window and the San Gabriel Mountains that lay gray and rocky in the distance. A brass Buddha statuette sat at its center, accepting Siripon's daily offerings in return for watching over the young couple. There was a spacious backyard already filled with fruit trees, a plot of turned soil that would serve as a garden. Kamron and Siripon imagined growing the plants from Thailand that they couldn't find in the local markets. They would make this place home.

Carrying his son into the house for the first time, Kamron said in English, "No one go to close the door on you." He whispered the words while holding the newborn to his chest, the baby squirming for the darkness in the crook of Kamron's arm as if he could find in his father the shelter his mother had taken away. The words were a promise Kamron knew he couldn't keep. Instead, they became a hope.

He had confronted closed doors all his life. One day when he was a child, his father left the house and never returned. His mother remarried and found her son too much of a troublemaker to keep in her new home. She sent him to boarding school after boarding school, each one expelling him for fighting with other students. And when he finally arrived in Los Angeles, the woman who had agreed to be his hostess would not let him in.

"I've made better arrangements for you, Yai," she said dryly, using his familiar name even though they had never met before. "You can stay with the other Robin Hoods."

Kamron was delivered to a one-bedroom apartment that two other men from Thailand had already claimed for themselves. They were all staying in America beyond the limitations of their tourist visas. One took the bedroom, one took the couch, and Kamron was left with a sleeping bag spread out on the kitchen floor. The first day he went in search of groceries, he returned to find the apartment door locked even though he hadn't been given a key. He sat in the hall, head slumped, elbows propped on his knees, until the others finally returned.

Kamron found work as a custodian in a Hollywood motel until the manager closed the door on him after hearing rumors the police were snooping for undocumented staff. He worked in a meat-processing plant removing the bloodied liners tacked to each slab of beef until the owner closed its doors forever. He ended up at the Axon Steel Corporation, working as a tube bender, his hours on the floor surrounded by red-hot metal and chemical cleansers that he dipped his hands into too many times a day. This was the life of the Robin Hoods. They stole from the rich and gave to the poor. They stole from America and gave to Thailand. They were thieves because they didn't have the proper visas. They had come as tourists, but they stayed as shadows.

Kamron assumed Siripon would close the door on him when he first saw her at a party. She sat on a sofa surrounded by friends, but she was the quietest person in the group. She wore a sleeveless silk dress. Her hair had been pulled back neatly into a bun. A plate of food balanced on her knees, and she took small bites from it, careful not to spill.

"Are you from Bangkok?" he asked her, leaning in while the others were distracted by karaoke. "I miss home terribly."

"Phet Buri, ca," Siripon said. "But I'm not a stranger to homesickness."

"It's a savage kind of pain, isn't it? Like your heart is being stretched."

"But you can't give in. You have to keep moving. Have you found decent work? Something that fulfills you? And you should make friends—I wouldn't have lasted here a month without my classmates."

"I'm Yai. Would you be my friend?"

She pursed her lips. With the outermost prong of her fork, she reoriented a lettuce leaf that was dangling off the edge of her plate.

"Do me this favor, please?" he said. "I don't know anyone else here. I only tagged along with my roommates because I needed some Thai food in my belly."

"Then, aren't *they* your friends?"

"Would you call someone a friend if they stole clothes out of your suitcase?"

"You're being ridiculous."

"I'm telling you the truth. They're both wearing my clothes. They're both probably wearing my underwear!" He straightened the collar of his checkered flannel, a shirt he knew was too casual for the occasion, but at least it was not yet tattered. "Honestly, I don't have a single person I can trust in this preposterous country."

"All right," Siripon relented. "Nobody should feel like they're here alone. I'm Noi."

The other nurses pointed out the humor: Kamron's familiar name meant "big," while Siripon's meant "little," both chosen by their parents because of their sizes at birth. Once they started dating, he struggled to convince himself that he was deserving of Siripon. She told him she cared for him, and he worried she would change her mind when she knew him better. After all, he drank too much, a habit he developed as a teenager. And he constantly felt his anger seething beneath his skin, the damage of his childhood, his loveless family. At least, he hoped those were the causes. He tested her devotion. He requested tiny adjustments to the meals she prepared for him, seeing how willingly she complied. If he suspected another man was attracted to her, Kamron asked Siripon not to talk to anyone else and watched to see how disappointed she got. He waited for her to see through his schemes, but she was not the suspicious type. She opened doors instead of closing them. She opened a door for him in Los Angeles, and a home grew on the other side. She opened the door between her legs, and now they had a son.

On Siripon's insistence, they named the baby "Rattawut" after a distant relative of Kamron's who was said to have served as an adviser to the king. She said the name proudly when she introduced the baby to her friends. She sang it alone to him in his nursery, her voice out of tune but earnest. The name didn't stick with Kamron, who found it too grand for such a small person, too serious for such an uncoordinated body. He began calling him "Ben."

"Where did that come from?" Siripon asked the first time she heard Kamron use it.

"From nowhere," Kamron said. "From my own imagination."

The truth was that Manda had used it first—he wouldn't reveal that to his wife. Siripon was too protective of the baby, careful with all her decisions regarding him. She would be suspicious if she knew her sister had come up with the name on a whim. But it suited the boy. Ben. And it was better still because it had nothing to do with Kamron's side of the family.

He appreciated having Manda in the house. She was more direct, while Siripon was often too subtle. She was more relaxed, while Siripon was too uptight. Their first few weeks together, Kamron was surprised when Manda helped herself to a beer, something Siripon had never done. He mentioned it to his wife when they were in bed, and Siripon shrugged. "She was drinking when we were still teenagers," she mumbled, her eyes already closed. As she drifted to sleep, she complained about having to pick up after Manda, and though Siripon didn't bring it up, he thought of how she cleaned up after him too.

They passed Ben from one to another as if he were an ember in a cold house. He made their faces glow. He warmed the dark corners of their hearts. He also turned their schedules to soot. Siripon would transfer to the night shift once her maternity leave ended. That would allow her to be home during the days, sleepy but available for the baby while the other two were gone. Kamron took an earlier shift at Axon, leaving the house before sunrise and coming home in the late afternoon. He would be there for Ben during the evenings, along with Manda, who requested a part-time schedule for her new job at JCPenney.

Days when they all worked, Kamron had Ben to himself during a brief window after Siripon left and before Manda returned. It came around sunset, the time announced by the flocks of wild parrots that circled overhead, their calls loud and screeching like the sound of broken glass being swept into a pile. On one of these evenings, awed by the life he had created, Kamron promised his son he would stop drinking. He ushered Ben through the house, lit golden at this hour, as he pointed out everything they owned. "I give the world to you," Kamron said. "If you want it, you take it." Outside, night settled, and the parrots grew quiet, their calls replaced by the shadowy song of crickets. Alone with Ben, Kamron felt the relief he craved when the others were around. The baby didn't care that Kamron had fought his way through school or that he had come to America as a Robin Hood. Ben knew nothing about Kamron beyond this short time they spent together, the few heartbeats they shared. He poured the last of his beers over the thick roots of a camellia bush and followed the bitter fumes up into the night. The hazy expanse of the galaxy shone above them, the same stars his ancestors had seen. He could love Ben with that prehistoric instinct. It brimmed inside of him and terrified him. If he put all his love into the room of his son, what would happen if Ben closed the door on it? Kamron did not have an answer.

5

On her first night home, Siripon called Phet Buri to announce that the delivery had been successful. She had yet to sleep for more than an hour, and the distance felt like an added strain on her body, even when the voices came on the other end of the line as if they were beside her. The family was delighted that everything had gone smoothly. The loss of Siripon's brothers still lurked in the dark urns of their hearts, but no one would admit to being afraid of death. They would only celebrate life, cackle at it, relish in the baby's struggle to make sense of the world, because struggle meant vitality.

Suddenly, Siripon broke down, unable to hold the enormity of her responsibility. Through sobs, she listed all the ways she would fail at raising the baby.

"You will be a fine mother," Gimjaa said. "You've been a mother ever since you were born."

"When parenting calls for strength, you must simply be strong," Pradit said. He asked if he would be called "Bu," and they chided him, told him he would be called "Tha" because he was part of the maternal lineage. Gimjaa herself would be called "Yaay," while Kamron's mother would be called "Yah."

"Of course, he won't be talking for a while," Siripon warned them, hoping they wouldn't be disappointed. Her sense of duty was amplified. She brought the receiver to the baby's mouth, relieved when he started to wail.

Kamron did the talking when they called his family in Bangkok. His voice softened, tinged with a desire to please that reminded Siripon of how he was during their early days together. The Chiwitchaiyas had been silent after hearing about the wedding—no one calling to congratulate them, no one sending them gifts, so that Siripon had cried the following day, certain she was despised by in-laws she had never met. Kamron tried to convince her that everything was fine, that silence was sometimes the best response from his family, but Siripon couldn't be soothed. Now she was grateful they wouldn't return to Thailand until Kamron's green card application was approved. She had initiated the process when they married, but it could take years to complete.

"You'll have to send us a photo of the little one," Kamron's mother, Jaidee, said toward the end of their conversation.

"Yes, I'll put it in the mail this week," Siripon replied. The request at least signaled some interest on her mother-in-law's part. "He looks just like your son. You'll see for yourself."

"Ja, ja," Jaidee said. "I suppose we will see."

After the call ended, Siripon reminisced about the life she shared with Kamron when they first met. Their courtship lasted for six months, from August to January, summer to winter. Soon after the party, he learned that she didn't yet have a car, and he waited for her each day in the parking lot of White Memorial, ready to drive her home after her shift. Siripon was suspicious of his intentions in the beginning. But as the weather grew cold and the evenings grew foggy, she was happy to see his blue Datsun waiting with its engine idling, the billow of steam drifting up from the exhaust pipe.

During their first weeks in the new house, Siripon was relieved they didn't have many belongings. As she adjusted to her expanding body, the open rooms made vacuuming easier; the empty shelves were quickly dusted. She and Kamron tried their best to find nice furniture. Still, the glossy velour of the garage-sale sofa exaggerated the grease stains on the walls. The smoked-glass coffee table was too large for the room. The crack in the Formica dining table caught her attention like an eyelash in her field of view.

She hadn't taken any of it for granted. In her letters home, she told her family how grateful she was. She and Kamron settled into a comfortable routine. When they both worked, she prepared breakfast before their early shifts and made sure they both had lunches to take with them. The two came together again in the evenings, quickly washing off the grime of the day before sitting down for dinner. If she didn't have to work, Siripon tended to the house. Each task had helped to make her surroundings seem more fixed, more stable, so that soon she thought of the place as a dependable thing.

6

Siripon splayed the baby naked on the changing table. Her face was grim. She warmed the bell of her stethoscope with her breath and pressed it to Ben's chest. "What could it be this time? Congestive heart failure? Is that it? Look at these swollen arms. Look at these thighs and ankles." Ben giggled against her gentle pinches. A mound of bubbles pushed up past his lower lip. "Are you choking? That must be where my keys have gone." She dabbed his mouth, thumped him between the shoulder blades with the flat of her hand. Each day was another batch of dire diagnoses. Everything that was cute about him transformed into a symptom. It was the game they played whenever Siripon put on her uniform in preparation for work. She used her fake fears to push away the real fear that came from abandoning him.

Since her maternity leave ended, she worried she hadn't prepared the others to take proper care of Ben. But she told herself she had to relax, she had to trust. After all, Kamron could fly Ben through the house, spinning around corners and dipping into dark rooms with surprising agility. Manda treated Ben as if he were her star pupil. She carried him out to the new garden populated by the seeds she brought over from Phet Buri. She explained to Ben the intricate processes of photosynthesis and nitrogen fixation, complicated pathways Siripon no longer remembered. On top of that, Kamron and Manda would be together. She would help him, and he would help her.

At White Memorial, the sound of babies crying was almost too much for Siripon. She lactated for weeks after returning, her coworkers handing her tissues to tuck into her bra whenever the material got wet. On quieter nights, they forced her to nap in one of the empty hospital rooms. Siripon always resisted, arguing that the quiet hours only gave her more time to worry about what was happening at home.

Her friends from Phuket managed to keep up with her. The night-shift nurses had their first children within a couple years of Ben's birth. It was as if something had switched collectively in them—they were all reaching a certain age; they had all been able to save enough money. The new mothers met in the cafeteria, exhausted, conversations swirling around feeding and sleeping and crying and changing. They said that Siripon was the luckiest among them—she was the only one who had a sister helping.

"You don't think Ben will be confused by it, do you?" she asked, revealing another reason for her anxiety. "He won't think Manda is his mother, will he?"

The nurses urged her to relax. There were pheromones, they said—the baby would know. They also whispered that they understood her fear. In the same situation, they would be worried too.

Siripon's parents had called together when they delivered the news that Manda was coming to join her. There had been a tragedy at the school where Manda taught, they explained. A student had died, and she couldn't bring herself to return to the classroom. Siripon didn't have a chance to get any details about what exactly had happened.

"You'd be helping her," Gimjaa said. "And she could help you when the baby arrives."

Having a family member beside her would be comforting to Siripon, even if it was Manda. She agreed to the arrangement, though she wasn't sure she had a choice. This was how her parents had always operated—they solved two problems with one solution.

When Kamron came home that evening, Siripon had a hot plate of rice and a tray of sizzling fried pork belly waiting for him. She took his empty lunch box and brought him a chilled can of beer as he removed his boots and hung his Buddhist amulet on the corner of the shrine, thanking it for keeping him safe another day. She was five months pregnant by then, and she made a show of struggling to slip into her chair.

"My parents asked if we might host my sister here," she said, nervous. "She could come in a few months, just in time for the baby—assuming the visa is approved. It might not be. You know how those things go." The house was as much hers as it was Kamron's. She had been the one to work with a real estate agent and the one who made the down payment on it. Kamron's salary was less than half of hers, so she paid the majority of the mortgage. Still, she felt she had to get his permission.

"Is this the troublemaker?" he asked, not looking up from his food.

"I never called her that, not seriously." Siripon regretted telling him about Manda mocking her when they were children, though it had been a luxury to share her side of the story without anyone discounting her. "Besides, I'll need help soon," she said, continuing to make her case.

"Never mind the reason. It won't hurt to have another person around." He reached over to pat her hand. The matter was decided.

Perhaps he was grateful to have inherited a new family, she thought. He had never shared much about his own, other than to say that his father abandoned them and his mother remarried, taking Kamron and his sister to live in a new house in Bangkok before Kamron moved out on his own. He hardly ever called home, and he wasn't the type to pen letters. Only a couple times a year did he mention wanting to talk to anyone there.

Washing the dishes that evening, Siripon grew anxious over everything she had to accomplish. She would have to fill out sponsorship forms. She would have to get the guest room ready while also preparing the nursery. Later, she would have to entertain Manda until she established a routine of her own. Siripon's mind was distracted with the growing list when Kamron came up behind her.

"Your skin is glowing, Noi."

"What are you saying about skin?"

"*Your* skin. Your skin is glowing. You have the most beautiful skin I've ever seen." His hands reached under her dress, and she squirmed. She had assumed he wasn't attracted to her because she was getting larger—it was only the third or fourth time they made love since Siripon told Kamron she was pregnant. He had come to her that first night too, smiling while kissing her, so that their lips couldn't seal properly. He had said they were celebrating the addition of the new baby. After the news about Manda, Siripon wondered who he was celebrating. Manda was always the more charismatic one, the one who could win people over. Siripon had seen Kamron be drawn to that. He often looked at other women at parties, the boisterous ones, his attention pulled away, even when Siripon tried to draw him back.

But that night, she told herself she didn't have anything to worry about. She was a hardworking wife, and she would be a devoted mother. She had also noticed that men were more attracted to her than to either of her sisters. They each had their gifts, and hers was prettiness, if nothing else. She surrendered her body to her husband, feeling more beautiful as he grew more passionate. She let go of him, stretching into the darkness before her hands came back to steady herself. She could rest assured. The sum of Kamron's and the baby's love was enough to buoy her heart. She would welcome her sister in this state of love, and Manda would be folded into it; she would feel the security of the family around her.

7

Manda said the November day she arrived in Los Angeles marked a triple birthday. First, her new life began in this foreign country, where she had to sleep in a different bed, speak a different language, and find a different line of work. Second, Ben was born, the baby demanding her constant care even though she had not been responsible for his conception. Third, the seeds she carried over—seeds her mother and younger sister painstakingly sewed into the hem of her skirt so that they would not be found by customs—began their germination. On nights when Siripon left for the hospital, Manda carried Ben to the garden and pointed out the new plants unfurling among the old. The boy thought in symmetries, so that he wasn't interested in one leaf unless there was another growing opposite it. He also wouldn't drink a bottle of milk unless it was accompanied by a bottle of juice. Manda supposed he saw her and Siripon the same way: a pair of mothers devoted to raising him.

She loved the boy as much as she had ever loved anyone. The realization came to her while she was pulling weeds. One muggy summer afternoon, tired and overwhelmed, she looked over to where she had nestled him on a blanket, and the sight of the boy suddenly revitalized her. She felt as if she could breathe him in like fresh air.

"My little Ben," she called out. The nickname came unexpectedly, the baby reminding Manda of Benjama Thep Uthit School, the place she left to help raise him, the place where so many children had come into her life.

In the beginning, she whispered the name into the boy's ear, worried the others would be upset if they knew. But Kamron overheard her and liked the shortness of it. A few weeks later, Siripon tried it out, calling the baby with it to see if he turned his head. Manda had been quietly delighted. She felt she had a claim on the baby just as the others did. And why shouldn't she? They were the same family, the same blood. They each had the same responsibility to ensure he grew up to be a fine young man.

The garden was bordered by the Harveys' cinder block wall to the south and the Minnuchs' rusted chain-link fence to the east. The western edge ran along the plywood shack Kamron used to store equipment and supplies: the toolbox, orange coils of extension cords, the lawn mower with its smelly canister of gasoline. The northern edge of the garden was lined with a little picket fence he had built, a swinging door at one end through which they could enter. Over three years, Manda worked the soil until it was dark and fertile, and the plants thrived: holy basil growing along the Minnuchs' fence, three varieties of eggplant on islands with troughs running around them, long beans and bitter melon creeping up networks of twine, and bird's eye chilis displaying their offerings like inverted flames. Siripon was grateful to use the herbs and vegetables in her dishes, and Kamron was happy to survey the greenery. But neither of them worried over the garden's threats the way Manda did. There were the snails, the ants, the rats, the birds, the opossums, the raccoons, all of which ravaged her small plot of land if she wasn't careful. The pests seemed to sense that this was an exotic place—these plants did not belong here.

She caressed the velvety leaves of her holy basil, folded one over, and crushed it between her fingers to release its spicy fragrance. It was only with constant care that her plants survived in the dry climate of Southern California. And her troubles weren't limited to pests. On the rare occasions when Siripon entered the garden, she pruned things back to nearly nothing, irritated by the overreaching branches and unruly vines. Kamron adjusted the knots of twine lattice Manda had carefully constructed; he shifted the heavy paving stones that she arranged to be able to step from one row of plants to another without muddying her sandals. She also had herself to blame. Only last week, annoyed by aphids clinging to her cherimoya saplings, she had plucked the plants out of the ground and tossed them all into the garbage bin. It had been a fit of frustration. She laughed at herself later, when she was getting ready for her shift at JCPenney and felt the loss of all her hard work. How had she come so far from her position as a science teacher? She once lectured on the periodic table. Now she cursed at insects.

As Ben grew older, Manda recruited him to be her apprentice. Three years old, the boy listened, mesmerized, as she told him the names of the things she grew. She pointed out differences in the shapes of leaves, the new buds forming at the ends of branches like tiny puckered lips. She lectured him on the importance of water, carbon dioxide, and sunlight to make things grow. He paid attention to all of it.

"He's stuck on you," guests said. They giggled when they saw him clinging to Manda's pant leg, embracing her instead of either of his parents. "You're clearly his favorite."

"And watch this," she replied, stepping into the garden and waiting for the guests to follow. Immediately, Ben blocked their way. He held out his hand and shouted, first in Thai, "Yoot!" then in English, "Stop!"

"A guardian for my little kingdom," Manda called over. "I tell him to protect my corner of the land, and this is what he does."

She welcomed the visitors who came to the house. She had not made many of her own friends—only Aunt Seamstress, the older woman who had sat beside her on the flight over from Bangkok—and Kamron seemed to have made no friends at all. Siripon's nurses brought their growing families every few weeks, so that a cozy community developed. On days when they were to arrive, Manda harvested her garden, and together, she and Siripon prepared dishes in the kitchen while Kamron grilled the chicken and pork that had been marinating for a week. The household earned a reputation for serving the most authentic meals. Their friends came to expect the family to host all of the holiday parties.

Aunt Seamstress came over on quieter days. She and Manda had grown close despite their age difference, drawn together, Manda suspected, because they both had a tendency for sternness and managed not to judge the other for it. Aunt Seamstress's face was blunt and chinless, and she never wore makeup, so that the only adornment she offered was a pea-sized mole that grew in the fold of skin stretching from the side of her nose to the corner of her mouth.

Manda was grateful for all that Aunt Seamstress did to comfort her during the flight over. She had been crying, and Aunt Seamstress, quickly finishing her chant to a Buddhist amulet she cupped in her hands, had assured her that everything would be all right. "I sobbed my first time!" the older woman admitted. "It was so bad I worried they were going to carry me off the plane. But trust me—it will get easier. This is my third trip back."

"You must have been one of the first," Manda had said, accepting the woman's tissue and drying her eyes.

"I moved with my daughter. She married an American, a soldier. They always get their way." She had introduced herself, explaining that she earned money by taking on sewing projects from her neighbors. That was how she got her name. She wrote down her address and telephone number on a scrap of paper and told Manda to keep it safe. Later, when Manda panicked over the customs declarations because of the smuggled seeds, Aunt Seamstress coached her through the immigration line. "I'll be right behind you," she had assured her. "When those guards ask their questions, you look them straight in the eye and answer with confidence. If you pause, if you show any sign of hesitation, they'll strip you naked and search your most intimate parts."

On her visits to the house, Aunt Seamstress brought her granddaughter to keep Ben company, and the four picnicked in the yard with bowls of rice and fried eggs or a batch of pan-fried noodles. The women encouraged the children to play together. The two were nearly the same age, both born in the Year of the Horse, Jessica a summer baby like Manda was. A secret plan had been hatched. The women would coax the children into falling in love. Manda and Aunt Seamstress would become sisters, and they would both have the young couple to care for them in their old age.

"It would only be fair," Manda said. "After all, Siripon and Kamron have each other. Who do I have?" The women laughed. Manda often made fun of the married couple, recounting their squabbles for Aunt Seamstress's amusement. Kamron was such a crude man that Manda was surprised Siripon was attracted to him to begin with. Once, when the sisters were still living in Phet Buri, Siripon had declared she could never fall in love with anyone who sweated.

Manda placed a bowl of shrimp chips on the grass mat, watching the children push their hands in at the same time, their stubby fingers almost touching. She was convinced they would make a good pair. They complemented each other. Ben was quiet and inquisitive, content with whatever others suggested for him. Jessica was more of a leader. She knew how to ask for things. She made up her mind with confidence.

"Look there," Aunt Seamstress said, pointing out something the children had done. "There, again. See? It looks like he's about to smooch her."

The children had crawled to an overgrown corner of the lawn, a narrow incline that the mower couldn't reach. They were pulling up dandelions and plucking them bare. But what looked like a kiss was only Ben trying to blow away some of the seed heads that clung to his hand.

"A false alarm," Manda said.

"A close one," Aunt Seamstress replied. "Just a couple more inches."

Manda hugged her friend. Aunt Seamstress had also been responsible for getting her to apply for the job at JCPenney. She thought Manda would feel better if she made money of her own—more than once, Manda had complained that she felt bad for living in the Chiwitchaiya house without paying rent. Unfortunately, the job still didn't allow her to help much, especially after taxes and the funds she sent to her parents. She had planned on getting her teaching credential, but after only a single English class at a nearby community college, she decided she didn't have the patience to master the language.

"All these figures of speech," she complained. "They don't mean anything. 'Piece-cake?' What's a 'piece-cake'? Or 'what-a-hanging'? How am I supposed to know 'what-a-hanging'?"

"Myself, I worked in a police station when I lived in Bangkok," Aunt Seamstress said. "That's why you'll never see me slouching."

The information surprised Manda, though it explained why Aunt Seamstress wore no makeup. It was also true that she had exceptional posture. Sitting on the mat in the yard, the imaginary line stretching from the back of her head to her tailbone was completely straight.

That afternoon, she mentioned the temple, as she often did. "Perhaps I could pick you up tomorrow," she said. "If for no other reason, you can go there to find a man. All of the attendees are upstanding. We don't tolerate anyone who has lost their way for too long." She had been married once herself, but her husband had been dead for several years.

Manda was thinking of how she would refuse, but she got lucky. Their conversation was interrupted when the children got into a quibble and Jessica began to cry. The women separated them, Manda wondering if maybe they weren't compatible after all. It would be better if Ben was the outspoken one and Jessica was more submissive—that would be more traditional. Either way, romance was so fickle. She thought of the few dates she had gone on while she was at university. There was a rumor among her friends back home that a man named Channarong—the person Manda had been with the day Siripon left for the airport—had also moved to Los Angeles. Manda could probably find him if she wanted to: One of the nurses' friends must know him, or maybe Aunt Seamstress could ask among the temple guests. But Manda didn't bring it up with anyone in America. It would be easier if she never had to deal with men again. She could grow old and move in with Aunt Seamstress. Ben and Jessica could take care of them. That wouldn't be such a bad life.

She plucked Ben up from the grass, brushing his shirtfront clean. Feeling his weight, his softness, both of which felt so perfect, she was reassured of his innocence—Jessica must have been the troublemaker. Or if it was him, then she forgave him; she understood that it was an accident, whatever had happened.

They snuck into the garden, where the lush green hid the yard and the guests, hid even the yellow house where Manda so often felt judged by the others. The long beans had grown tall enough that their tender shoots seemed to touch the sky. She turned on the hose, washed Ben's face, then set the end into one of the dry runnels she had dug. Water pooled and caught Ben's attention. He cocked his head to listen. It must have been the trickle he heard, the music of it. He manipulated it with his fingers, changing the pitch and giggling. Every day, Manda was surprised by how his mind grew more sophisticated. She felt lucky that she was the first to see it.

8

The nurses came to celebrate the New Year. They brought their families and too many jackets that Ben had to heap onto his bed. They brought cartons of panettone and fruitcakes uneaten from Christmas. They said, "Sawadee," and "Wadee," and "Wadee, ja," and Ben pressed his hands together to greet them.

The nurses were all Thai. The nurses were all women. The nurses all knew that, if they came to the front door, they would have to remove their shoes to walk through the main house and then put them back on again once they stepped out the back door. So, they came into the patio through the gate, the handle clanging to announce their arrival. They sent their husbands to the barbecue to keep Kamron company in his cloud of smoke and ashes. They sent their children out to play in the yard. They stationed themselves in the kitchen and rolled the sleeves of their blouses and dug for knives and ladles and pestles and graters to help finish the feast. Ben played hide-and-seek for a while, crawling beneath the dipping branches of the apricot tree and holding his breath so that none of the other children would notice him. But soon, bored, he came inside and bellied himself onto the kitchen counter, where he watched the nurses cooking, their voices rising above the percussion of their utensils.

He was enchanted by the world of women. He studied the way they dressed and styled their hair, the way they created comfort for their families, the way they counteracted the clunkiness of the men. He longed to learn their methods of transformation: bulbous papayas shaved down into needles, crudités arranged into patterns on cut-glass platters, pungent pastes pounded into fragrant sauces speckled with chilis and herbs.

"Ignoring the other kids. Do you plan to be a chef, then?" the nurses asked. "Or maybe you want to own a restaurant?"

"He will be a scientist," Manda insisted. "Look at the way he examines everything."

Ben's aunt was always explaining who Ben would become. She explained who he already was. Her words had a way of shaping him, so that if he didn't fit them before, he came to fit them afterward.

"I will be a scientist," he said, nodding. He wasn't sure what that meant or when this would have to happen. He was in the first grade now. That was part of the Outside. His teacher from the Outside was Miss Donovan, who decorated the bulletin boards with penguins, her favorite animal, a bird that couldn't fly. She didn't talk about how to become a scientist.

Ben often found himself moving between the Outside and the Inside. Outside, his name was Rattawut. He wore blue jeans and polo shirts and Velcro shoes that he kept on all day, trying to ignore how they baked his feet. He ate lunch out of a brown paper bag. He spoke English, the words coming out like a script he had to memorize for a show. Inside, his name was Ben. He wore shorts and T-shirts and sandals that came on and off a hundred times a day. He ate meals with multiple dishes: fried things and raw things and spicy things and soups. He spoke Thai, a language warm and wet as a newborn fawn, a language that stretched and twisted until it was soaked with feeling.

"He's the smartest student in the class, but nobody knows because he's so quiet," Manda said. "By the time he started first grade, I had already taught him everything he needed to know to graduate from second grade." Manda was his teacher from the Inside. She didn't care about penguin decorations. She taught him about plants and how they used sunlight to grow. She taught him about the anatomy of frogs.

Ben sat quietly, agreeing without agreeing. His mother never defined him like that. Siripon always told him he could be whoever he wanted to be, if only he worked hard at it. Her love felt different from Manda's love. It was total and unwavering. He was careful not to take too much of it, afraid she would give it all to him and have nothing left for herself. She dropped a batch of egg rolls into oil, wincing in the wok's splattering halo. He wished she would tell Manda that he didn't have to be a scientist. He wished his mother would tell the nurses that he could be anything he wanted to be. But it was only Manda who spoke up. Her will was stronger. She refused to compromise. He was never afraid of using up her love because he knew she kept some of it for herself.

The dining table grew full of plates and bowls that clinked together when anyone walked by. Kamron came back inside smelling faintly of Kingsford lighter fluid. He disrupted the world of women, so that they stopped paying attention to one another and started giggling around him. He turned on the cassette player and danced to the music, his tongue clicking, one elbow jutting out from his side like the chicken wings he had just finished grilling.

"Only one thing would make this night better," Kamron said, and for the first time in his life Ben saw his father reveal a mysterious can from behind his back. He plucked it open. He brought it to his lips and tilted his head back, his Adam's apple undulating.

"Dear, dear," Siripon said, watching him with a smile that wasn't happy. She held a plate full of som tum, and it tipped in her hand. Dressing dripped onto her toes.

Ben had grown up hearing that Kamron used to drink and that he stopped when Ben was born. It had been a gift to Ben, a promise made because his father loved him. But now Kamron chugged the beer and then another. The liquid in his hand became gulps in his throat and sloshes in his belly. He sang to the music, his voice crooning with too much emotion, too much manufactured love. He tried to pull the other nurses up to join him, complimenting their beauty and their grace.

"Oh dear," Siripon said. She stooped down to wipe her toes.

Kamron, as if apologetic, danced toward her. "I've been good for a long time, haven't I? I've been good for as long as Ben has been alive. Son, how old are you?"

Ben didn't answer. He had a sense that it was a trick question, that if he told the truth, it would somehow be wrong.

"Boy, remind me how old you are. Eight? Nine?"

"Six," Ben said.

"You've gone back to your old habits, then," Siripon said.

"Do you see what I have to deal with every day? It's always my fault. I'm always the one to blame!" Kamron crushed a can and tossed it into a pile that had collected outside the plate glass window. Ben understood that it wasn't his father's first beer after all. Maybe he had been drinking all afternoon. Kamron grabbed the rest of the six-pack he had snuck inside and flung it at the little window in the door. The glass shattered. Shards fell and broke into more pieces on the floor. Two of the cans burst open, and little jets of foam shot out of them, making them spin.

"Is that how you want it? You think you're the only one who can get mad?" Siripon yelled. She hooked her arm behind the food and swiped it off the table. Plates broke. Bowls catapulted their contents in different directions. Those that were overturned trapped pockets of darkness against the linoleum.

The music played, but everyone sat as if they didn't hear it. Ben looked at his mother, then his father, then his aunt Manda, then the other guests. Everyone was silent. He came to a new understanding. There was the Outside, the Inside, and a deeper, angrier dimension that lived in places like the shadows of overturned bowls. Here were situations that weren't explained in English or in Thai, situations that were allowed no words at all.

He watched his mother turn around and go into the kitchen. It was a night when time was supposed to move forward, from 1984 to 1985, but everyone seemed to be thinking backward, from today to yesterday, when Ben's father wasn't drinking. They were thinking back to when Ben was born.

"Go check on your mother," Manda said. The nurses turned to look at Ben with sympathetic expressions on their faces. He felt himself being shaped by his aunt again. She was creating a version of him that was sent into the middle of things he didn't understand. He crept into the kitchen and found his mother standing beside the stove. The flame was on, but there was nothing cooking.

"Mom, I'm sorry," he said. He took one of her garlic-smelling hands and pressed it to his cheek.

"No, this is not your fault," Siripon said. "Do you understand? You are not to blame for your father. Look at me. Do you understand?"

Ben looked up at her face and managed to nod, though he didn't believe himself. She sighed and then nodded too. He understood that she was hurt, but she would not show it anymore that day. She would not show it because she was not allowed to be sad when she was supposed to be happy. This was another lesson to be learned from the world of women. They had to be strong. Stronger than men. The two walked back into the next room and the party that no longer existed. Soon they would be saying "Happy New Year."

Following Sister

1

The children were told to wash their faces. They were to leave their school uniforms on, the nicest clothes they had, and gather on the stairs. It was 1970. A boy in the neighborhood had found a camera left by one of the soldiers in the city, someone who had been transferred to Saigon, and Gimjaa convinced him to bring it to the house. She wanted a family portrait.

It would be their first photo. As far as Manda knew, there had never been a reason for them to have their picture taken; there had never been a reason for them to be remembered. The boy pointed the dark eye of the lens at them. Manda imagined what the camera would see: her mother's broad and mournful face, her father standing at attention at the end of the banister, the children—Manda, Siripon, Tassanee, Kiet—barefoot and fidgeting.

"Neung, song, saam!" the boy counted. Manda thought about what the camera wouldn't see. Gimjaa's pelvis was misshapen, fragmented and healed improperly, like a bridge constructed in haste. Pali symbols were tattooed along the perimeter of Pradit's back; they had been responsible for keeping him alive during the Second World War. The ghosts of Manda's lost brothers, one older and one younger, mocked her from behind the rain jars. The camera wouldn't see Manda's own frustration overwound by the thought that she was as good as either of those brothers, that though she had been born a daughter, she had the spirit of a son.

Her brothers' ghosts were a constant standard by which she and the others were judged. Though neither of them had reached the age of two—the firstborn malnourished and dying shortly after birth, the second losing his battle with hemophilia at the age of one and a half—Gimjaa often described them as being even-tempered and clever, quiet and pristine. Potential was always like that. It did so much without ever doing anything. Manda rose from her position on the stairs, freed, relieved, as the boy explained that he would try his best to develop the film even though he had never done it before.

Later that night, the two eldest sisters pressed their ears to the wall and eavesdropped on their parents in the next room. Outside, cicadas pulsed, geckos hiccupped, and the cattle farmers across the road emptied the last of their Singhas and turned off their tinny stereo.

"Close your eyes and you can hear them better," Manda whispered.

"They're saying something about the Outer Country," Siripon replied. Eleven months younger than Manda, and far more obedient, she was the child least accustomed to staying up late. She let her small chin rest on Manda's shoulder, the movement like the landing of a delicate bird. Manda would have twisted away if she wasn't distracted by what they overheard. "The Outer Country" could be any foreign land, but in their house, it meant America. Someone was being sent overseas.

"If they try and make me go, I'll run away to Bangkok," Manda said.

"You, Pi Neung? Is that what they're planning to do?"

"Who's the oldest? Who graduates in less than two months? Who always has to do everything first?" Manda crawled back under the mosquito net. No one understood the burden of her position in the family, the curse of carrying her names. "Neung," the number one, marked her as the firstborn. And "Manda," or "Mother," was a constant reminder that she was responsible for everyone else. It was a source of amusement among most of the people who met her. "Why would anyone name you that?" they asked. If she was in the mood, she explained that it hadn't been intentional. "Manda" was simply the only word Gimjaa could think of when it came time to fill out the registry, her mind still delirious with fever. If Manda wasn't in the mood to explain, she simply told people to mind their own business.

The village had already lost others to America: friends of cousins, cousins of friends. The US was desperate to fill jobs. It turned people into airmail letters and long-distance phone calls, words instead of bodies. Manda would have no way to refuse her parents' decision. The Thrakoontong family was poor. Pradit had been a respected soldier, a lieutenant colonel in the Royal Army, but now he worked as a delivery man transporting packages throughout the district. He took his rickshaw as far as Ban Lat and Cha-am, thirty kilometers away, to deliver crates of palm sugar or padded boxes of orchids to hotel owners trying to attract GIs. He spent his meager earnings quickly, first donating to the temple, then funding his children's schooling.

"If the spirit is nourished, the body will follow," he regularly proclaimed.

"The body can't follow if it's too weak to walk," Gimjaa countered.

The family was fortunate she was an excellent cook. She transformed scraps into elegant dishes despite gnarled hands that already showed signs of arthritis. To pay for necessities, she fried curry puffs and battered bananas for her children to sell at the night market. On weekends, she erected a tarpaulin beside the bus station and cooked in the back while her daughters attracted customers to the front. Father and mother, philosopher and pragmatist, the two complemented each other. They raised their children under these dual ideals, demanding rigorous study and nightly physical labor, skills they were told would have come easily to their dead brothers.

The next day, Manda didn't bother to pay attention in class. She wouldn't have to care about trigonometry or Arrhenius acids because she wasn't fluent enough in English to land a good job in America. She had heard stories of people toiling in manufacturing plants, where demanding bosses didn't care if anyone was educated. Maybe to survive she would have to depend on an American husband—if she could find one. She imagined a foreigner letting her into his home, into his bed. She imagined what it would be like to lie beside his hairy, pale body.

The idea of attracting a man had always felt alien to Manda. All her high school friends were boys, but she didn't give in to their offers to kiss her or grope her in the back of the movie theater. She knew they wanted nothing more than to experiment, to satisfy their curiosity in preparation for real romance later. The boys didn't want Manda. They wanted pretty girls, delicate girls, sympathetic girls, subservient girls. They wanted girls like her sister.

They were smoking beside the ductwork that slithered out of the cafeteria. Manda went to them as soon as the day was over. "My parents are sending me away," she declared. "They're forcing me to go to America." She waited for their condolences, their shared indignation. They only shrugged. "Ay ngo! What kind of idiot would be scared of that?" Here was the benefit of knowing boys—so few of life's problems were a source of despair. They closed in on her, their steps cocky, their cigarettes bobbing between their lips. They convinced her of the luxury of flushing toilets and blue jeans, democracy and Hollywood movie stars. They told her about the freedom of speech, something that wasn't offered in Thailand. Then they blew cigarette smoke in her hair.

She circled the campus on her rattling bicycle to get the stink out. Her friends constantly played pranks on her, but they comforted her too. Everything they said was true. America offered opportunities. Riding home, she imagined herself in a modern house with electrical appliances quietly completing her daily chores. She imagined going to the movie theater every night and stopping afterward at a restaurant for a hamburger and french fries dipped in ketchup. "It will be exciting as hell," she said aloud, though she didn't believe her own words.

Everyone was home by the time she stepped into the courtyard. Siripon sat pub peab–style on the lacquered platform where they ate their meals. She always did her homework there, only steps away from where their mother worked in the kitchen, where their father attended to his rickshaw, and where Tassanee and Kiet played. In the middle of the commotion, she pursed her lips and tried to focus. If the afternoon was particularly chaotic, she plugged her ears with her palms, all while refusing to go off on her own. It was as if her only reason for working hard was for people to know that she was working hard. Manda often mocked the behavior. Surrounded by her friends, she sat with her legs folded to one side, her eyes squeezed tight, her palms crushing her ears. "*A* squared plus *b* squared equals *c* squared!" she shouted.

Today, Siripon bowed her head ingratiatingly as if someone important but invisible stood over her.

"What's going on with you?" Manda demanded, stepping into the shade of the awning.

Her sister didn't answer. She pressed the pad of her finger against her lips, an attempt to suppress a smile.

"Never mind. I don't give a damn anyway." Manda kicked off her shoes and climbed the stairs to her room. She spread her own homework across her bed. She always claimed the upstairs for herself in the afternoons, forbidding anyone to even walk down the hall where the floorboards creaked. She began her work, but her thoughts returned to her move. She told herself she could always come back if she needed to, that her mother and father would welcome her home once they saw what a stupid idea it had been to send her away in the first place. Maybe after all that hardship, her parents would coddle her, spoil her, finally care for her more than they cared for her dead brothers.

The smell of dinner drifted through her window. Manda followed it downstairs, anxious for the announcement of her departure so that she didn't have to play dumb any longer. She climbed up to her spot on the platform. The surface was laid out with mounds of slivered vegetables, rice noodles, and a pot of nam prik that no one else in the village could rival.

"Siripon gets the first helping," Gimjaa said.

"Why should she get special treatment tonight?" Manda asked.

"And what concern is that of yours?"

Manda glared as Siripon lifted a bundle of noodles and centered it on her plate. She ladled the thick nam prik on after it, moving her hand in a prim little circle as the sauce dribbled from her spoon.

"Siripon is such an angel," Manda muttered. "Siripon is such a good, good, *good* girl."

"Go on, complain like you always do," Gimjaa said. "If you must know, your sister doesn't get many more meals with us. She'll be in the Outer Country soon enough."

The others grew quiet, not even daring to look up from their empty plates. Siripon bowed her head in that ingratiating way again. Her reason for doing it had become clear—she knew she had taken something that didn't belong to her.

Nobody ate much that evening. Eventually, Siripon gathered the dishes and washed them before they all had to leave for the night market.

"Our arrangements will be readjusted," Pradit said, pacing in front of his children as if they were troops awaiting orders. "Next week, Tassanee will do the dishes. Manda and Kiet will go to the market. Siripon will stay home and study—I've already ordered her books."

The journey to America would take years of preparation. Siripon would have to earn a degree; she would have to gain work experience; she would have to find a sponsor and apply for a visa. For their parents to know all this meant that they thought it through long ago. The conversation Manda overheard the night before was the last of several that must have taken place. Had they considered sending her at any point? Did she ever stand a chance of going? She packed her baskets with curry puffs fresh from their bubbling oil. Each hot bundle was a burden in her hand. She had probably held twenty of them every night for the last five years—140 puffs a week for 260 weeks. She walked through the crowded night market, furious that the baskets were cutting into her shoulders. She ignored any requests for food, no longer caring if she brought home any money or not. Soon she decided to leave, unwilling to serve when she wasn't appreciated. She slipped between some busy stalls, preparing to step into the road, but a hand took hold of her before she let her weight down. She turned back, surprised. It was the boy who had been at the house the day before—the photographer. He handed her an envelope.

Manda waited until she was hidden behind the shadows of the market's scaffolding before she pulled out the picture. She saw the faces of her family and her own frightened face. She *was* frightened—that was the truth of it. She was frightened to move to America, and she was frightened to stay in Phet Buri. She was frightened of living a new life, and she was frightened of being trapped in her old one. She tore the image, separating members, separating limbs, splitting faces and minds. She let the scraps scatter over the ground, and she threw her baskets down after them, the curry puffs spilling into the dirt. She was about to abandon her basket altogether when Siripon arrived.

"It will be okay, Pi Neung. We don't have to tell anyone. You can take half of my money. I'll say someone cheated me and I didn't notice in time." Siripon stooped down at Manda's feet to clean the mess. Without looking up, she whispered a quiet apology.

2

The sisters shared two memories that floated up in their consciousness when they thought of each other. In one, a boy in the schoolyard dangled a snake above Siripon's head. The gesture was a blatant attempt to terrify her and an expression of his love. The teachers didn't notice. They were too distracted by the chaos of play. Only Manda, aware of everyone, ran to her sister's defense. She shoved the boy, left him sprawled on the soccer field, face red, belly exposed. A cloud of dust rose around him, and when it cleared his brother had arrived. Manda charged again, but the larger, oafish boy didn't budge. A crowd gathered. She cast out her vilest insults. He punched her in the chest, the pain so cavernous she couldn't breathe. Still, she shielded Siripon, bracing for another blow, grateful that her friends were running over to help. The larger playground battle erupted. Children on both sides were kicked and pummeled. Clothes were torn. Blood was drawn. It didn't end until the teachers arrived to pull the crowd apart by ears and elbows. Only Siripon remained unscathed.

There was a second memory at the food stand. The sisters sold miang kham behind their counter. They formed rounded cha plu leaves into cones and filled them with needles of toasted coconut. They placed in a little wedge of lime, a cube of ginger, a slice of chili, and a single dried shrimp. Poor, they were instructed to include only half a peanut in each pouch. But a handsome boy approached, a boy who had caught Siripon's attention every Saturday for a month and a half because of the sweetness in his eyes. She snuck him whole peanuts, tucking them into their coconut nests and covering them quickly with dark sauce in the hope that no one would catch her. Manda noticed her sister smiling at the boy. She traced Siripon's submissive pose from her bowed head to her furtive fingers, where she spotted the crime. She informed their mother. Gimjaa told her husband. Pradit beat Siripon with a switch—twice across the back for wasting money and twice across the bottom for flirting, each strike leaving a raised red welt that wouldn't go away for a month. Between strikes, he grazed Siripon's goosefleshed skin with the tip of the switch as he reminded her of what she did wrong. The sensation worked like hypnosis, like a brainwashing technique he might have witnessed in war. "You should be grateful to Manda for keeping you out of trouble," he said. "You should thank her for having such a watchful eye."

Siripon didn't have much time with her siblings after the decision was made to send her away. The collection of English books grew each time Pradit returned from his trips to Bangkok. She sometimes wept when she looked over at them, or worse, while she was studying them, so that the foreign letters swam across her vision like startled fish. Practicing, she worried her words were incomprehensible, that she would fail in America and disappoint her parents. "Please, I would like to purchase a bag of rice and a dozen eggs," she repeated. "Please, can you help me find directions to my house? I am lost." Manda mimicked her in front of their friends. She turned down the corners of her mouth and yammered similar phrases: "I need rice! I need egg! I am lost!"

This is the price of service, Siripon told herself, trying not to care. But of course she cared. She wanted to please everybody. She came home from school and asked if she could do the laundry. She volunteered to ride to the market to pick out fresh tilapia. She peeled cloves of garlic without crushing them, arranging the translucent skins into a neat pile like a sheaf of tiny scrolls curled one inside the other. When she climbed into bed at night, a flush of heat rose from under her collar, her proof that she had done all she could for the day. Somehow this ability had fallen to her. Only she had been provided with the strength to serve.

Siripon spent her senior year studying double, once for Phet Buri and once for America. Manda had already moved to Bangkok, where she was pursuing a degree in the natural sciences. When Tassanee began cleaning the kitchen and Kiet left for the night market, Siripon returned to her prison of books. She had not stepped foot beyond her neighborhood, and yet she was tired of being so far away.

Sleepy, crying, she wrote in her diary: *Tell me, why was I chosen to go? Why am I so easily removed from the family? Why am I the only one who always has to work so hard? Mother and Father don't love me as much as they love the others. Maybe I'm not really one of them. Maybe I'm illegitimate. Maybe they purchased me.*

She went to bed and dreamt she lived in an enormous conch shell. Sea urchins invaded whenever she tried to rest. They scraped pores into her home through which the boiling sea entered, dousing her, scalding her flesh. She woke to discover her diary shifted from its usual spot beneath her bureau. The binding caught the light behind the rim of carved wood. She reached for it and found it weightless. A hollow had been left between the covers. In place of her secrets was a Buddhist statuette carved from black stone and a message on a slip of paper: *A good daughter would not be thinking such things.*

Siripon shut the book and pushed it back into its dark corner. She assumed her father was responsible, but she was too frightened of the confrontation to ask. Under his gaze, she tried harder to please him, working and studying each night to the point of exhaustion. She suffered from insomnia. She lost weight. Her heart felt as if it was constantly racing. Relief only came after she graduated from high school and boarded the bus headed south to Phuket. For two years, she would attend the Mission Hospital, a nursing school run by Seventh-day Adventists. When she graduated, it would deliver her to a temporary job in

Bangkok and then to a permanent position in the US. She bowed to her family through the window as their figures grew smaller, then smaller.

The Mission Hospital had strict demands, but Siripon didn't mind them when the other nursing students so willingly helped. They all had the same story. They were working toward America so that they could provide better lives for their families. Siripon was happy to work long shifts, to study each evening, to wake up to the same breakfast of rice porridge and pickles, the same lunch of curry and papaya, the same dinner of rice with tofu and eggplant. She found comfort in the daily replacing of linens along the rows of hospital beds, the newly washed sheets and pillowcases that gleamed on their lines beside the ocean. She liked the thoroughness of patient assessments, the tender inspection of each ailing body.

Everyone at home agreed the job suited her. Neighbors left messages asking her to help cure their diseases. Gout, arthritis, hypertension, hypothyroidism, insomnia, fainting spells, asthma—the list grew so long Siripon wrote it down and carried it with her to classes. She took meticulous notes and reported them to her parents during her weekly phone calls so that the information could be relayed to the others. But the calls also brought with them a sense of dread. Each time she spoke to her parents, she was tempted to apologize for what she had written in her diary. She tried to detect any trace of anger in their voices, but she could never be sure. The more she worried, the harder she worked, as if her debt of service grew with each missed apology. Her teachers praised her performance, especially her phlebotomy skills, and later her ability to start intravenous lines. They offered to write her letters of recommendation so that she could choose where she lived in the US. Her reputation followed her to Bangkok, earning praise from the charge nurses and the patients. When the end of the program approached, her parents arranged for her to rent a room in Los Angeles. The weather there would be similar to Thailand, they said, though the winters would be cold.

Siripon returned home one more time before leaving for the Outer Country. Seeing her mother after such a long time away, she took Gimjaa's hands and rubbed them warm. She stretched and massaged Pradit's feet. She told Tassanee to make sure that she did everything their parents asked of her. She told Kiet to stay out of trouble. The morning she was to depart for the airport, Siripon sat with her parents one last time on the lacquered platform as they looked through her paperwork again. Still, her mind returned to her diary. In the hours before her ride was to arrive, she considered opening it again, bringing the statuette with her. But she didn't dare to touch it, to let it into her American life. Instead, she took her guilt overseas. It became her mission to please her parents, to ensure that she could make them proud of her, even after what she had done wrong.

3

A shadow like a large bird flickered across Manda's body. She looked up through her dorm room window to catch an airplane passing. Siripon would have departed by now, on her way to her American incarnation. Maybe it was her. Manda turned back to her grim reflection in the mirror. She touched her pencil to her eyelid, completing the dark line she had begun. "Jing jing, what's the point?" she asked.

"She's having second thoughts again," one of her roommates complained. The women had been responsible for arranging a date for Manda. She was to meet a man named Channarong, another graduate student at Phet Buri Teacher College. She had prepared all afternoon, bathing, shaving her legs, styling her hair. Several borrowed dresses lay like alternate personalities on her bed, but only one fit her well enough to wear. She rose to put it on.

"No need to rush," the others urged. "You don't want to seem desperate."

"Did any of the others call me desperate?" Five years had passed since Manda moved away from home, and she had yet to find a man who didn't disappoint her. These graduate students weren't as interesting as the boys she grew up with, the only ones who had rivaled her intellectually, the only ones she had bothered to befriend. They were scattered throughout the country, attending different universities, pursuing different fields, but they still wrote to her. Hopefully, college hadn't turned them into bores.

Manda missed her time as an undergraduate. She had thrived on the rigor of her classes, the challenge of exams. They presented her with the opportunity to show everyone what she was capable of. In graduate school, she rose to the top of her class, but with each passing term she worried that she would have to leave it all behind. Phet Buri felt smaller each year. She knew she was outgrowing it.

She found Channarong waiting by the entrance of the night market. He was tall, well-groomed, and just plump enough for his sharper features to be softened. He greeted Manda politely before weaving through the crowd for some bowls of shaved ice. When he returned, he held them both out to her so she could choose the one she preferred.

"Everyone seems to agree you're the smartest one in the department," Channarong said.

"Maybe I'm the most practical," Manda replied. "It isn't difficult. Teaching just requires common sense."

"You don't give yourself enough credit."

"If a student isn't working hard enough, you motivate them. If a student's causing trouble, you calm them down. If a student isn't intelligent, you teach them to blame their parents."

Channarong smiled at the remark. He took Manda's hand and led her closer to the river. The sound of the market was replaced by the babbling of water. But as she stepped down the embankment, Manda realized her borrowed dress was too tight after all. It resisted her thighs as she descended. In her bowl, condensed milk seeped through the layers of ice and pooled at the bottom.

"I heard your sister is moving to America," Channarong said.

"She left today. If I was a better sister, I would have gone home to say goodbye."

"You didn't want to see her one last time?"

"Who knows what I want?"

A faintly fetid odor rose from the mud beside the water. Manda and Channarong moved carefully over the ground, avoiding the softer patches. He described the laundry business his father owned and the pharmacy where his mother worked. Manda tried to pay attention, but her mind drifted back to the airplane she had seen cutting across the sky. By now, it would have traveled thousands of kilometers.

They tromped beside the river for a long time. The mud sucked at their feet. Manda noticed how easily Channarong moved. He was a strong man. He was handsome and kind and ambitious. Still, she wasn't attracted to him. She suspected there was something missing in her, an absence of the desire to love someone romantically. Whenever the pressure to be in a relationship arose, she thought about how much easier life was without a man. She wanted to establish her career. She wanted friends. She didn't want to waste an evening naked in bed just for some temporary pleasure.

The conversation dried up by the time they returned to the night market. Beneath the awning of a noodle stand, Manda spotted her roommates eating. Their table was brightly lit by a naked bulb overhead, so that they seemed to be the center of attention.

"You are someone I would like to know better," Channarong interrupted. "Maybe next week I could take you out again?" He leaned down to kiss her, but Manda reacted as if a fly landed on her cheek. Her hand caught his face, and he stepped back, embarrassed.

"Thuy! I'm so sorry," she said. Her friends were giggling.

"You're a hard one to figure out," Channarong answered. "Don't you want to give me another chance?"

"Let's end things here," Manda replied. "I'm not used to doing so much walking."

4

From her class of two hundred, Siripon traveled to Los Angeles with seven other nurses. They grasped hands as they made their way through the airport, letting go only at customs, when each had to show their documents to the immigration officers on their own. If Siripon felt close to the other women during their years of training, she grew closer to them still in America: new sisters to replace the ones she left behind. Maybe they were even better than her real sisters, because they carried the same burdens she did. They understood.

She began work at White Memorial Medical Center, and her cohort shrank further. Only three nurses shared the day shift with her, six-thirty a.m. to six-thirty p.m., seven days out of every two weeks. She met with them on breaks if the patients cooperated. The women gathered at a corner table in the cafeteria and shared their lunches. Siripon had learned to distract herself from sadness by keeping busy, but among her friends she let her emotions show. They spoke of home, sometimes crying together, and then they cheered one another up as best they could before returning to work.

White Memorial was in Los Angeles, in a neighborhood called Boyle Heights. Siripon heard the *pop-pop-pop* of shootings every week, but the gangs didn't harm the nurses; they knew a day would come when the nurses would eventually have to save them. During the first year, the women rotated through each department. Siripon assisted with surgeries and then with the ob-gyn. She preferred the pediatric units. She was good with the babies, and they responded well to her. She came to know the families whose children were chronically ill. They, too, had come from other places. They said her name with different accents, and she liked the feeling of being translated by them, as if each were adopting her into their family.

Her hostess in the Outer Country was Kun Luk, a woman Siripon loved immediately. On the evening of Siripon's arrival, Kun Luk swung open the door of her small house in Monterey Park as if she had been watching for the taxi out of her peephole. She batted Siripon's hands away and paid the fare before carrying the suitcases up the narrow flight of stairs herself. Inside, the table was set with a plate of rice and a second plate with pieces of fried chicken on one side and slices of cucumber on the other. "I don't have much, na?" she said, smiling. "But we will make do. And later, I can show you the bus route to the hospital."

All of Kun Luk's siblings were still in Phet Buri, and she had not seen them in years. When she arrived in America, she knew no one. She worked in a food-packing factory to make a living. "Bags and bags of chips," she said, describing the salty treats to Siripon, who had never heard of them. Dozens of puffed-up bags were lined up in a cupboard. Siripon sounded out the name printed on each one: "Laura Scudder." After dinner, Kun Luk tore a bag open so that Siripon could have the chips for dessert.

Kun Luk was like Siripon: They both preferred to keep busy. On their days off, they went to the Bangkok Market. They had to take two buses to get there, but once they arrived, they were happy to be surrounded by the ingredients of home. They made curries and fried fish and chili paste that they ate with raw vegetables. When they couldn't find ingredients, they substituted them with things in the American markets: bananas instead of plantains, carrots instead of green papayas. Once, in search of a substitute for cha plu leaves, Siripon plucked a leaf from a neighbor's avocado tree and crunched it between her teeth, too curious to worry whether it might give her a stomachache.

Usually, they ate alone. Once a month, Kun Luk permitted Siripon to invite the other day-shift nurses over. The two would cook for the small group of friends, proud to be able to play hostesses. They also brought food to parties. Siripon had not grown up going to parties; the village where she lived had not bothered with parties. But here in the Outer Country she embraced them. She put on the silk dresses her mother had insisted she bring with her, garments the family paid a small fortune for in case she should have to look her best for a special occasion. She entered the crowded rooms and mingled. She found the hosts and offered to wash the dishes. The parties helped to keep her homesickness at bay, but every now and then, she was reminded that other people were hurting more than she was. She would catch one of the guests staring off vacantly—their hand might pause while reaching for a ladle. "I bet I can read your mind," she said, offering a sympathetic smile while her own sadness suddenly swelled again. They were all together, but they were still alone.

5

Siripon sent news home every two weeks. The tissue-thin letters arrived at their parents' house in Phet Buri, and Gimjaa read them aloud to Manda over the telephone, first while she was at Phet Buri College, then at the teachers' apartments near Benjama Thep Uthit School, where Manda found a job as a science instructor.

Everyone back home was surprised that Manda was an excellent teacher. They knew that she was intelligent, but nobody expected her to be hardworking and disciplined. She was among the strictest teachers at Benjama, and yet her students loved her. They loved her *because* she was strict. She didn't treat them like children. She demanded that they live up to their full potential.

Manda kept an atlas in the top drawer of her desk. Sometimes she opened it to a map of California and felt how far away it lay. *They have accepted me in the pediatric intensive care unit,* Siripon wrote. *The administrators told me I have a knack with babies, and I prefer them over the older patients, who always find something to complain about. As for Kun Luk, she cares for me like a daughter. I try to be a good guest. I conserve heat and water to keep the bills low. I cook and clean. I made her a set of cross-stitched pillowcases that she displays in her living room.*

All of Siripon's letters ended the same way: *You have nothing to worry about. I hope I am making you proud.*

Listening to her mother read, Manda wondered what Siripon didn't tell them. Surely there had been mishaps and obstacles, but her younger sister never spoke of such things.

The envelopes were accompanied by money orders, one hundred American dollars that Pradit cashed on his way home from his deliveries. He donated a tenth to the temple, where he asked the divine spirits to keep his overseas daughter safe. He and Gimjaa invested the rest in the future. They built up funds to send the other children to college. They bought a scooter to replace Pradit's rickshaw. They plumbed running water to the bathroom so that they could refill the tub without having to carry over jugs of rainwater. But near the end of summer, Siripon's contributions were cut in half without any explanation. Gimjaa suspected her daughter had met a man. She confirmed it with Kun Luk—on Siripon's nights off, she went out with a stranger and didn't return home until midnight. The money was being used to buy makeup and new dresses.

To Manda's amusement, Gimjaa began her nightly phone calls to Los Angeles, making sure Siripon was alone in her bed so that she wouldn't ruin her reputation. Their mother's tone was casual at first, but soon she became more pointed, demanding to know who the man was, where he came from, and if he was able to support himself. They learned Kamron's name and that he had grown up just outside of Bangkok. They learned that he went to America on a tourist's visa, but that he now worked in a metal factory. This information appeased Gimjaa. Each time she called to read out a new letter, Manda heard contentedness in her mother's voice.

Less than a year had passed when Siripon sent a photograph from her wedding. In it, she and Kamron stood in front of gold lamé curtains with their fingers shyly intertwined. She wore a modest white gown with lace covering her arms. He wore a black tuxedo. There was no bridesmaid or best man in the ceremony, only a few guests. The entire event, including a dinner, cost them only fifty dollars.

You will like Kamron, Siripon wrote. *He's quiet like our dear father.*

Manda couldn't know if her sister's observation was true. Men could be quiet for so many different reasons. She studied Kamron's face and thought she recognized something dark in him, something unlike anything she ever saw in her father. But she kept her thoughts to herself.

Her parents were pleased enough by the wedding; they were happy that Siripon had found someone who would help her in the Outer Country.

"And you? When will you find a husband, huh?" Gimjaa asked Manda one evening. "Isn't it about time?"

"I can't think of anything worse than being tied to a man," Manda replied before returning to her lessons.

The Garden Kingdom

1

Students were waiting for Manda on the bridge, their bodies silhouetted against the sunset—thin limbs and white shirts floating over the river like the pale skin of lanterns. It was April. Heat and humidity seared her skin. She never understood how she tolerated it from one year to the next except that she was willing to suffer through so much for the children.

"I thought six of you were coming." She set her bucket beside the sloping edge of the river. Inside, chloroform lapped against the metal siding.

"Jaroen didn't show up," the children said. "We can take his share." Their expressions were smug as they pressed their hands together and raised them to their foreheads.

Of all the boys to be unreliable, she thought. This year, Jaroen had been her favorite student at Benjama School: industrious, enthusiastic, and not overly fussy. Fussiness was a quality she abhorred in people, especially in men. "So be it. If it's five, it's five," she said.

The students linked arms and scaled down the embankment. At the water's edge, they beat the reeds and lily pads, and around them, scattershot, the frogs emerged—black spots that disappeared so fast they might not have been there at all. Nets reached out and arced back. Quick bodies were stilled. Only eyes and vocal sacs trembled. It was an hour's work, three dozen muddy frogs pushed into the chloroform vapors. Manda told the children to secure the bucket well to her bicycle, to make sure the frogs couldn't escape like they did last year. She gave each of them five baht for their labor. Then she chanted to release them from this sin she had asked them to commit.

She was relieved to have gotten the task done without being distracted. Earlier that afternoon, her mother had called, and Manda still felt wounded by the conversation.

"How many times must you make me hobble over to the telephone?" Gimjaa had complained. She had been trying to reach Manda for two days, but each time she rang, Manda had been out.

"Well, how was I supposed to know you were trying to reach me when I'm forty kilometers away, Mother?"

"And you argue with me on top of it. Honestly, I have no idea how I've put up with you all these years. Why can't you be more like Siripon? She always tries to please her parents. She's pregnant now. Going to give us our first grandchild. I would have told you sooner if I could have."

Manda felt an evaporation of the pride that accompanied being the eldest sister, the clever sister, the charismatic sister. She had never really thought about having a baby of her own, but now she saw an opportunity missed. Siripon had not been in America for more than three years, and she had already gotten married and pregnant. Manda was twenty-five, and she hadn't lost her virginity.

"Such great news," she said, though there was no rise in her voice. "Siripon must be making you so proud."

Gimjaa's laughter came over the line in small raspy swells. She explained that the baby was due in November. "I'll tell her to stop sending us money completely. She needs to start saving for the little one."

"Everything for the baby," Manda said.

Perhaps Gimjaa sensed her eldest daughter's disappointment then, because there was a pause in the conversation, and when it resumed, her words were more tempered. "Someday your time will come, ja."

"I have all the children I can handle," Manda insisted.

She rode back toward campus, surprised to see Jaroen emerge from a stand of sugar palms. He was panting and sweaty, his rib cage pushing out beneath his shirt with each inhalation. Moonlight caught a wildness in his eyes.

"You timed it perfectly if you were trying to miss all the work," Manda said, drumming her fingers against the lid of her bucket.

"I'm sorry, Ajan. I got lost."

"You're going to lie to me too?"

"It's the truth, Ajan. I had to take a different way, and I made a wrong turn. Do you want me to . . . ?" He took the handlebars of her bicycle and swung a leg over to pedal. It was something he had done for her before, when she had stayed after school to help him prepare for an exam. It was an act of service they both kept to themselves.

They ascended the dirt runway from the river shore, turned onto Kiri Ratthaya Road where the surface was paved and the tires could get more traction. The city had settled for the night. The restaurants were dark. The metal grates were pulled down over the storefronts. Only one figure lingered—a man. Though he was beside them for no more than an instant, Manda worried. "Leaw, leaw," she whispered. "Faster, faster." But Jaroen didn't speed up. He went along as if everything was as it should be. Manda caught the boy's scent lifting off his body, something like cedar and ocean brine. Instinctively, she knew it was the perfume of sex.

"Do you know that man?" she asked.

"We're almost at the apartment, Ajan." There was restrained excitement in his voice. As they came into view of the campus, she watched Jaroen's legs pedaling, his arms stretched to the handlebars. His body celebrated a triumph, and she knew it involved the man they had passed. Something entangled them, so that their being in the same place was more than a coincidence. She wrapped her arms around Jaroen's waist, wanting to protect him.

2

The Chiwitchaiya household didn't plan a New Year's party as 1986 approached. On the afternoon of December 31, Siripon slept in after a night at the hospital, and Kamron picked up an overtime shift at Axon. Manda worked in the garden, freeing her plants from the overturned buckets she used to shelter them from the frost. She wore blue jeans and a thick holiday sweater that was quickly getting spattered with mud. Her manager had handed them out for the holiday sales, and she didn't expect to wear hers out in public again.

The sun slipped behind a sheet of clouds and turned pale. At the house, the curtains were still drawn over the windows. Ben had gotten into the habit of bringing her something to drink in the afternoons, but today he had not appeared. She rinsed her hands and feet, resolving to make him play outside after lunch. Some fresh air would do him good.

She found him balanced on the spine of the living room sofa with his arms outstretched. On the television screen, his latest favorite movie played: *Staying Alive,* a John Travolta film Kamron had ended up with after a white elephant party. Manda admitted that Travolta was an attractive man. His co-star was a beautiful British woman with luxurious brown hair. Both of their bodies were so elongated, so equine. Manda couldn't compete. Her ancestors were short, stocky, and furry-legged. Her own belly pressed against the waistband of her jeans.

"No 7 Up for me, huh?" she said, needling Ben with a knuckle. "Today you don't love your auntie."

"I love you," Ben said. His head dropped, but only for a moment.

He had his old baby blanket knotted around his waist, and he waited for a cue. "Watch me," he said.

Travolta, panting and sweating in an absurd leather loincloth, rose above the stage on a smoking pedestal. He reached down for the British woman—her character's name was Laura—and motioned for her to jump up to him so that they could execute their final lift.

"Come on . . . Come on." Travolta was panicking. "Come on!"

"I can't!" Laura said. The pedestal was getting too high, and she was dizzy after being slid across the stage so that he could perform an impromptu solo. But she pushed herself up. She ran and leapt, splitting her legs and flaring her arms. Simultaneously, Ben jumped into the air, splitting his legs and throwing his arms up. He landed, smiling, with a boom so loud the heating ducts rang throughout the house.

"You'll wake your mother. Just wait and see," Manda warned.

Again, the boy feigned guilt. But a moment later, he pointed the remote toward the VCR and rewound the tape to repeat the performance. Manda went to wash her hands for a second time, scraping the dirt out from under her fingernails. As she looked at herself in the mirror, she thought of Ben poised in the air, his small body trying to command the stage. He wasn't pretending to be John Travolta. He had imagined himself as the British woman with the mane of brown hair.

Manda went back to where Ben was poised on the armrest. She drew him to her.

"What are you doing?" she asked.

"Just dancing," Ben said.

"And who were you pretending to be while you were dancing?"

"Laura," Ben said.

"Not Tony Manero?"

He shook his head.

"And why not? He's quite handsome and talented." She readjusted him on her lap so that they faced each other. He was still so young, so pliable. "Ben, you don't want to be a girl, do you?"

He considered it. Maybe he sensed something in her tone that made him cautious. He nuzzled his head into her shoulder, but he didn't speak.

"Oh, it doesn't matter one way or another," Manda said casually. "So?"

He curled his hand in the tightness of her sweater. "Sometimes," he said.

Manda realized she had been worrying about Ben in the back of her mind, cataloging his movements and decisions. His mannerisms were too exaggerated and prissy, and he had a tendency for particular toys: a dollhouse one of the nurses had purchased for him, two little stuffed bears in red and green overalls. Her love for him must have masked her suspicions so that the realization never surfaced before. Now the thought that something might be wrong with him made her anxious.

"I need to get cooking or your mother will nag, nag, nag," she whispered.

At this, the boy seemed relieved. He lingered beside Manda for a moment longer and then returned to his performance, though the second reminder that his mother was asleep convinced him to move more quietly.

That evening, Manda watched the family around the dinner table. Siripon was overly attentive, wiping the boy's mouth and cutting his food into little cubes. Kamron ignored Ben, his gaze drifting to the cabinet by the door, where he stored his bottles of Jim Beam—he had graduated from his cans of Budweiser. Ever since he had started drinking again, he seemed more content to be alone with his glass as he wandered around the patio.

Ben was sent to bed, and Manda gathered the others back to the table. She would be direct—there was no point in mincing words. "Your son dressed up like a woman today," she said.

"What are you saying about my son?" Siripon's face was already clouding over from lack of sleep. Her schedule never seemed to offer her enough rest.

"Ben," Manda said, lowering her voice and looking into her sister's eyes. "I caught him today, right over there—cross-dressing. He had that blanket tied around his waist. He was dancing like the woman on the television screen."

Kamron had been stepping into his sandals so that he could escape outdoors. He set his glass down and turned back toward the table.

"It's not normal," Manda continued. "A boy needs to act like a boy."

"You're jumping to conclusions," Siripon said. "Anyway, what harm can a little thing like that do? He was playing. He's just a child."

"Exactly right—he's just a child," Manda replied. She counted on her record of winning arguments with Siripon when they were children. Her sister always backed down, especially after Manda laid out her case thoroughly and systematically. "It's because he's still a child that now is the time to intervene. We must keep him from going down the wrong path. It's bad enough he has to grow up Thai in a country full of farang. Do you want to pile something else on top of that?"

"Things like this sort themselves out," Siripon said. She was being more stubborn than usual. "Children don't know the difference between boys and girls at this age."

"He's already in the second grade. The other kids are aware enough to bully him, believe me. You know how a thing like this gets treated. And what if he should become attracted to another boy, huh? What if he should try to kiss someone? The other parents would banish him from the place." She looked over at Kamron, hoping to have his support, but he refused to take sides. His gaze followed a moth that had come in while he stood in the doorway. It bumped along the ceiling.

"You listen to me, both of you," Manda continued. "I've been around plenty of children. You need to do something about this. If you let it fester, the problem will get worse."

"Just leave him alone," Siripon said. She got up wearily from the table and trudged toward the bedroom.

"You're not going to do anything?" Manda called after her. "Are you so soft that you won't even help him?"

Her sister didn't turn back. Kamron stepped outside, still without a word. But he came back later, clumsy and heavy-footed.

"Is it serious?" His voice was gruff.

"And why didn't you say anything to her, huh? You just let me go on by myself. Is he *my* son?"

"You know Siripon won't punish the boy."

"Who said anything about punishment? Ben doesn't know any better. No—it's not punishment he deserves; it's a remedy." She rose and looked Kamron in the eye. There had been a time when she was intimidated by him, but that insecurity, that weakness, had faded. He had a temper, but he was cowardly too. "For years I've watched you become a mockery of a father to that boy. You were so quick to go back to drowning in alcohol. It's no surprise he's straying. He doesn't have a proper role model."

Kamron opened his mouth as if to speak, but Manda refused to let him interrupt.

"If you don't want your son growing up gay, you better act like a proper father. Help me get us through this, and don't say a word to your wife."

3

Jaroen planned to be a teacher. "Like you, Ajan," he told Manda. They met after class to prepare for his college entrance exams. The room smelled of formaldehyde and the stale, fetid cavities of dissected bodies. She pressed a piece of chalk into his hand and directed him to the board, where she tested him on the great discoveries: Gregor Mendel's peas, Charles Darwin's finches, Albert Einstein's theory of special relativity. Jaroen summarized concepts clearly and without hesitation. His mind was a room full of drawers in which everything was in its place.

"Ajan, I'm tired of the other boys and their games."

Manda was not paying attention. Her gaze was down at a book, checking the accuracy of something Jaroen had diagrammed.

"I've been meaning to tell you," he said. "Sometimes I go out to the rice fields. I watch the animals—the way they move, the way they hunt. Oy, Ajan, the boys came up all around me."

"Boys?" She looked up, noticed a scrape on his elbow that had only begun to heal.

"I was watching a heron—the prettiest one I've ever seen," he said. "It was standing in the water. It was perfectly still." He sobbed hard. She stepped to the door and locked it, and they sat alone until his breathing calmed. He said, "They cornered me in the bathroom. They said I want to suck them off. They said I want to take it from behind."

Maybe if Jaroen had been Manda's son, she would have embraced him. Instead, she told him to wash his face so that the other students wouldn't see him crying. Watching him at the sink, his hands catching water and moving up to his face, his face fighting to be stoic but crumbling again in tears, she loved him more, but she respected him less. She did not want her favorite student to be weak.

There were three bullies, and they were long-limbed and well-nourished boys. Their faces had the unblemished sheen of people who had never known hardship. In class the next day, Manda waited for them to speak out of turn, and it did not take long. She called them to the front of the class and told them to hold out their hands. They all loomed over her, beaming, their palms open as if they were waiting for a gift. She raised her ruler and brought it down on the first boy, content when she noticed goosebumps rising along his arm. His face grew sober.

"That hurts, Ajan," he said, as if she had gone too far in a performance meant for the other students.

"Did you think I couldn't hurt you?" she replied.

For a week they retaliated. They spoke out of turn. They fell over one another, toppling desks, sending trays of instruments crashing to the floor. Each time, Manda called them to the front of the room. She delivered seven strikes for every misdemeanor they committed, until the number seven took on its own ominous presence in the classroom. Students whispered that seven was Manda's favorite number; they joked that the answer to her test questions was always seven. But her ruler never failed to surprise the boys with its shock of pain.

It was late on Sunday when her bus delivered her to the dormitory after a weekend with her family. She found her roommates sitting in front of their empty dinner bowls, deep in conversation. Before Manda could put away her things, they told her Jaroen was missing. His parents hadn't seen him since Friday.

Manda's mind went first to the bullies she had been battling. She rode to each of their houses, apologized to their parents for interrupting so late at night, and asked to sit with each boy privately. Alone with them, her expression grew stern. "Did you do anything to Jaroen? Did you go too far?"

They stared back. They almost convinced her that they were innocent. At least, she believed that *they* believed they were innocent.

"Just because your parents are in the next room, don't think I'm afraid to raise my voice," she said.

Two of the boys stayed cold and detached. The third wasn't as careful. "Jaroen makes his own trouble," he said. "Maybe we'd leave him alone if he wasn't meeting pathetic men in the city. It's disgusting. How do you know that isn't where he is, huh? Your star pupil. Trust me, he's probably on his hands and knees on some man's bedroom floor."

"Take me to them," Manda demanded.

The boy laughed. "I'm not a kathoey," he said. "Just because I know your boy gets plowed doesn't mean I go there to watch."

She rode toward the river. It was past midnight, her way illuminated by the half-moon over her shoulder. The path, which she had thought nothing of before, was now full of places where danger could hide. Every few meters, the light was obscured, leaving shadows that could have been plant or animal or man. At the turnoff from Kiri Ratthaya, she parked her bike under the dark web of a plumeria tree and went to the streetlamp where the man had been. Only a few houses were visible. Tube lights glared from a cinder block patio, their buzz merging and separating with the pulse of cicadas that surrounded them. She crept toward the faint odor of cigarette smoke that drifted up from behind the wall. Crouching with his head lowered, a man traced figures with a stick into the hard-packed dirt just beyond his open door.

Manda took a breath. "What have you done with Jaroen?"

The man looked up, bleary-eyed. He took another drag of his cigarette.

"Tell me right now," Manda said more bravely. "Where is Jaroen?"

The man held up his knobby hands, half shrugging, half surrendering. Manda could tell by the way his head dipped that he was drunk. He looked nothing like the man she remembered, even in that flicker of memory. This person was wiry and hunched over. His hair was white, and his eyes were circled by deep wrinkles. She considered apologizing. Instead, she simply walked away.

It was the same for the other houses. She encountered more people who could not have been the man she searched for. In another lit courtyard, a pair of dogs rushed her, snapping and snarling at the gate, chains around their necks rattling against the wrought iron. Soon the lights inside the house turned on. Voices approached. Before anyone else could yell at her, Manda hurried back to her bicycle and the road that could show her nothing more than where she had come from.

4

The garden in winter wasn't as generous, but Manda filled two bags with what she could gather and brought them to Aunt Seamstress as an excuse for arriving unannounced. She dismissed her friend's gratitude for the gift, and the two exchanged New Year's greetings.

"I can't let my guard down for a second," Aunt Seamstress said, beginning as she always did, by praising her granddaughter. "If I make a mistake adding the tip at a restaurant, who do you think corrects me? Jessica is the sharpest mathematician in her class."

"Ben can recite any biochemical pathway you name," Manda countered. "No one appreciates that in elementary school, but he'll be applying for college soon enough."

"You should have brought him along."

"Another time, another time. Today, actually, I was hoping to discuss a sensitive matter with you," Manda said, lowering her voice. Then, realizing she was frightening herself, she laughed. "Oh, I'm sure it's nothing. Just a child playing a game."

"You'll have to explain yourself, Sister."

"I found Ben yesterday, alone in the living room. He was wearing a blanket around his waist. Perhaps it was nothing more than a costume—he was dancing along to a movie. But he was leaping up in the air, fluttering his fingers—" Manda's voice trembled. She didn't like to discuss intimate matters outside of the household, even with her only friend. But she also couldn't help feeling that she needed to do something to save her boy. "Aunt Seamstress, should I be worried?"

"I imagine it's nothing, Sister. Like you say, it's just children playing their games. The other day, Jessica asked if she could wear one of her father's neckties! Can you imagine that?"

"A necktie is one thing, but a skirt is another. I thought I was lucky to be raising a nephew."

"If you're concerned, it never hurts to make an offering for him. Come with me to the temple. It has been a few weeks since you've gone."

Manda had considered this, but she sensed an offering was insufficient for such a serious matter. How many times had she slipped money into a donation box or served her favorite dishes to the monks only to receive nothing in return? She got to the point of her visit. "You are so much more knowledgeable on religious matters than I am, Aunt Seamstress. I wanted to ask if you might be able to recommend someone who could help more directly."

"I'm not following you, Sister."

"I wonder if you might know someone who can—someone who would be able to treat him."

"Sister," Aunt Seamstress said, "those kinds of things shouldn't be done lightly."

"I reflected on the matter for hours, Sister. Last night I barely slept. I know I don't have any children of my own—maybe that leaves me unqualified. But I worry for Ben like a mother worries for her son."

"Of course you do. You love him—anyone can see that. But maybe in this matter his parents would be better off deciding."

"They aren't strong enough, Sister. I've tried to talk to them—I went to them first. They only dismissed me."

Aunt Seamstress patted Manda's hand and then held it as she thought to herself. She shook her head and sighed, seeming to come to a decision. "It is a curse for a woman to love a child who isn't her own. I know that personally." Her voice had softened. She reached for her address book, looked up a phone number, shook her head again, and copied the information neatly onto a scrap of pattern paper. "Don't tell your sister where you got this, na? I would hate for her to think I snuck behind her back."

"I will handle her," Manda said. "Siripon is a loving mother, but in matters like this, she can be too timid. I just want to get it taken care of as quickly and quietly as possible."

"Yes, yes, of course, of course." Aunt Seamstress pushed the scrap of paper into Manda's palm. "You have what you need. Now, enough. Really, how is it we stumbled onto such a troubling topic? In a few weeks, we won't remember anything about it."

"You will have to try the chayote I brought you," Manda said, happy to move on to lighter matters. "They are the perfect texture, not too firm and not too soft. Cook them tonight—I've brought enough for the whole family."

Manda called the number as soon as she was sure no one in the house could overhear her. The telephone rang several times before someone answered, a man with an almost inaudible mumble.

"Sawadeeca," Manda said. "May I inquire if I have reached the temple of Ajan Lien?"

"Unh, unh, unh," the man said.

"I hope I have the correct number. I would like to request the ajan's help."

"Unh, unh," the man repeated.

"Can you understand me?" Manda began to second-guess herself. She had felt buoyed after her success with Aunt Seamstress, but now she grew frightened again. Growing up, she had been aware of other Buddhist practices her parents had warned the children to avoid. They involved cloudy jars with mysterious blobs inside them that disappeared if you were stingy with your offerings and spirit houses posted beside entranceways where ghosts were thought to dwell. "There is a boy . . . my nephew," she said. "I would like to request Ajan Lien's help for him."

A muffled sound came through the line, then a long silence. Manda was just deciding to hang up when another voice came on. This man was also hard to hear, but his greeting was friendlier. She asked again if she had reached the temple of Ajan Lien.

"Yes, yom," the man said. "I am Ajan Lien, though I don't live in a temple."

"I'm sorry, I didn't mean to assume. Please forgive me. But I am so relieved to have found you. I'm not sure where to begin, except that I have a nephew, a young boy, a child—" She explained what she had seen: the blanket, the mannerisms, the toys. The image of Jaroen's face appeared before her, a glimpse of him crying in her classroom. He and Ben had the same expression when they revealed themselves to her. They were equally vulnerable, equally fragile.

The monk listened silently; he paused for so long that Manda wondered if he was still there or if her words had been wasted. "Your boy is possessed by the spirit of a girl," he finally said. "She is probably lost, perhaps not even aware that she has died. Spirits like that can find their way into a child, but we must remove her, guide her beyond this life."

"It's possible I haven't described the situation fairly. I would hate to be mistaken. Perhaps you could examine him first to be sure."

"It is more common than you think," the ajan said. "But we should act quickly. I can come to help him tomorrow night."

Manda closed her eyes in relief.

The next evening, Manda anxiously waited for Siripon to leave for work before telling Ben to change into his temple clothes.

"Are we going there at night?" he asked.

"It's something more special than that, ja. A monk is coming here to see you."

Ben's eyes grew wide, but Manda was quick to soothe him. "This is a special monk, and he has magic that will make you even better than you already are. Now, go and change, or we won't be ready when he gets here!"

She finished washing the dinner dishes and rushed to change as well, stopping at the back door to look for Kamron outside. His dark figure lurked in the corner of the patio. He had been irritated when she told him about her plan, but he had relented. It was typical of him. He didn't want his son to be gay, yet he refused to take responsibility for the solution.

Manda dusted the statuettes on the shrine. She removed a bouquet of withered flowers and lit incense in their place. A motorcycle rumbled in front of the house, and she crept to the window. Darkness. So rarely did guests come to the front door that she had forgotten to turn the porch light on. She flipped the switch to find that the monk and his companion had already arrived, their figures suddenly upon her.

Ajan Lien looked to be in his thirties, too young to have acquired the knowledge necessary to perform this task. His scalp had not been shaved in some time, so it was covered by a layer of black stubble, and one arm was adorned with a sleeve of tattoos: warriors and demons from the epics Manda had been taught as a child. The man with him was considerably older. His cheek and mouth were scarred, almost as if he had once been a fish that was hooked and then freed. Manda invited him in, but he held up his hand, declining. He said he would return later.

She led Ajan Lien to the shrine room. The monk surveyed his surroundings without any expression.

"I hope everything is suitable," Manda said.

"Yes, Ajan," Kamron said. "If there is anything we need to change, just let us know."

"May I ask which direction is east?" the monk said. Oriented, he sat on the floor and straightened the folds of his robe around him. From an orange satchel, he lifted out several objects and arranged them in a half circle to one side. "And the boy?" he asked.

"Yes, Ajan, here he is," Manda said.

Ben had come out in his new outfit. He had washed his face and smoothed down his hair. But upon hearing himself summoned, he shrank back, escaping to the living room where she had caught him in the first place. Ajan Lien coaxed him in again. Ben lowered himself to the floor. He crawled on his knees to the monk and put his hands together to greet him.

"Good, good," the monk said. "Now, come and lie down."

Ben turned to Manda, his eyes questioning.

"Do what the ajan says," she whispered. "Follow his directions and be a good boy. Don't disappoint me."

Ben lay down. His arms were straight along his sides. He looked like a wooden doll that had fallen over, an abandoned Christmas toy. The monk unfurled a large white sheet. It billowed over Ben, so that for a moment Manda worried he was gone, that she had been duped as part of some sinister trick to abduct him. She searched for his features as the material settled, seeing the small peaks of his nose and feet, the roundness of his belly. He was still there, and yet she longed for him.

She eased herself down, realizing her throat had caught. The pain of losing Jaroen was still acute. She had found him the morning after her pointless bicycle ride back toward the river. Her class was scheduled to perform a chemical titration, and she had hurried to the storeroom to get supplies. It stood in the far corner of campus, a lonely walk from the classrooms. She had pulled the door shut behind her before bothering to turn on the lights. Things had been rearranged. Where a collection of amber bottles usually stood, a shelf had been moved haphazardly, leaving a clearing in the center of the room. She peered over the counter. There was a patch of blue. Pant legs. She made her way over, pushing things aside. The boy was on the ground. He didn't stir, even as she knelt beside him. Foam collected in the corners of his mouth and around his nostrils. She screamed. Later, she wouldn't be able to remember if she had called him her child or her son. Beside him lay an empty bottle of pesticide. She lifted him. His head fell back. She reached into his mouth in the hopes of making him vomit, but his body did not react, even to this violation. Finally, she sealed her mouth to his and inflated his lungs only to watch them deflate again.

In the shrine room, Ajan Lien chanted. The incantation was alien to Manda compared to the lines she recited at the temple. As he spoke, his voice droning, he pinched and crimped a sheet of paper until it formed a box, a cradle. The monk shaped another sheet, this time tearing and twisting it. Tiny arms appeared. Tiny legs poked out of a conical dress. It was a girl. He lay her in the box and placed them both on Ben's chest.

The boy whimpered. His wide eyes glistened from behind the open pattern of the material. Manda urged him to be quiet a little longer. But looking down at him again, she felt a sense of dread come over her. She realized the sheet covering her nephew was a burial shroud, its edges intricately embroidered. She put her hands together and closed her eyes, praying that the monk could be trusted. If she had made a terrible error in judgment, if she had placed Ben in danger, she didn't know what she would do.

The strange chanting lasted for a long while, until finally the words were familiar again. The monk lit a candle and dripped wax into a bowl of water. With a bundle of reeds, he sprinkled the water over Ben and the small paper figure that balanced on top of him. Then he lifted the box and the girl and held them out to Kamron. "Burn them," he said.

Manda's gaze followed her brother-in-law as he left the room. The image of the shroud and the fire brought her back to Jaroen's cremation. It had been a rushed affair, his parents too grieved to organize anything formal. Out of pity or a shared sense of shame, hardly anyone attended. Afterward, Benjama School invited monks from Maha Samanaram Ratchaworawihan Temple to come and cleanse the school. They processed through the halls and sprinkled mon water in each of the classrooms. At the chemical storeroom—the quiet, tainted darkness in the corner of the campus—the monks painted the elongated Pali symbols of blessing over the transom. Manda had been afraid of seeing Jaroen's ghost that day. She worried he would follow her after he was untethered from the site of his death. That evening, she accepted her parents' offer to send her to America. She no longer wanted to be around the children, to have to witness their vulnerability. She was grateful for the distance.

"It's fortunate you contacted me in time," Ajan Lien said. The monk blew out the candle, and the ceremony seemed to drift away with the thin trail of smoke. Manda took Ben's hand and helped him up.

"We weren't too late," the monk continued. He placed his hands on Ben's shoulders. "It may take a few days for the spirit to leave his body, but be patient. Watch for signs of her departure."

"What sort of signs might we encounter?" Manda asked.

"These things are impossible to predict, yom," Ajan Lien replied. "You must pay attention to anything out of the ordinary. It could be as subtle as a gust of wind or as obvious as a figure walking out the door."

"Will we see her?" She was growing frightened.

"It could be anything, anything. Keep an open mind."

She thanked him and paid what they had agreed, what amounted to four of her paychecks. The monk left, and Manda and Kamron carried Ben to bed. He was quiet, dazed, looking up at them but saying nothing. Manda covered him in a blanket and said good night. She and Kamron sat together in the living room without speaking. The television was on, a detective show, though, lost in their own thoughts, neither of them paid attention to it. Around midnight, they heard Ben groaning in his bedroom. He was twisted in his sheets, his forehead damp with perspiration. Manda woke him and asked if he was all right.

"I don't feel good," he said.

They led him to the kitchen. They offered him a glass of water only to have him shake his head. Kamron wet a small towel and pressed it against Ben's forehead, but he pushed it away.

"I feel sick," he said. He ran to the bathroom and vomited.

5

Ben's night swarmed with things he didn't understand. He realized he had not been physically hurt by the monk, but he had been frightened and was frightened still. Under the cloth, he had felt as if he was trapped, as if a spell was keeping him from escaping. The monk chanted in his relentless rhythm, formed the little figure that did not want to come into being. Ben understood that something was wrong with him, something to do with the paper girl, and he tentatively traced it back to his conversation with Manda only a couple of days ago. He was aware that he had answered her question in a way he shouldn't have; he knew he wasn't supposed to want to be a girl. But he had decided in the moment to answer honestly. He had wanted, simply, to be himself.

His father's arms smelled of smoke as they carried him back through the lit hall and into the darkness of his room. The room had changed. The house had changed. The walls no longer protected him. Threats came in through the doors; they seeped in through the tiny openings around the windowpanes. Threats were invited in by the arms that carried him and the arms that tucked his blanket up to his chin. He closed his eyes. He tugged his mind back to a recessed place within him to escape his fear and confusion. Soon he was asleep.

In his dream, the paper girl appeared. She was alive now, no longer the little figure newly twisted together. She was his size, a child equal to him, the other half to his whole. Faceless, voiceless, she gestured for him to follow her. She was in a hurry. They ran out to the garden, to where his father had carried the echo of the girl only a few hours earlier.

Smoke billowed and covered them. Embers crawled up stalks like angry ants. Flames engulfed leaves, blackening and shriveling them until they became shadows of ash. The girl urged Ben to keep moving. They were running away. They would never come back again. The flames threatened to catch her; they danced around her dress. Ben looked for water. He found the dry end of the hose and followed it back, hand over hand, toward its source. Time was running out, but the hose kept going with no end. Heat pressed upon them. The paper girl left. She ran into the darkness, and he was alone.

He awoke and threw up again. A puddle of yellow froth—all that could come up from an empty stomach—seeped into his sheets. Manda coaxed him out of bed and cleaned him up. He was pliant for her, closing his eyes, stooping his head down into the cold water. She brushed his teeth, wet and combed his hair. She stripped his bed and put the sheets in the wash.

All morning, Ben wanted to stay by Manda's side. He understood that she had the power to make things happen. He lay with his head in her lap, docile, even after his mother arrived home.

"Your boy is sick today," Manda said. Her tone was casual. She didn't mention the monk or the ceremony. "He must have eaten something that didn't agree with him."

Ben was about to object, but he doubted himself. Everything that happened felt like a dream. The monk's visit merged with the paper girl coming to life.

Siripon pressed her hand to his forehead. "You're cool, at least. You can come and sleep in my bed if you want."

Ben shook his head. His mother felt too ethereal. Only Manda was solid. She knew what he had been through, and perhaps only she could fix it.

They watched morning cartoons that turned into game shows. Ben had a sense that he and his aunt were waiting for something, though he did not know what. He fell asleep and then woke up with a start, worried that the monk was standing over him.

"Maybe I'll leave you alone for a bit so I can check on the plants," Manda said.

The announcement made Ben feel sick. He ran to the toilet and threw up again.

Siripon came out of her room after noon and told him to get something into his stomach. She brought him his favorite, Chicken in a Biskit, crackers that looked like little quilts. She gave him two at a time until the plate was nearly empty.

Four days passed, and Ben was still throwing up. Siripon called his school to report that he was sick. Kamron grew more attentive. He checked on Ben in the dark morning hours before leaving for work. He told Ben silly jokes translated from Thai, jokes about women seducing dumb men, jokes about jungle animals fighting over fruit.

Manda encouraged Ben to come with her to the garden, to breathe in fresh air, to get his blood circulating.

"Still not feeling well, ja?" she asked. "What did you eat to make you so sick? Or maybe you got it from one of your friends."

He nodded, even though neither of these things could be true. He had not eaten anything that the rest of his family did not eat. He had not seen his friends since his winter break began. She was defining him like she always did, telling him who he was before he knew it for himself.

One morning, as a surprise, she took him to the toy store in the mall. "A secret trip. We don't have to tell anybody," she said. She constantly complained that she didn't earn much money, so Ben knew this was an unusual treat. The place was still adorned with Christmas decorations. Candy cane garlands wrapped around pillars. Plastic elves and reindeer prepared to deliver gifts. He walked solemnly down the aisles, dazzled by the brightly colored packages, the possibilities inside. He liked the Transformers best, cars that morphed into robots. He settled on a yellow VW bug called "Bumblebee." It was smaller than the other trucks and sports cars; it was friendlier.

"What about this one?" Manda suggested. She pulled down a blue Corvette stingray. "Tracks."

"Bumblebee is the one that drives Spike around," Ben said.

At home, he built a racetrack out of the couch cushions and navigated Bumblebee through it the rest of the day. He didn't mind that he hadn't seen his friends since before Christmas. He didn't want to see his friends if something was wrong with him.

"I'll ask around at the hospital," Siripon said, trying to diagnose him. She muttered possibilities, tapeworm and another word that sounded like "resuscitation."

Each night, Ben went to bed trying to figure out what had happened. Each morning, he woke up without answers. Night, morning, he threw up from the confusion. Night, morning, he threw up to release the pressure built up inside of him. Night, and he went to bed again, tugging his mind back to the recessed place. The memory faded in layers, like gray veils slipping away, until one morning he awoke and remembered nothing of the ceremony.

6

But Ben's vomiting did not stop. Weeks passed. Kamron paced the yard, jaws clenched, footsteps clumsy, sloppily counting and re-counting the nights as if they were phantoms slipping through his hands. "She thinks she knows what's best," he said to himself, remembering Manda's reassurance that she could take care of the situation. He could not say why he had permitted her to arrange the ceremony, but he knew, too, in a way he despised, that he would permit her to do it again if she told him to. Ever since she had moved into the house, Kamron had felt her condescension, her unspoken belief that she knew more than he did about what was best for his son. He had come to accept it. He accepted it because he doubted himself.

Ben still had an appetite. He still had the energy to play. But every day Kamron heard from Manda how many times his son ran to the toilet to vomit. Her voice was urgent and frightened. Her voice was conspiratorial. "Calm down," he said, wishing they were done with it. He brought Ben back to the bathroom, cleaned the boy's face and arms with the washcloth. He wet and combed the boy's hair. He wondered what more he could do, telling himself that at least he was there; he had not abandoned the family the way his own father had. And he thought of why his father had left, if maybe the best thing he could do was leave.

The January nights lasted too long. His alarm went off, and he groped for his clothes without turning on the lights. In the shrine room, he prayed and replaced his amulet around his neck, thinking that, somehow, he was protected while his son was not. Maybe, he thought, his job was to teach his son how to be strong. But he did not know where his strength came from unless the source of it was his anger. Through the kitchen window, he saw Siripon pull into the driveway hours earlier than usual. She had not thought much of Ben being sick in the beginning—she saw far worse at the hospital. But lately her face was wrinkled with worry.

"Still the same?" she asked.

"Maybe a little better last night. I don't know, Noi."

She was no longer tender toward him, not since he began drinking again. These days, her warmth was reserved only for Ben. Kamron imagined the two together in the quiet hours before she went to bed, mother and son, and the happiness between them.

He clipped an old receipt to the back of the Datsun's visor, a hiding place the women would not accidentally discover. Each morning, before leaving for work, he marked another day passing without Ben getting better. Three weeks had passed when he decided they would call Ajan Lien again. After Siripon left for work, he held the receiver out to Manda.

"He said it would take time," she argued, but he could tell that she was anxious too.

"It has taken long enough."

"I'm sure if he was worried, he would have reached out to us."

"Let's not lie to ourselves, Neung. You think he's given Ben a second thought since he took your money? Suddenly, you're as naive as Noi. That man can't be trusted—I knew it as soon as he walked through the door."

Manda took the phone. She dialed and waited a couple of minutes, but no one answered. They ate dinner, she called again, and still no one answered. Now a deeper fear crept up in Kamron. He dialed the phone himself, refusing to hang up until someone answered. Finally, a man picked up, but it was not the monk.

"I need to speak with the ajan," Kamron said.

"Gone," the man said. "Back to Thailand."

"Then when will he return?"

"No, he's not returning. He moved five days ago. Six days, maybe. Six. He took everything with him."

"I need to find him. Which temple will he be staying at?"

"There are so many, Brother. I don't know where he might end up."

Kamron pressed his forehead into the receiver and surrendered to its dull pain. If Ajan Lien had returned to Thailand, they might never find him again. Kamron couldn't ask his family to help. He wouldn't tell anyone what happened.

That night, alone, he stopped in front of the shrine. The ordeal had to come to an end. He placed his hands together, bowed, but he didn't know what he would pray for. He did not wish that he had done nothing, surrendering the boy to his homosexual tendencies. And yet Ben's current suffering was hurting him too. Kamron questioned his own religious commitment. After all, these ceremonies were constructed on faith, and he had not believed fully. He had hesitated. A side of him had always doubted religion—maybe that was why he had suspected the monk in the first place. Maybe his doubt prolonged Ben's suffering. Or maybe the timing of the ceremony had been a coincidence and Ben was truly sick. What would the Buddha permit? How much of a fool was the divine spirit willing to make of Kamron? The spiritual realm was beyond his comprehension—he had always known this. The forces that worked against him were too powerful. He closed his eyes and thought. In the end, he asked for peace. He did not need to see things clearly, to be able to distinguish right from wrong. He only wanted the tension to release, the days to soften.

"Dad?"

He turned. Ben stood small and lonely in the doorway. He was dressed in star-patterned pajamas that made Kamron long for a simpler time.

"Time for bed yet? Did you come out to say good night?"

The boy looked down at his feet. "Can I sleep on the bathroom floor?"

"Don't be silly. Why would you want to do a thing like that? People sleep in bedrooms, on beds, not on bathroom floors."

"Please," Ben said. He looked tired. He looked like he was on the verge of tears.

"Fine, then." Kamron unzipped a sleeping bag and spread it out on the tiles. He laid Ben down and draped a sheet over him. "Just for tonight. We're not going to make this a habit."

Ben looked at him, pleading, and Kamron lay down beside his son. He offered his arm for Ben to rest his head on. Only when he was pinned in place did he realize the light was in his eyes, but soon he drifted into sleep. Later, waking up to the sound of Manda tapping at the door, he did not know what time it was. He glanced at the top of Ben's head, the whorl of hair circling counterclockwise at its center. His son was making little noises, like the mewing of a kitten.

7

Siripon was comforted by the sulfurous, ammoniac smell that permeated the fourth floor of White Memorial. It was an atmosphere of medications as intricate as the bodies they were meant to preserve. For ten years it had accompanied the sanctuary of her job, ever since her first days in the Outer Country. She reached down to take Ben's hand. A month had passed since he first got sick, four weeks of daily vomiting, stooping at the toilet every few hours—that sound of hollowed strain. Siripon had hoped the illness would go away, and when it didn't, she asked for ideas, first among her friends, then among the other nurses on her floor, then among the pediatricians. They suggested acid reflux, hiatal hernias, even fish bones that might be lodged in the folds of his throat. Dr. Kay Magarian offered to examine him without an appointment.

The doctor was tall, five-eleven or six feet compared to Ben's four. Her practiced cordiality kept him on his best behavior. She peered at him through the small lenses of her bifocals. She asked him to open his mouth to let her look down his throat. She lifted his arms so that she could palpate his abdomen.

"You're a healthy young man. So why are you throwing up?" Magarian asked. "We may not know what's going on with you, but we can at least get you back to school before you forget everything you've learned."

Ben slumped down at the end of the examining table. He wrung his hands, an old man's mannerism.

"He says he didn't eat anything strange," Siripon offered.

"Let's watch him for a few more days," Magarian replied in a calm voice. "If it doesn't slow down, bring him in again." She handed Siripon a note declaring him not contagious.

In another week they were back at the hospital. This time in radiology. Far from the bustle of the pediatric units, Siripon didn't feel as comfortable among the muted, shielded rooms. It was a place that made no attempt to soothe its patients beyond the reassurance of safety—the posted signs and warning lights glowing patiently above the doors. Through a tinted window, she watched Ben in his booties and hospital gown. A technician handed him the cup of chalky barium he would need to drink to help with the imaging. In Ben's hands, the paper cup looked too large, the liquid too much for him to get down. But he managed it, stopping once only to catch his breath between gulps. The technician positioned him on the table and swung the cyclopic X-ray generator in front of him. On the monitor, the white tube of his esophagus emerged. Siripon forced herself to look away. Anything she saw would only make her more nervous.

She considered that she might have to deal with a serious illness. She saw it all the time—parents who suddenly had to arrange for acute care, chronic care, monthly procedures. The task always seemed impossible at first, but almost everyone adapted. That was the power of parental love. She told herself that, whatever it was, she would handle it. Somehow she would have to.

When the procedure was over, she took Ben to visit her unit. The two entered to find a small crowd gathered around her newest patient's crib. "Oh, Fernando, he awake?" Siripon asked. The one-year-old reached out for her and squealed. She had played with him for hours on his first night there.

"Perfect timing," Kathy Rubio, the charge nurse, said. "It's amazing this kid still has a smile after all those surgeries."

"I bring mine today." Siripon nudged Ben forward. His body resisted, still weary from the experience.

"And what's the matter with yours?" Kathy asked.

"Just a little test." Siripon put her finger to her lips. She had told them all about Ben's peculiar illness, but she didn't want to bring it up now, not when it might embarrass him. Kathy tugged on his chin and told him he looked more like a man every day. The remark felt like an order rather than a compliment, and Siripon laughed. She reached down and stroked Fernando's cheek. There was barely any skin to touch between the oxygen tube and the yellowed patches of medical tape that held them in place. He had been sick since he was born, and there was a good chance he would not survive the year. "So sweet," she said as Ben crept up to the bars of the crib and looked in. At first, the baby's blanket concealed the colostomy bag protruding from his abdomen. But he turned to reach for Siripon again, and the blanket slipped away.

"What's that?" Ben asked in Thai. He had taken a step back, startled.

Siripon explained. She watched him watch the baby, wondering what he was thinking.

"He's cute," Ben offered.

"A little ray of sunshine," Kathy said. "Your mom wants to adopt him. How do you feel about having a little brother?"

Siripon didn't deny it. She wouldn't have minded having another child in the house. She and Kamron had tried to have more, but nothing ever came of it. Now she only wished she could bring out some of Fernando's qualities in her son. She wished she heard Ben laugh more often.

Five days passed before the results from the radiology lab arrived. Siripon called Dr. Magarian, who reported that everything was normal physiologically. Her voice lowered. "Do you think it could be anything else? Maybe something happening at school that you aren't aware of?"

Siripon let out an exasperated sigh. "What you saying?" she asked. "Never mind, never mind, I know you got to ask your question." On one hand, she was relieved that nothing was wrong with Ben's body. But the mystery of his vomiting still went unsolved.

She would not have time to think about it that night. The beds in the PIC unit had been full all week. Past the swinging doors, the nurses from the day shift rushed around her. They nodded without stopping to chat. She entered the break room, refrigerated her containers of rice and curry, and turned on the coffee maker for her second cup of the night. Its *click* and *whir* served as a dose of caffeine even before the coffee was ready.

"Fernando coded at three," someone called over from the center station. Siripon stepped out to see a crowd gathered around the distant crib. Between the nurses in their pastel uniforms and the family members pressing in, she could barely make out his small figure. She drank down the scalding coffee and went to him. His abdomen inflated and deflated, a stuttering rise and weak fall below his brown-blue rib cage. His eyes rolled into focus when she appeared, and later, she would be grateful for this final connection.

Work was hectic until two a.m., when Siripon took a break for her last cup of coffee. She heated her food and divided it into paper bowls for the others—they complained if she didn't give them all at least a taste of her cooking. When they could, the others entered and took their share. No one spoke. They enjoyed the lull that often arrived around this time. It was a deep exhale, when exhaustion overcame pain. The little bodies breathed and gurgled. The bedside machines pumped and chirped. They were eating when Fernando passed away.

Siripon got a ride home with Jerlie Bautista, a nurse from the neonatal unit. The two had become friends after Jerlie repeatedly asked Siripon for help getting IV lines started on the tiny newborns. Siripon had maintained her reputation for finding veins—sometimes they even paged her in geriatrics. She could see the faint color on the skin, feel the faint rise. Then it was just a matter of tracing it down.

The carpooling was a favor to Jerlie too. She recently leased a Land Cruiser so she could be higher up on the road, but she got intimidated driving the hulking vehicle by herself. She was short. They both were—just over five feet tall. After Jerlie got a new trim that made her hairstyle similar to Siripon's, the other nurses began calling them "the twins."

Jerlie exited the freeway, the concrete barriers giving way to gas stations, then to the small businesses that led to home: the doughnut shop with its neon OPEN sign that never turned off; the florist, still dark, revealing only glimpses of pale blooms in the window. When she turned onto Caroline Street, Siripon felt relief and confinement. She needed rest, but she wanted to sit with Jerlie longer. She wished they had another five miles before she had to get out of the car.

"Thank you. You know I need this today," Siripon said.

"I'm so sorry you lost your baby."

"But what we can do?" They grasped hands. There was some truth to them being called twins.

The curtains of the house were still drawn closed, making it look asleep like the others around it. Ben would be awake by now, but he didn't like the glare from the large front windows when he was watching his cartoons. She walked up the path toward the front door, tapped her wedding ring against the window, and his face appeared, expectant, through a slit in the curtains. It was a routine that she loved, a pleasant welcome before she became engrossed in the responsibilities of the house. He ran to the door, twisted the rusted lock, and let her in. Every day, he had the same welcome enthusiasm, like the greeting of a puppy. She fantasized about him coming to her with the same beaming smile for the rest of their lives. But no, she wouldn't hold on to him too tightly. She would send him to college. She would make sure he reached his full potential. That was her duty as a mother.

He stepped in to hug her, but she held out her hand.

"I am covered in germs today," she said, pushing down the memory of the night's commotion. She refused to dwell on Ben's disappointment. Lately, she worried that he was growing up to be too soft. A little practicality would do him good.

"How's Fernando?" he asked.

Siripon pretended not to hear. Ben had been asking about the baby every morning. But she suspected his curiosity came from insecurity rather than any sincere interest in the boy. "Did you eat breakfast?" she asked.

Ben shook his head.

"I can pour you some cereal."

"Something warm," Ben said.

She already knew what his preference would be. She stumbled to the kitchen, scrubbed her hands, and dug out two frozen hash brown patties from the freezer. As the heating elements of the toaster oven buzzed and reddened, she picked out a load of laundry from the basket and carried it to the washing machine. She would ask Ben to move the clothes to the dryer once the cycle was over, but he would forget. This was a routine that had played out more than once.

"Is Fernando doing okay?" He crept up behind her. The missing hug from earlier made him needy. Balancing first on the rim of the laundry basket, he bellied up onto the dryer so he could look down at the open door of the washing machine and the jumble of clothes she pushed in.

"He gave me the biggest hug last night," Siripon said, careful not to cry. She couldn't bring herself to tell him that Fernando was gone.

"What's wrong with him again?"

"His digestive tract doesn't work," she said. "That reminds me. Your test results came back, and you're fine. So why are you still throwing up, huh?"

Ben was quiet as he thought through this problem. From the kitchen, the golden smell of the potatoes reached them. Siripon sniffed the air to make sure there was no burnt undertone. She wished she didn't have to stay awake to flip them over.

"When you're a little older, I should teach you to make these yourself," she said as they went back into the kitchen. She pulled down the squeaking door of the toaster oven and released a small swell of heat. At the suggestion of new responsibility, Ben withered more, not wanting to think of independence this early in the day. Siripon didn't know whether her nights at the hospital affected his development, if he would be more secure if she was in the house each night as he fell asleep. She could tell that he was growing closer to Manda as a result. And though she tried to persuade herself that her own feelings didn't matter, she fought the urge to pull her son back to her. Ben's happiness and well-being were the most important things, not her jealousy.

With a fork and a fingertip, she flipped the patties over. Ten more minutes and they would be done. Ben hovered beside her for a moment, but music from the television drew his attention back to the living room. When she finally slid the hash browns out of the toaster oven, he seemed to have lost interest in breakfast altogether. He lay on his stomach on the shag carpet, propping his head up with his forearms. The Pink Panther sauntered across the television screen. She placed the plate of food and a cup of water behind him on the coffee table.

"Eat them while they're warm. You know where the ketchup is."

"I threw up again this morning," he said. "I'm sorry, Mom. I don't know what's wrong with me." And suddenly he was crying.

Siripon sat down. She broke up his food into bite-sized pieces and held one out to him, sighing as he opened his mouth and waited.

She took him to Dr. Sutro. His office was in a complex of identical Spanish-style buildings surrounded by overwatered African lilies and ferns. Siripon had called home twice to talk to her parents, but she said nothing about taking Ben to see a child psychologist or anything about his sickness. On one hand, she didn't want to worry her parents. On the other hand, knowing them and their expectations, she didn't want her parents to think less of Ben.

Sutro was another tall doctor. He answered the door in khaki pants and a cerulean cardigan, Mr. Rogers–like, but Siripon had been around enough doctors to know he would be just as comfortable in a white coat. He squatted to get eye level with Ben and offered his broad hand. "It's a pleasure to meet you, Rattawut."

Ben offered his hand as if it were an injured bird. His eyelashes were still dewy from having thrown up in the corner of the parking lot.

"How are you today?" the doctor asked.

Ben shook his head. He stepped back, out of the shadow of the office awning, so his shoe sank into the soft, muddy lawn and left a little print.

"He shy one," Siripon said.

"I don't mind if you're shy, Rattawut. You don't have to say anything if you don't want to. But I hope we can get to know one another."

Inside the office, the floor was covered in a thick green rug that absorbed the sounds of the street traffic. The place smelled of old glue and something faintly spicy, tobacco or the lingering aroma of zucchini bread that had already been eaten.

"Rattawut, do you know why you're here today?" the doctor asked.

"Call him Ben, maybe," Siripon said. "We call him Ben."

"Ben? Rattawut? Well, they're both nice names. What would you like me to call you?" the doctor asked.

Still nothing from the boy. Siripon led him to the couch and told him to sit down. She had tried to explain that Sutro was a different kind of doctor. He wouldn't poke Ben or drown him in barium. He would just want to talk. Ben had been skeptical of this, and Siripon feared it was her fault, that her lack of faith in therapy had inadvertently rendered it useless. She tried to keep an open mind. There was no harm in trying.

"Here's what's nice about spending time here," the doctor said, undaunted. "While you're with me, you can do or say whatever you want. No matter what, I won't be mad. And your mom won't be mad either. Will you, Mrs. Chiwitchaiya?"

"No," Siripon said, smiling, unsure if the question had been rhetorical.

"Does that sound good?" the doctor continued. "Sometimes we just need to talk about things that are going on inside our heads. Here, do you want to see something?" He leaned in closer and pushed his nose sharply to the left with his index finger. As the skin stretched, a raised scar no longer than a quarter of an inch became visible beside his right nostril. "Do you know how I got that? One day, a boy just about your age swung out and cut my nose with his fingernail. Do you see it? But no one got mad, not even when that happened."

This seemed to bring Ben some relief. The doctor asked him to describe his family, and the boy listed Siripon, Kamron, and Manda as he counted them on his fingers.

"Isn't it nice to live with so many people who love you?"

Ben nodded. The faintest smile played on his lips, but he resisted it.

"Can you tell me how you've been feeling?"

Ben shook his head.

"Is there anything that has been happening that you want to get off your chest?"

He shook his head.

"Tell him. It okay," Siripon said in English. Then in Thai, "Just try it, son. Let's see if this can help."

"Rattawut, do you know what stress is?" the doctor asked. "Have you ever heard of that?"

Ben nodded his head. "It's like when you have to do something, and it's just waiting there for you to do it," he said.

"Or sometimes it feels like pressure," Sutro said, "like something building up inside of you."

Ben nodded.

"Ah, wait. I have some toys," the doctor said. He stepped to a closet and lifted out a canvas bag. He poured the contents onto the small table in front of them, where they rattled against the glass. It was a collection of miniatures: little chairs, little tables, little ovens, little beds.

"Look, this like what we have," Siripon said, holding up a small orange kitchen counter.

"But ours has two doors, and this only has one," Ben said.

"Tell me more about yours," the doctor tried.

"We put our phone on it. And there are phone books underneath."

"Shall we open the doors and see if this one has telephone books underneath?"

Ben hooked his finger into the tiny drawer handle and pulled it open. When he saw that there was nothing inside, his face dropped. He put the toy down and tucked his hands under his knees.

"Shall I go see what other toys I have?" the doctor asked. "What kind of games do you like to play?"

But Ben had decided not to speak anymore. Siripon sensed his resolve. He didn't even bother to shake his head or shrug his shoulders. For the rest of the hour, he sat in silence as the second hand of the clock ticked away. Siripon whispered her apologies on their way out. "He be less shy next time."

"Yes, well, perhaps you'd like to try someone else," the doctor said. "It's all about finding someone he'll be comfortable with. He wants someone he can talk to. I can tell he needs it."

"He talk to me," Siripon said, angry that she had gone through a dozen interviews only to have to start her search over again. Driving home, she thought back to her own childhood, to the arrival of her brother, Kiet. Siripon had been only seven, but she remembered the family gathered around the newborn baby. He was unwrapped and splayed on a courtyard bench like a prized cabbage. She hadn't been able to discern the problem then. She knew that boys were different from girls, and the thing that made them different was right there in front of her like a mushroom sprouted between Kiet's legs. It wasn't until nursing school that she examined a baby with undescended testicles and understood.

Villagers had stopped by the house when the news got out about Kiet's condition. They stood him on the table and pulled his pants down, coaxing him into filling cups and bowls for them. His urine was an aphrodisiac, they said. Old men drank it down, their eyes full of hope and mischief. In the evenings, when everyone had gone, their parents chuckled at how silly it all was. But at least Kiet's deformity was real. Ben's illness was less comical. Whatever was wrong was in his head, the result of him growing up in America.

It occurred to her that she was only making the situation worse by calling so much attention to it. They had planted the seed in Ben's mind that something was seriously wrong when maybe nothing was. Why did they make such a fuss about it? Children were able to move past these things.

From the produce drawer of the refrigerator, she freed two plastic bags, letting their contents tumble out onto the shelf. She folded each bag in half and then in half again lengthwise, then she rolled them into tight triangles, tucking in the ends so that they would not come undone.

"Put them in your pocket," she said. "If we're out somewhere and you need to throw up, just use the bags."

Ben inspected the neat bundles. He slid one into his right pocket and the other into his left. Throughout the week, Siripon didn't bring up the vomiting again except to replenish his supply of bags. Each time she did, Ben watched, his eyes and nose reaching just above the countertop where she worked. Soon he was able to fold the bags himself.

8

The fifth-grade classrooms of Warren Way Elementary School were perched higher up than the others. A dozen concrete steps led to the front doors, and through the back doors it was twenty steps down to the grove of magnolia trees that provided the only shady corner of the playground. On the first day of school, Ben walked the perimeter of the rooms looking for out-of-the-way corners he could reach in a hurry. His face was still tear-streaked from the morning's argument with his mother because he hadn't wanted to come. It was the same argument he had with Siripon every year.

As the start of the day approached, the commotion and laughter from the other children grew. Ben didn't join in; he didn't seek out the few friends he hadn't seen all summer or compare his clothes and school supplies with those of the other children. Instead, he went up the steps early, in through the door of his new classroom. Mr. Gorlund, his new teacher, whistled "Take Me Out to the Ball Game" as he pinned a border of corrugated cardboard around a bulletin board.

"You caught me unprepared," Gorlund said. "I usually like to wait for the first bell before I let everybody in." His tone was nice enough, businesslike to acknowledge that his students were the most senior at the school.

"My name is Ben. I wanted to let you know I throw up when I get nervous." The lines were well rehearsed, identical to the ones he had used with other teachers the last three years. The performance was a contrast to his first days back at school, when everyone assumed he was sick despite the doctor's note. Multiple times, the nurse had called his mother, waking her too early to demand she come and pick him up. Weeks had passed before they finally relented.

An expression of recognition passed across Gorlund's face. He offered his hand. He was the tallest teacher at Warren Way, and Ben only came up to the hips of his gray corduroys. "I have a seat for you right over here by the back door."

The news calmed Ben. He saw that all the seats had been preassigned, that they didn't follow any order he could discern. The others might not even know he had gotten special treatment.

When the rest of his classmates came in, he was seated with his hands tucked beneath his legs. Already, and even though he knew most of them, the presence of so many children made him insecure. Gorlund announced that they would go around the room to introduce themselves, and Ben imagined the attention focused on him, the other children scrutinizing everything about him. Spit pooled behind his lower lip and dribbled down his chin. He slipped out and made it all the way to the bottom of the stairs, to the shady grove of trees, before throwing up. A wall of overgrown ivy mobbed the chain-link fence, and he let out his breakfast into the tangle of vines, the fragments separating layer by layer as they fell.

Mr. Gorlund winked at him when he returned to his seat.

The first morning was always the hardest. Ben ran out four times before lunch: once before the introductions, once before the Pledge of Allegiance, once before it was his turn to read from the first chapter of the geology textbook, and once when they each were supposed to guess how many Jolly Ranchers were inside a jar. He wasn't always able to make it to the bottom of the stairs in time. He resorted to throwing up over the handrail from the top of the landing, so it rattled the dry leaves below. Through the crack in the door, he could see some of his classmates watching and trying to understand what was wrong with him. He believed nobody in the world knew as much about throwing up as he did, how simple it was to open your throat and let go. The other kids acted like it was such a big deal, like it was so gross. During recess, they poked their wormy fingers into their mouths and mocked him with that *gak, gak* sound. It didn't make any sense to Ben. Why would one part of your body violate the other when, really, everything just wanted to function as one, to help itself empty when it needed to? And afterward, things felt calm. Afterward, he felt as if he could accomplish anything. The habit had become a part of him long ago, his way of succeeding.

Fifth grade quickly distinguished itself from the lower grades. Mr. Gorlund focused on nutrition, the value of milk and liver because of all the vitamins they contained. Ben wasn't used to eating a slab of liver and drinking a glass of milk. He didn't know how the apportioned meals he colored in on his diagrams were supposed to align with what his family ate at home. He didn't want worksheets with plates divided into three compartments. He wanted meals served family-style, bites taken one spoonful at a time from shared bowls and plates.

During PE, Gorlund made the class crawl over the dome of colored bars and inch, hand over hand, across the fencing that lined the backstops. The others giggled, embarrassed at their teacher's unconventional exercises, but Ben quietly complied, not wanting to call attention to himself, even when his belt buckle got caught on a loose screw and he had to undo it while upside down. He had a natural talent for acrobatics. He excelled at running and jumping so long as no ball was involved. When it came to kickball and soccer, he couldn't predict where the objects would go after he struck them. He didn't understand the shorthand his classmates used during the sports games, terms they picked up from the pros. He heard the same things himself when his dad watched television, but Ben usually spent those hours fuming as he waited for the remote control to be turned back over to him—he never bothered to pay attention. Luckily, there were enough children like him, friends who played freeze tag or crawled around the jungle gym. Some of them didn't even ask him why he had to throw up all the time.

Gorlund told them about spelling bees. Leading up to the first competition, Ben waited to find out how the insects were involved, if they would be released when he wasn't expecting them. The students arranged themselves around the perimeter of the room. Ben took a position close to the door and watched as words were assigned to each of them in turn. "Agreement." "Scarcely." "Splutter." The rounds were simple enough; he only had to visualize the word on the page and then recite what he saw. As his turn approached, he ran to throw up and came back ready. "Temperature. *T-E-M-P-E-R-A-T-U-R-E.*" He worried that the others might think he was cheating, that they might accuse him of having a vocabulary list hidden outside the door. He made a show of wiping the spit from his mouth to convince them that he was sincere. "Ambulance. *A-M-B-U-L-A-N-C-E.*"

The words grew more challenging, but the students had a chance to study them all beforehand. When they made mistakes, they were asked to return to their seats. The remaining competitors dwindled; Mr. Gorlund whistled for them to gather at the front of the room. He wrote their names over their heads, the chalk dust falling into their hair like donations of dandruff. If Ben wanted to run out now, he would have to weave through the narrow paths between pushed-out chairs and lolling backpacks. There was the threat of him tripping, losing control in the middle of everyone. He bit his thumbnail, unable to stop, even when saliva dripped down his wrist. He thought of the plastic bags secure in his pockets—he had switched from produce bags to Glad-Locks, even though his mother complained that they were too expensive. He liked the assuredness of the yellow-and-blue-make-green seal, the tests they demonstrated with soup on television commercials. He hardly ever used them, preferring to run outside, but they still gave him a sense of security. When the next word came, he took deep breaths to get through it. "Rhinoceros. *R-H-I-N-O-C-E-R-O-S.*" And he won, though he didn't understand how. How could anyone *not* win when all the words were provided for you and all you had to do was remember them?

Weeks later, after multiple spelling bees, Mr. Gorlund called Ben up to his desk. He flicked a formal letter out to him with a playful whistle. The school was selecting students for the district competition, he explained. Ben would be one of Mr. Gorlund's representatives.

Manda was overjoyed when Ben announced the news to the family. Everyone was happy, but only Manda raised her fists into the air and shouted. "I'm going to write home about this," she said. "Our little genius has truly mastered the language if he can keep up with the Americans."

"He *is* American," Siripon said, not bothering to look up from her cutting board. She sliced the rind thinly off a pineapple and then began to remove its eyes with precise diagonal cuts, leaving a spiral pattern in the flesh. She had explained it to Ben before: Anyone who was born in the country was American. But Ben understood what Manda meant. Even if he was born here, he wasn't like his friends. So much of school was foreign to him: the liver and milk, the spelling bees, the Christmas music, the presidents' holidays. For Valentine's Day, someone had brought in a cherry pie that everyone else said was delicious, but to Ben it tasted like hot medicine. In class, teachers asked him questions, and he replied with answers he knew were not quite right but matched how everyone else answered. According to Mr. Gorlund, cheetahs ran seventy miles per hour. That was American thinking. When Ben was at home, with Manda, he could talk about how some cheetahs must run faster and some must run slower. Some probably twisted their ankles during a hunt and couldn't run at all, at least for a while. Others probably played dirty and let the rest of the cheetahs catch the prey before they swooped in for leftovers. This was Thai thinking—honest thinking with all its complications. The teachers never discussed honest thinking; they fit everything into neat compartments.

The students gathered in the cafeteria among its beige linoleum and collapsible tables, its gloomy curtains dragging their black hems across the stage. The place smelled to Ben like canned green beans and Wonder Bread—more American things. He wished his mother would serve them at home, pack him a ham sandwich for lunch instead of a Tupperware container of rice and chicken. He wished he could look like his classmates with their pale skin that matched their light hair. Stepping onto the stage with the other competitors, he shuffled to align his toes exactly with the closest edge of masking tape that had been placed on the floor. Bonnie Stewart sauntered by. She stuck her finger in her throat, pretended to gag, and then called him "Puke Boy." Ben made no response. It was a name he heard a lot, and he guessed it should bother him, that he should be hurt by it. But it didn't hurt. Ben didn't associate himself with "Puke Boy." It was only a costume someone else forced him into, something he could take off at the end of each day as he walked home from school.

Besides, he didn't think of what he did as "puking." That was such an ugly word, sticky and mucosal. "Puke" and "barf" and "upchuck" and "ralph"—none of these words described what he did. Neither did the nice, clean words the doctors used: "vomit" or "regurgitate." In Thai, there were two choices. The crude word was "uok," which sounded to Ben like the start of the act, the initial constriction of his throat, but not the whole thing. The more formal word was "ajean," which was closer but still not right. It made him think of kanom jean, the thin rice noodles that his mother swirled in water and then bunched into neat loops that she arranged on the plate like links in a chain. No, only "throwing up" described what he did, the act of ridding his body of the heaviness that made him feel so trapped all the time. He threw up to feel better. He threw up to survive.

The teachers sat in a row in front of the stage while the students who had not been selected to compete giggled behind them. Most of the children didn't care about the competition and weren't even watching, which was a relief to Ben as he awaited his first turn. Mrs. MacGregor, one of the other fifth-grade teachers, explained in her soft Southern accent that the top two winners would compete next month at Aster Reid against the other students from the district, strangers and their strange parents watching.

"And finally, we remind you to be careful. Rushing can lead to mistakes," Mrs. MacGregor said. "Miss Anderson, we will start with you. Your first word is 'chimera.'"

The progress in this spelling bee was slower than the smaller competitions he was familiar with. He watched impatiently as Mrs. MacGregor congratulated Eric Bodey for correctly spelling "punctuate."

"Mr. Chew-it-cha-ya," she said, each syllable imbued with a new strangeness. He thought of the contest, the simple recitation of words he knew with certainty. There had to be a twist, a reason why the other children thought it was so difficult.

"Mr. Chiwitchaiya, your word is 'jungle,'" Mrs. MacGregor said. It was a simple word. But as he prepared to speak, an image came to him. He saw Bonnie Stewart with her finger in her throat, and perhaps the hundreds of other people at other schools waiting to put their fingers in their throats. They would know him only as "Puke Boy," no matter how many words he spelled correctly. He didn't want any of it.

"Jungle. *J-U-N-G-E-L.* Jungle," Ben said, and without waiting to be told he was wrong, he went to sit down among the others on the crowded lunch tables.

When he got home, he ran to the bathroom, even before he could tell his family what happened. For a moment, he wished he had tried to win the competition. He would've told his dad first, and then his aunt, who would maybe have cooked him a special dinner. He delighted in the idea of saving the good news for his mom until last, until everyone else already knew it so that his joy of sharing it with her would be amplified by all the people around them.

But he hadn't won.

He had given up.

He sat back on his haunches, grateful for the bathroom. It felt like the cleanest room in the house, welcoming him with its white tiles, its soaps, its gleaming fixtures. Through a small, square skylight, the sun streamed in and bounced off the mirrors and the shower door. The clear pool of water in the toilet bowl was ready to accept whatever he had to offer it. This was the secret passageway for his anxiety, his escape to the sea. He *was* the world's expert. He could warn people about the dangers of throwing up a stomach full of water, the way the pressure from his diaphragm made it shoot past his mouth and go out through his nose. If it was morning, sometimes there was nothing but the dribble of bitter yellow bile and dry heaves. They came out of him like growls, and with each convulsion he felt sharp pains like wires poking into his rib cage. There was the sickly cold feeling of throwing up ice cream, or the pain of throwing up a peanut butter sandwich, when the lumps of bread glued together by the peanut butter came out as logs that stretched the walls of his throat. That came with something he would never admit—that when these lumps pushed up, he felt as if his body were built in reverse, as if his mouth were actually the other end, and he felt like the most disgusting boy who had ever lived.

Today, it was bits of ground chicken, pinkened by the chili paste he had eaten with it. After his initial purge, he locked the door. He pushed the rugs off to the side to reveal the cool tile, and he lay his body on the coolness as he had for the last three years. He did not worry about whether or not this was normal behavior. In the bathroom, he was alone and unjudged. There was no one to intrude on him, no one to question him. There was no time. His mother knocked on the door, and it was his decision whether or not he would let her in. This afternoon, he heard the fatigue in her voice, the frustration. She was his favorite person in the world, even though all of the guests who visited the house said that Ben was "stuck" on his aunt Manda. Siripon was his favorite, but he could not tell her for fear of hurting his aunt.

"What happened this time?" Siripon asked.

He didn't answer. He waited to see if she stayed on the other side of the door. When he finally did open it, her forehead was wrinkled. Still, she held two Chicken in a Biskits in her hand. He ate them slowly, the two crackers pressed together, the wavy edges aligned. This would be a comfort to him for years afterward, when he faced the stresses of adult life on his own. He'd keep a box of the pale crackers in the cupboard of every place he lived, and when it all became too much, he'd take it down and eat them, two crackers at a time, a little pair, like a mother and a son.

Sawan

1

Gimjaa watched her grandsons huddled under the new light switch. They giggled in terror, wanting to turn the lights on but afraid of getting electrocuted.

"I told you not to take so long bathing. Now it's too dark to match your pajamas," Tassanee said with an air of haughtiness. She came to help, drying her hands meticulously on her apron. She had been the one to warn them about the dangers of the current coursing through the Phet Buri house.

"Scary, scary, scary," the children chanted.

"Don't make me nervous," Tassanee said, laughing and covering her face with her hands so that her jagged teeth wouldn't show.

"And why did you install the lights at all?" Gimjaa rasped. Her face was upturned to keep her red chaw of tobacco and betel paste from dripping out of her mouth. The lights were senseless, a foray into the future by people who had no need to venture there. The family was fine without ceiling lights, without the washing machine, without the television—luxuries paid for by her daughters in the Outer Country. They all would have been better off if Siripon and Manda had never left. Gimjaa hoisted herself up and flipped the switch. The rods winked on, illuminating the boys, naked and wet. Grateful, they went about their routine, spared for another night.

Lately, each of Gimjaa's days passed like a puff of steam. It was morning; it was dusk. It was morning; it was dusk. She felt the strangeness of the family's new technology as if her body were growing foreign limbs.

Here, the lights like a glaring new scalp. There, the washing machine like a knotted stomach. And the original pieces of her—her eldest sons and daughters—were lost in the past. Siripon and Manda had been gone for several years now. The boys had been gone for a lifetime.

Gimjaa's grandsons turned on the television and flopped onto their bellies, entranced by the attractive news anchors reporting on the royal family's visit to France. Even when Tassanee placed a bowl of peeled grapes beside them, they ate without acknowledging the treat, their hands floating blindly to the bowls, where they grasped the translucent globes and sucked them into their mouths.

"Lie that close to the screen and you'll go blind," Gimjaa warned, knowing the boys would ignore her. They were ten and six, her dead sons reborn a generation later—sometimes she believed this. They renewed her desire to live at a time when she did not much care about herself. Seeing their vitality, their stubborn drive to grow, she felt responsible to help them. She knew already that Paitoon would never amount to anything. He would find an unattractive sweetheart at a young age and forget about his career. Niran was cleverer. He would get into trouble as a teenager—just as Manda had—but once he got that penchant for mischief out of him, he would become shrewd and successful. Her eldest grandson, Ben, was eleven now, though she had never met him. Her daughters said he was a shy boy, smart but quiet, and Gimjaa assumed by the description that she wouldn't like him.

"We haven't heard from them in too long," she complained to her husband.

Pradit moaned. Another asthma attack had come. He sat at the dining platform with his forehead balanced on his stacked fists. He didn't need to ask to know his wife was talking about their daughters. She brought them up every few days as if they were the subject of a long conversation that never ended.

"They used to write to us every month. Now it's as if their fingers have been lopped off," Gimjaa said.

Pradit grunted. Tassanee placed a bowl of grapes beside him, and he sat upright to eat them. He and the grandsons all had a peculiar way of chewing, using only their front teeth, so that their faces puckered and elongated.

"Are the grapes sour?" Gimjaa asked. Seeing that her daughter was preparing to bring her some, she shook her head. "*You* have them. What does an old lady need grapes for?" She was content to see the children clean and powdered after their baths. She was content to be with her husband, who moaned gently at his perch. After thoughtfully eating his grapes, he found the nearest towel and went to take his own bath.

I should guilt those daughters of ours, Gimjaa thought. *I should tell them if they don't come and visit soon, they will miss the chance to see their parents alive.* It was an exaggeration. She had diabetes, but she managed it without needing anyone to give her injections. Her arthritis was tolerable, especially in the dry season, and though she could not straighten her fingers to their full length anymore, they were still functional enough to use a mortar and pestle, to apply talcum powder on her skin, to swat at mosquitos.

In the bathroom, water splashed against tiles. Gimjaa counted eight bowlfuls poured over her husband's body. She imagined his stooped tattooed back and withering legs beside the water basin, his downward-pointed nose and lavender-colored lower lip that was always pushed out, his penis that hung down limp. She believed Pradit deserved a peaceful life after serving all those years in the military and then working as a delivery man to support the family. He tolerated his asthma without complaint. He was faithful. He was dignified. He was a good man.

Beyond the window the sky was a gray drape behind the black network of tangled branches. The contrast was hard to discern with all the light that reflected against the glass. She drew her attention back into the room, to the image of herself sitting on the floor and the empty seat on the platform where her husband had been a moment ago. She would not bathe—she was too tired. She would go to bed when Pradit did, follow him again. They would lie side by side, their hands lightly touching for another brief night.

2

Gimjaa tried to wake Pradit for their morning meal, but he didn't respond. He lay face up with his hands resting on the softness of his belly. His feet jutted out from the bottom of the thin blanket. "Be lazy, then," she complained, crawling out on her own and eating two bowls of porridge with candied pork. Then, handing her empty bowl to Tassanee to be washed, she had a revelation. "Go and look in on your father," she said. "He might be dead today."

Tassanee rushed into her parents' darkened room. She shook her father, and when he didn't respond, she screamed for her husband. Udom went in after her, quickly ducking under the mosquito net to where the still body lay. He pressed his fingers against Pradit's carotid artery and quickly came to the same conclusion.

The news of Pradit's passing traveled through the neighboring households, then from the village to the city—a doctor was dispatched to examine the body. The news went from Phet Buri to America, where the household in Los Angeles was awakened in the middle of the night by a telephone call. Siripon got up, irritated and tired. She heard her brother's crying and coaxed him to calm down long enough to explain what happened. Her heart hollowed. Her first thought was that Pradit had not been proud of her. She had worked so hard for the family her entire life; she had served them. And yet she had never been good enough. The sorrow came—sorrow for her father; sorrow for her mother, left behind; sorrow for Tassanee and Kiet, forced to handle the arrangements. The distance had frustrated her since the day she arrived in Los Angeles, but in that moment, it felt immense and impossible. She walked back to bed to tell Kamron the news. He had been snoring loudly and was startled awake by her voice.

"Already?" he said. Pradit had been only sixty-eight. He was the first of their parents to pass away, though Kamron couldn't be certain of his father's whereabouts. Kamron grew sober. He wrapped his arms around Siripon, but she didn't close her eyes.

The next morning, her face puffy from lack of sleep, Siripon decided she needed to iron. She brought out a pile of her uniforms and pulled the first of her shirts over the padded board. She began with the front panels, careful to flatten even the small patches between buttons. She ironed the back and the sleeves, pressing to sharpen the creases. She was caught up in her work when Manda came out of her room.

"He's gone," Siripon said without looking up. She refused to let herself cry.

"Who? What are you talking about?" Manda asked.

"Our dad. Who else?" Siripon said.

Manda remembered the previous night's ringing telephone, surprised she hadn't guessed that it was a call from Thailand. Sadness overtook her as quickly as the realization did, so that her face gave the impression of crumpling in her hands. She ran to her bedroom and slammed the door. Her sister had been so blunt. She was supposed to be gentle and sweet, but she had a way of shattering Manda. Ben knocked. He tiptoed into the room, his hand lingering on the doorknob, unsure. She pulled him into her, trying to find comfort in their mutual pain.

But the boy didn't understand.

"What does it feel like to die?" he asked. "He was breathing one second, and then the next second he wasn't? And then his heart stopped? Do you die all at once, or do your arms and legs die first? And then your body, and then your brain?"

Manda was annoyed by his insensitivity. She didn't understand how he could be so cold—he was as cold as his mother. No, she wouldn't get angry at him. She understood that Ben had never met his grandfather, nor had he met death. "You do not have a grandfather anymore. He is gone forever," she said, hoping to arouse his sadness. She brought his head to her chest, held him, and soon he began to cry.

They interred Pradit's body for a year. Manda wore black mourning clothes every day, even at work, careful to adorn her outfits with patterned scarves and bright jewelry to avoid looking too glum for the customers. Siripon wore her usual uniforms to the hospital, reserving her black clothes for days at the temple. The family made regular offerings to ensure Pradit's journey to Sawan. Their friends joined them, arriving with donations and trays of Pradit's favorite foods. They mourned in black and in white. They mourned for him and for themselves, realizing they might soon lose their own parents, and they would not be home when it happened.

The year passed with frequent calls to Phet Buri. The family exchanged photos of their temple visits, relatives posing with grim faces, eyes that had recently held tears. The siblings spoke quietly of their mother, wondering how long she would survive now that her husband was gone. Manda's pain became more acute. She knew she had been a disappointment to her father, a lost cause for too long. What had he thought of her on his last night alive, knowing she had not established her own family or career? What did he think of her now? This was how Pradit haunted all his children. They questioned what he thought of them and believed they had never done enough to please him. They imagined him standing in front of them, his back rigid, his face stern, judging.

3

They were on the last bus to arrive at the Phet Buri station—it was almost midnight. Two days had passed since they left Los Angeles, the hours lost somewhere among the shifting time zones. By the station window, Siripon stood, arms crossed and expectant, waiting for Tassanee and Kiet. When their dusty pickup pulled in, she noticed, even at a distance, how much her siblings had changed. The four of them were not young anymore. They had inherited this life.

The reunion was noisy. They embraced one another, examined one another, teased one another, their happiness tempered only by the knowledge that Pradit was gone. It was another reminder that what was left behind was their responsibility. The father had died. The mother had lived. The Thrakoontong family was taking on its next reincarnation.

She looked out at the uneven road as they made their way to the house. The air swept over her, carrying the sweet burnt smell of the hay fires that kept mosquitos away from the cattle. The landscape was dense with forest growth that occasionally opened to slate-colored ponds still in the moonlight, houses darkened to silhouettes. The truck slowed at the familiar corner. Tassanee honked the horn, and footsteps approached; Udom's dark hands slid open the gate to reveal the courtyard. Here was the place where Siripon had so often been overworked. Manda had constantly angered Pradit, but he was always quick to forgive her. Tassanee and Kiet had been treated more leniently because they were younger. Only Siripon had been made to do everything. She had obeyed. She had served.

They found their mother slumped inside the newly enclosed section of the courtyard. She sat bleary-eyed, as if she was lost in time, coming out of her trance only when they were upon her, when their voices called out to her and their hands touched her. Then her eyes glinted, though she was slow to smile. She greeted them sadly. She embraced them with the knowledge that her husband was gone.

"We are here now," Manda said, embracing Gimjaa. She held her mother's face and ran her thumbs over the wrinkles that covered it.

Siripon bowed before hugging Gimjaa. She presented Ben, pushing him into her mother's arms. A mission had been accomplished by bringing the two together. It was as if her only job had been to deliver Ben like a precious stone carried in from the mines. The first son lived. The first son was not a ghost.

Exhausted from travel, they reminded themselves that they would have more time to talk the following day. They filled their stomachs with bowls of rice and curry, washed their faces, and settled among the empty beds for the night. In the morning, the siblings gathered in the kitchen to discuss practical matters before the others awoke. Pradit's cremation would be a large and expensive affair. It would last three days, drawing people in from across the district, friends and distant relatives, veterans and their memories of war.

"You didn't cash the money order I sent you," Siripon said. "You're taking charge of all the preparations; there's no need for you to pay for them too."

"I know the distance can't be helped, Pi Noi," Tassanee said in a weary voice. "As for the cost, I'd never beg you for more money."

"Begging! What a choice of words. Nobody said you were begging. It's just easier for us to save in the Outer Country." Siripon knew she was calling attention to her sister. She immediately regretted it. The trip alone had used up too much of Manda's savings. Along with the plane ticket, she had insisted on purchasing gifts for the family: Levi's jeans and Folgers instant coffee for the siblings and cousins, tennis shoes for their mother, video games for their nephews. And when the ceremony was complete, they would have to donate more money to the monks.

Siripon had already decided she would carry the brunt of the financial burden. She didn't complain.

The rest of the day was spent getting settled. Ben was a stranger to life in Thailand, and Siripon took it upon herself to show him how to brush his teeth with water from the rain basins and how to bathe and use the squat toilet. She gave her mother a thorough physical exam, worried after hearing that Gimjaa had not been sleeping since her husband's death. She had gained weight, and her diet was terrible, according to the others. Siripon blamed herself for this, just as she blamed herself for her father's death. She was a nurse, and yet she had not looked after their health well enough; she had not made sure they were taking care of themselves.

For lunch, she constructed a salad out of greens she bought at the local market. It was nothing like what they would find in America, but she had to make do. She placed it in front of Gimjaa, telling her that she had to finish it before she could eat anything else. Her mother wouldn't have it. In protest, she pushed the bowl off the table, the leaves falling around her feet. Siripon shook her head. With only two weeks in the country, she didn't know if she would be able to change her mother's habits. She washed the dishes and helped Gimjaa lie down on the cool linoleum. She washed all of the bedding and shook out the mosquito nets. She scrubbed the floors upstairs and downstairs. She swept the courtyard. When she was done, she insisted that Tassanee drive her to the bank so she could arrange for a money transfer. Then, on the way back, she stopped at the market to purchase enough food to sustain them until they left for the temple the next day. Walking the narrow, bustling aisles, her mouth watered from all the scents that surrounded her, all the things she had been missing. But she wouldn't let herself overindulge. It was not why they had come. Evening arrived, and she felt the familiar heat rising from underneath the collar of her shirt. Once again, she had done all she could to help.

4

Manda glimpsed the crematorium, stark white against the darkness of the mangrove trees. Its steep gables and golden spires could have passed for ordinary temple structures, but a chimney, tall and narrow, stood out like the tail of death that hadn't been tucked away.

In the courtyard, men on ladders were hanging a banner with Pradit's name and portrait over the entrance. Workers in the crematorium building dusted benches and arranged them in rows facing the dais. Others, mostly women, prepared food in the kitchen and out on the deck beyond the kitchen entrance. Their work filled the place with smells and noises, nourishment for the people who were expected to come. Manda was proud that her father should command such respect. He had always been humble about his accomplishments in the military. She had heard of them only in fragments, heroic stories from fellow soldiers revealed before Pradit was able to stop them.

The family joined the procession moving down to the mausoleum. Pallbearers slid the coffin out from its yearlong bed, the wooden panels beginning to warp at the seams, though they still hid their contents. It was carried solemnly back, accompanied by two rows of monks walking ahead of them, their hands together as they chanted. Manda felt Pradit's ghost hovering above them like a shadow of a dark bird. She wanted to avoid the dead—her father, her brothers, Jaroen—but she did not know when or in what form they might appear. She cast her eyes downward; she quieted her thoughts to keep from offending them with her fear.

They returned to the crematorium. The other family members placed their hands together and bowed as the coffin was carried into a small building closed off from view. They dispersed to help with the remaining preparations, but Manda stayed behind, compelled by the need to witness. She followed the monks inside, stopping just before the door to the room where her father had been delivered. The chanting continued, the low drone of a dozen monks moving in unison, phrases broken only when one monk paused for breath before joining in again. The soft thump of bare feet moving. The sound of wood scraping. There was a faint odor of dirt so subtle it seemed to be beside her at first—a coating of dust that had collected on her clothes during the drive up the windy mountain road. But the smell grew stronger until she realized it was her father's corpse, finally exposed. The image of him as she had known it disappeared. In its place was a gray and rotting body, a face sunken and hollowed, its cavities serving as nests for the decomposers. It was a thing she couldn't love. She hurried out in search of air, in search of distance, but there too she was disturbed by her surroundings: her mother sitting with a hopeless expression on her face, the villagers thin and sweating, the meat roasting on skewers—all of it was mortality and death.

"Please don't frighten me," she pleaded. "I respect you, but I don't need to see you."

She had been worried about encountering her father's ghost since she learned of his death. Even on that first day, when the pain of the loss was still sharp, she couldn't tamp down the fear that he would visit her. That night, she coaxed Ben into her bed, crammed him in beside her on the small twin mattress. His body had been hot, a furnace that intruded on sleep, but she preferred that to being alone.

She went in search of Ben, needing the reassurance that he was unharmed in the face of so much decay. He paced in front of the cremation chamber. Beside him a group of musicians were preparing their instruments for the long performance.

"Are you being taken care of, or has everyone abandoned you?" Manda wrapped her arms around him, pulling him in closer to her.

"What's this door?" Ben asked. Only the front face of the chamber was visible, the rest of the structure set behind the wall. A smoke stain trailed up from a small arched door in its center. Within the door, there was a smaller panel that had been left open. Ben bent forward to look inside. He leaned in so close he touched the metal with his nose, marking himself with a black smudge of soot.

"You should be playing with your cousins," Manda said. "We brought you all this way to meet them."

"Are they really going to light Kun Tha's body on fire?"

"It's our way of paying respect to him," Manda said. "We will cremate the remains and collect the ashes."

"Aren't you supposed to bury people in cemeteries?"

"And why should we do it the foreigners' way when we have our own customs here?"

"I'd rather lie down in the grass than get lit on fire."

"Come, now. Where are your cousins?"

"They don't like me."

"You're not allowed to say they don't like you when you haven't even let them get to know you. Now, follow me. Stop making a fuss." She listened for the sound of children. The laughter and screams drifted toward her from a distance—they were more signs of life and vitality. She spotted the group beyond the frontage road, eight children passing a soccer ball back and forth, Niran and Paitoon among them. They were lost in their game, seemingly oblivious to what was happening nearby.

"Go on, join in. You're only in Thailand for two weeks, and then you might not see them again for years to come."

"I don't care," Ben said. But even as he shook his head, he meandered over to his cousins. The children's bodies looked like lava rock as they raced across the clearing. They wore mismatched clothes, T-shirts that once boasted bright colors and bold logos but had now been worn and washed too many times. Meanwhile, Ben's skin was pale from too many hours inside. He had picked out his own outfit for the ceremony, a white polo and long khaki pants—he had brought only his best clothes for the trip. Manda was concerned that the long pants would be too warm, but they had served him well. His exposed arms were covered by hundreds of mosquito bites, overlapping red bumps that felt hard to the touch, but his legs had been spared. The children goaded Ben into trying to steal the ball. He made a few half-hearted swipes, but he kept his hands in his pockets, his face glum. The boy was different, lacking the assuredness that other children possessed. Manda was tempted to blame it on fear, but what did he have to be afraid of? The shadow of death passed over her again. She looked up at it. "If you're listening, Father, you should teach Ben how to be a proper boy. That's the one thing I can't do for him."

The only response was the blazing heat of the day.

In the afternoon, the guests arrived, many of them Pradit's age, soldiers who had served beside him, wives and children who joined in to honor him. They made their offerings of incense and money to the monks. They bowed to Gimjaa. They bowed again when the urn carrying Pradit's bones appeared. It was a heavy clay vessel, half the height of the men carrying it. They moved along a path of banana leaves to a pedestal. The orange drape that covered the urn was pulled away to reveal the bones inside. They had been cleaned. They were white and smooth, and they were arranged to look as if Pradit were crouching inside with his arms and legs crossed. The guests poured vials of perfumed water over the bones. "To bathe him," they said. Then the urn was moved into the crematorium. Monks ran sai sin string through its handles and wove it between their hands. The spool of string was passed down to the people who sat before the dais, each one holding it between their fingers. Everyone chanted together. The patient cadence of drums began. It was joined by the clack of the woodblock and the soft clang of finger cymbals. Notes on the xylophones climbed and descended.

"They're going to keep playing for three whole days?" Ben asked.

"We have to keep your grandfather's spirit entertained," Manda said. "We have to help him along his journey to Sawan."

"And if he doesn't go to Sawan, then he'll go to Narok?"

"Narok is only where bad people go, ja. We don't have to worry about Narok."

He had so many questions. He wanted to know it all. The bones were the only glimpse of his grandfather he had ever gotten, and so he couldn't imagine them covered in flesh; he couldn't imagine them needing sympathy.

"The other kids say Kun Tha had to be buried for a year so he wouldn't dance in the fire."

"Don't listen to them. That's nothing but an ugly superstition," she snapped. But there was truth to it; bodies freshly dead had been known to twitch in the flames, a mechanism of muscles still tightened. As a child, the thought of sitting up during her own cremation—suffering when she should be at peace—had been one of Manda's biggest fears.

"If everyone is going to stay awake, I want to stay awake too," Ben said.

"We'll all sleep when we can. You have to get some rest so you can help us tomorrow."

"I want to help tonight. What can I do?"

"We'll see tomorrow."

The evening drew on with a patient, reverent stride. Ten o'clock and the children and the elderly retired home, leaving with hired drivers who shuttled vans back and forth along the spidery roads. Later, well after midnight, the other guests left, some apologizing for not being able to return the next day. Manda tried to convince Ben to go back with his cousins, but he refused. Instead, she and Siripon prepared a bed for him on the floor of the temple hall, and Manda sat with him until he fell asleep. When she heard his heavy breathing, she rose and found her sisters washing dishes in the kitchen. Their arms moved wearily among the wet things. Beyond the doorway, others were cleaning larger pots and pans beneath spigots that ran water down into the dirt. Everyone seemed exhausted, and only the first day had passed.

"The dead manage to kill the living," Manda said.

"Don't joke like that, Pi Neung," Tassanee said. "I keep sensing him around us—watching and listening. Wait and see; if you're not careful, he'll appear."

"I'm not scared," Manda lied.

"It's a shame one of the boys didn't become a monk's apprentice," Tassanee said. "Udom insisted ours were too young." She spoke of a sacrifice in which a male relative of the deceased followed the way of the monk for three days to honor the dead.

"They're all too young," Siripon said. "You can't force them to do a thing like that. Shaving their heads, meditating all day, fasting—it's too much. Besides, what about Kiet?"

"You know how he is. He won't even entertain the idea."

"Then we'll have to do without."

"I'm just saying it would have been nice." Tassanee's voice had grown more pitiful. She paced around the room, picking up objects and then plopping them down in irritation. "I feel like we're not doing our duty."

"We're doing the best we can," Siripon replied. "Do you want us to sprout our own penises for the occasion?"

Manda felt a sense of disappointment over not having children of her own. She was the eldest, and yet she could offer no help. She glanced over at their mother, who sat quietly at the end of the table, close to dozing off. Gimjaa's gaze fell onto the pattern of the tablecloth as if she was hypnotized by it.

"This entire family is disgraceful," Tassanee said, unwilling to drop the subject. "Three boys and one grown man, and no one has the guts." And though her voice had been sarcastic to begin with, she was suddenly crying.

"Ja, what has gotten into you? Why is this thing so important?" Manda asked.

"And why shouldn't it be? Our father is dead, and no one cares!" She couldn't be consoled. She dropped a pile of dirty dishes from their evening meal into the sink. "No one cares! No one gives a damn!"

The others started to retort, but it was Ben's thin voice that caught their attention. He squinted in the bright light. "What is everyone talking about? I want to help."

"Son, you should be sleeping by now," Siripon chided. She tried to lead him back toward his makeshift bed, but he slipped out of her grip and took Manda's hand.

"Ben, we need someone to volunteer in a special way for your grandfather," Tassanee explained. Her eyes had grown bright and hopeful. "Do you really want to help?"

"Oy, stop it. You'll only confuse him," Siripon insisted. "He doesn't know what you're asking of him."

"Yes, I do," Ben said. "I want to help Kun Tha go to Sawan. I'm ready."

For a moment, Manda said nothing. But she realized if she was strategic, everyone would see the influence she had on the boy's upbringing. They would see that she had instilled in him the proper values. "And why shouldn't he do it?" she said. "If he wants to—if it's in his heart, then we can't deny him. Besides, he is surrounded by loved ones here. We will all be around to help him."

Manda took Ben by the shoulders. "Are you sure you want to do this? You'll have to spend the night in the back room without us. But if you do it—if you do this, your auntie will be so proud of you." He was still malleable. His reasons for volunteering didn't reach beyond his desire to feel useful. He nodded purposefully, glancing around the room for approval. He reddened when Tassanee clapped her hands.

"Think of how excited everyone will be," she said, smiling and revealing her crooked teeth. "Everyone will say what a wonderful grandson you are."

She rushed outside to ask the workers if the monks were awake. She wanted to know if she might disturb them for only a moment to tell them the good news. Gimjaa had perked up. She placed her hands on Ben's face and looked into his sleepy eyes. Only Siripon seemed to be upset. She sighed as she ran her fingers through her hair.

5

The next morning, Siripon bathed and changed and stopped in the crematorium to bow before her father's bones. A photo of him—his death photo—had been placed in front of the urn. In it, he was dressed in a white suit and standing in front of the military base where he had once trained. His face was grim and taut, just as Siripon remembered it.

Most of the guests had yet to return, and the rest of the place was quiet. The musicians played softly. Florists at the dais refreshed garlands of white roses below smaller chains of jasmine and crown flowers. Siripon crossed over to the eastern rooms and found her mother rising from her mat.

"How are your legs today?" Siripon asked.

"Don't worry about this dead wood, Noi. We have other things to attend to." She tugged her sarong away from the mat, revealing a small puddle that darkened the material where she lay. She had wet herself in the night.

They went to the bathroom, and Siripon bathed her mother. She surveyed the browned patches of skin around Gimjaa's thighs, her cracked heels, the burdened way she carried her weight. "You have to look after yourself, Mother. Promise me."

"Your boy is closer to Manda than he is to you."

Siripon didn't respond. She had expected the criticism to come eventually. She bent to powder her mother's legs before pulling her sarong up around her.

"He's quiet like you, though," Gimjaa said.

"Yes, I told you he was." She was unsure if her mother's remark had been a compliment, but it gave her a sense of satisfaction. At least Gimjaa saw something Ben inherited that Manda couldn't take credit for.

"And how is your marriage? I hear Yai drinks every night."

"He's a good husband and provider," Siripon said. "He holds a job and takes care of things around the house if they need fixing."

"He seems angry."

"Who told you that?"

"No one had to tell me. I can see it."

"Forgive me, but you're wrong, Mother. He's a decent man. I don't know how someone could have convinced you otherwise." As the words came out, Siripon questioned whether she was lying. She and Kamron had argued too many times recently, especially after Ben had gotten sick. The shouting matches always left her feeling tattered. But at times like this, when she had other things on her mind, he stayed quiet; he refrained from adding to her stress.

She led Gimjaa to the kitchen in search of food. Tassanee was preparing a large pot of porridge, and Ben sat quietly at the table. His hair was carefully combed, and he was neatly dressed. Siripon assumed he had gotten himself ready without anyone's help. She was proud of him, but she was concerned too. She considered trying again to change his mind about the ceremony, if for no other reason than to dispel her nagging feeling that he had inherited another trait from her: the need to constantly please others.

"Did you sleep?" she asked him.

"I dreamt about the music all night," Ben said. "It was like I was in a circus with clowns and acrobats and bears that did these dances."

Siripon was tempted to ask if he was troubled by it. The music had frightened her, especially in the middle of the night, when it took on a tireless quality. She was used to the night shift at the hospital, but here the late activity made her anxious. She examined her son's mosquito bites, content that they were healing. Other members of the family drifted in: Manda and Kamron, Udom with the boys. Tassanee placed the steaming pot on the table.

"I'm starving," Niran said, peering down into it. "I could eat that whole thing."

"Greedy little monsters," their mother said. "Why can't you behave yourself like Ben over here? Look how patiently he waits. And on top of that, he's willing to become a monk's apprentice, unlike either of you."

"Maybe he doesn't eat because he knows he'll just puke it up again," Paitoon said.

"Why would you say a thing like that?"

"He did it yesterday. On the field while we were playing ball. He puked up everything."

The boys made gagging sounds, and Ben blushed. He offered Siripon a single nod to confirm that his cousins were telling the truth. She hadn't told anyone in Phet Buri about what was happening. She didn't want to admit that she was unable to help her son.

"Well, maybe he wasn't feeling well," Tassanee offered. She pressed her wet hands against Ben's cheeks. "Are you better now? Do you need some medicine?"

"No, thank you."

"I don't want to eat next to him," Niran said. "Maybe we can take our food outside—"

"Boys! How can you treat your cousin like that? Don't tell me you've never thrown up. I remember cleaning plenty of your disgusting messes. Now, sit! Go on either side of him, and don't let me hear another word about it."

Siripon felt sorry for her son, but where else could he turn if not to his family? At some point, she would have to ignore the slights against her boy; she would have to let him fight his own battles.

It was not all bad. The news of Ben's sacrifice spread among the guests who had recently arrived. They stopped in to praise him, complimented him on his devotion. They even went so far as to say how good it was that he grew up in America so he could develop into such a respectable young man.

There were other comments. Some of the guests said that Manda talked Ben into taking the oath of the monks. Siripon shook her head and laughed. She tried not to entertain such ideas. But by the end of the morning, she was tired of hearing them. She thought back to the previous night, when Ben had surprised the group. He had spoken up of his own accord, but he ran to Manda for help. *I am still his mother,* Siripon thought. Always, she wanted what was best for her son, whether that came from her or Manda. But more and more frequently, she felt unreasonable. She wanted to make it clear to Ben that she was the first person he should look to. She needed Manda to stop interfering.

The formalities of the ceremony began again. Nearly everyone wore white now, even the workers who lived at the temple. The day was hot again and doubly busy with the preparations for Ben's ceremony. Siripon was looking for him when Tassanee caught her attention. "It's Mother. She says she isn't feeling well."

"What are her symptoms?" Siripon asked, frustrated by the pull in two directions.

"How am I supposed to know, Sister? I'm not the nurse here. So many things are wrong with her."

Gimjaa sat in a shady corner of the smallest building. Her face looked pasty. She fanned herself as she tried to catch her breath.

"Are you dizzy, Mother?" Siripon asked.

"I ate too much this morning."

Siripon pressed her hand against her mother's forehead. She was hot to the touch. "We'll get you some water. You have to try and calm down."

"I'm too lost without him. I don't have anything to live for."

"Don't talk like that. Think of your grandchildren. How would they feel if you were to disappear from their lives?" Siripon felt sorry for her mother, but she tried not to show it. Gimjaa always had a childish quality about her. She was one of the toughest survivors Siripon knew, yet she gave the impression that she couldn't take care of herself. They sat quietly until her breathing slowed. Siripon caught the attention of a passerby and asked her to bring them some water.

"You'll be all right here alone for a moment, won't you? I need to go find Ben."

"I can take Ben to change." It was Manda who spoke. She was guiding him toward one of the back rooms.

"I was going to take him myself," Siripon said. She tried to sound dismissive, but she could hear the annoyance in her voice.

"Stay, stay, Noi. If Mother is sick you should tend to her."

Siripon was up on her feet. She took Ben's arm and tried to coax him closer to her. "I'll take him to change and be right back."

"And why won't you let me do it, Sister?" Manda said. "You always spread yourself too thin."

The woman had returned with water. She tried to hand the cup to Gimjaa, but it slipped and tumbled to the ground, wetting her clothes again.

"Mother." Siripon stooped down to sop up the mess. "I'm sorry, Mother. Are you okay?"

"Go take care of Ben. I'm fine."

"I'll take Ben," Manda insisted. "He can change right over there. It's just a little thing."

"Go, go," Siripon said, nodding to her son. "But come right back to me when you're finished."

6

A crowd gathered around a clearing on the west side of the crematorium. Through a window, Ben watched more people arrive as his mother pinned his gown at the waist. It wasn't much more than a thin sheet, and he was nervous his body would be visible when he stepped into the sun. He covered himself with his hand, embarrassed, but no one commented, no one laughed. When they saw him approaching, they placed their hands together and bowed.

A chair had been set on the grass. Beside it stood a table on which a pair of scissors and a razor had been neatly arranged. Ajan Somchai invited Ben to sit down. The monk cut a lock of Ben's hair and placed it into an aluminum bowl that had been lined with a banana leaf. Ben's family followed, each person cutting a lock of his hair and placing it into the bowl. Then the other monks did the same. When they were through, a junior monk, Ajan Somboon, cut off the rest. He lathered Ben's scalp with soap and shaved it in sections, moving from ear to ear.

"Don't worry about what the kids at school will say," Tassanee called over to Ben. "They might not understand, but you're doing a good thing for your grandfather."

Ben wasn't concerned about his hair. His reputation had nothing to do with how he looked. "Puke Boy"—the name hadn't bothered him when the taunting began years ago. He had felt separated from it. But the words gnawed at him over time, following him from Warren Way to Third Avenue Middle School. He heard the name in the halls between classes. It was mumbled on the lunch patio as students found tables that were far away from him. Even his friends had grown comfortable teasing him if they passed by one of his dried messes.

"That happened during Mrs. Abood's English class, didn't it?" someone had said. "I could see it from my seat. I asked if I could close the door."

The heat of embarrassment never failed to creep up his throat. He was anxious for each day to end so that he could go home and leave school behind. His grandfather's death had been convenient. The cremation was a chance to escape even longer: two weeks for everybody back home to forget about him. He fantasized about the residue of his throw-up blowing away, all traces of it gone from campus by the time he returned.

The monks led him inside to change into the orange robes he would wear for the rest of the ceremony, the color meant to echo autumn leaves, things detaching from their source. Junior monks undressed him and wrapped the new material around him. They rolled the ends until it was snug along his side, and they wound the end of the roll over his shoulder and under his arm. He tensed when the men touched him, afraid his body would respond to the sensation of their skin against his. Since he arrived, Ben had been aware of the monks' bare shoulders and arms, how lean and muscular they were. It was the same at school; he stole glances at the other boys in the locker room, all the time pretending that his thoughts were like theirs, that what he saw meant nothing to him. He recited the vows of the monks, the pledge to disengage from the concerns of the mortal world. The guests bowed to him again, and he felt the embarrassment of being looked at.

Ben had asked his mother once if she would let him become a monk when he was older. He wanted her to know what he already knew: He would never be with a woman; he would never marry.

"Of course," Siripon had said. "I would be proud to have a son who devoted his life to Buddhism." But she didn't look up from the meal she was preparing, and later, worried she hadn't been paying attention, Ben brought up the subject again. Siripon acted as if she had never considered it before. She smiled regretfully. "Don't you want to raise a family? Don't you want to give me grandchildren?"

He had always been open with his mother on other matters, but he kept silent when it came to his feelings about boys. Time weighed down on him. Each year, the expectation that he should want to find a girl felt more pressing. Other students talked about going to school dances together. There were rumors of couples kissing or even having sex. He was relieved he rarely got pulled into the gossip. Throwing up was a convenience in one way, at least: None of the girls saw him as worthy of their consideration.

His day was filled with long meditation sessions, but he couldn't ignore his anxiety. In this country, and in this place, he didn't fit in, just like he didn't fit in at home. He was Puke Boy. He was gay. These things consumed his mind. Deep in the solemnity of the cremation, he imagined Pradit's ghost waking from his nest of bones. The old man looked down upon his own body, strummed his ribs, poked his fingers into the hollows of his eyes. He floated among the buildings, laughing at the music and dancing that must seem so trivial as he prepared for Sawan. Ben yearned to be a ghost. He yearned to escape with his grandfather to a higher plane of existence.

Evening came and he followed the monks to their quarters. They bathed and rested in their dimly lit rooms. Eventually, Ben fell asleep without dreaming. He woke to a sound of movement in the crematorium. The furnace was being prepared. Wood was arranged inside. The flame was lit. Four men removed the urn from its pedestal, and a while later the bones were carried back, covered in a white shroud. They were placed into the furnace, and the door was closed.

The crowd grew larger, five hundred or six hundred people arriving, so that they couldn't all fit inside at the same time. The furnace door was opened, and the guests filed by with offerings of sandalwood flowers that they dropped into the flame, the fire hissing with each new addition. There was no other color inside the furnace except for the orange glow. All the shadows had been lost. Ben watched the bones. Something familiar came to him, a sense that he could experience the cremation from beneath the shroud. Even as he sat on the dais, he was lying beside the bones, the shroud trapping him as his skin charred. He shut his eyes as if he could escape from it, but the heat surrounded him.

All day, he endured, fidgeting and waiting for it to end. Ashes rose in a plume above the chimney and drifted to the ground. The last of the food was prepared and arranged on the tables, and the monks chanted again to the attendees who remained. The third night passed, and the fourth day arrived. Ben changed back into his white clothes. He had not looked at himself since it all began, but now he stopped in front of a mirror and saw the shock of his exposed scalp. He ran his hand over it, felt the tiny bristles that were just coming back in. Soon it would all grow back, but for now he clung to the idea of being someone else. He did not want to return to school. He never needed to see the other students again. He went out in search of his family, anxious to hug his mother and aunt now that he could touch them again. Ash collected on his skin as he surveyed the ceremonial grounds. The valley below was dense and green with a vibrancy he had never seen in America. He wondered if he would ever feel the heat of Thailand again, if he would smell the trees and soil and wildness.

Forbidden Knot

1

Manda's face hovered in front of the television screen. She was waiting for a weather forecast, but instead the anchor was reporting on the political upheaval in Europe. The ticker scrolled across the bottom of the screen: *First parliamentary elections in Poland . . . NASA's* Galileo *reaches asteroid . . . Standard poodle wins Best in Show.* Around her, rain drummed against the roof and windows; it clapped against the leaves of the trees, the sound intensifying with each gust of wind. The winter storm had been relentless for five days. Drives to work were harrowing battles, the car wading through mud-flooded intersections, the windshield wipers slicing arcs in the blurry glaze that coated the glass, providing just enough clarity to permit her to lurch forward. She was annoyed, not only by the rain but by the realization that she had grown soft in America, that a little water was enough to ruin her week.

She walked to the guesthouse, where she would be able to see again what damage had been done to the garden. She looked, even though she knew what she would see, as if seeing it could minimize the damage. Despite the cold and wet, the kitchen door had been left open for ventilation. Siripon was preparing wontons for Ben's Boy Scout ceremony that evening. Aluminum trays covered the counters, and more were arranged on the dining table. They were lined with neat rows of pale uncooked wontons waiting for the hot oil. Siripon spooned filling onto more powdery wrappers. She wet the edges and folded them into precise little pouches.

"Let me know if you want my help," Manda said as she passed by on her way to the back window.

Siripon didn't look up. A small offense. It was better this way, Manda told herself. Who wanted to do monotonous work for people that wouldn't appreciate it? Still, she realized her position in the house had eroded after their father's cremation a year ago. Siripon's requests for Manda to watch Ben came less frequently. She was taking on more of the responsibility for her son, depriving herself of sleep to take Ben to his club meetings and orchestra practices. Even Siripon's definition of the word "family" had changed. The other week, she told Manda they were going to JCPenney to get a portrait taken. "A family portrait," she had said. Manda spent the morning getting dressed only to discover she was not invited to go with them. She complained to Ben about it later, but he wasn't sympathetic. "Mom just meant the main family," he said casually. The photo hung over the mantel now—Siripon in a red dress, the boys in gray suits, the three of them smiling as if they were perfectly complete. Manda avoided looking at it whenever she passed by. She purchased her own frame with her discount and slipped into it an old photo of her and Ben in the garden.

She looked across the yard through the gloom. Several of the plants were slumped over, the stalks unable to withstand the weight of the torrent. She didn't know if they would be able to recover. "You'd think they'd cancel the event," she said.

"They never cancel," Ben mumbled. He sat curled in a dining chair with homework balanced on his knees. He had grown even more sullen this last year, as if simply existing made him unhappy. Manda tried to catch his attention, perhaps offer him a wink, but he didn't look up at her.

"The restaurants lazy," Siripon said in English. "Other people fold one time. We fold two times. That's a real wonton." She held one up for Ben to see. It stood upright like a little boat on the island of her hand. She often spoke to Ben in English these days, another sign that she was pulling him away from Manda, whose English hadn't progressed after all these years. Manda glanced down at the table where her sister was working. The mix in its little bowl was pink and speckled with pepper and green onions. These days, Siripon used turkey instead of pork to fill the wontons. The other meats were suddenly too fatty and high in cholesterol to feed to her loved ones. There were no more pork broths for her soups, no more spicy beef pad kaprow. It was only turkey—turkey-stuffed omelets, turkey fried rice, turkey on toast with cucumber relish. She said that no one could taste the difference, that if she didn't tell the family she was using it, they would never know. Manda didn't argue, but she thought the dry, vapid flavor ruined the dishes—Siripon had simply accepted it. That was a side of her sister's personality Manda envied: Siripon never reconsidered decisions she'd already made.

As the ceremony approached, Ben went into his bedroom and emerged wearing his uniform. It was a combination of drab garments and bright adornments. Dime-sized medals jingled above a front pocket. A sash of merit badges ran diagonally across his chest. He slumped down onto the sofa, fiddling with a wooden neckerchief slide he had carved into an eagle. "I don't know why she's doing all this," he complained, nodding toward his mother on the other side of the patio.

"Your mom likes her homemaking. She's happy to cook and clean every hour of every day for you."

"No one's even going to know what wontons are," Ben said.

"Why wouldn't they?"

"They only eat American food. We should just bring a casserole."

Manda grimaced. She was tempted to suggest he quit the Boy Scouts, a thought that had occurred to her multiple times since he joined. She was suspicious of the mysterious men who were telling Ben how to behave. He was at risk of losing his culture if the family wasn't careful. But she restrained herself. It had been Siripon's idea to enroll Ben in the troop.

"You get to see new thing with the Scouts," Siripon replied when Ben first asked why he had to join. Manda guessed her sister was growing concerned for her son. Maybe she finally sensed that Ben was not like the other boys. He didn't play sports or go to school dances. His friends were all girls, members of his various clubs, groups that played music for residents of the local retirement community or discussed unsolvable math problems. He wasn't close to any of them, and he didn't seem interested in any of them. The fathers who ran the Boy Scout troop were retired Marines. They came together to promote their ideas of how young men should behave. The boys had to have their shoes shined and their nails trimmed and their hair cut short. They raised money by recycling newspapers, forcing Ben to scour the neighborhood streets every week collecting stacks that took up half the garage. During the annual Azalea Festival, he painted a cardboard box with bright letters, loaded it with sacks of peanuts and popcorn, and slung it over his chest to sell to the parade watchers. It was not so different from the nights at the street market that Manda and her siblings endured, their shoulders scarred by the heavy yoked baskets. Perhaps all Siripon wanted for Ben was the same childhood they had.

Ben didn't think of the Scouts the way the other boys did. When they gathered for their weekly meetings, he sat off to the side with his handbook open in his lap. He was the only one who passed all of the patrol leader's tests: Morse code messages, a quiz on marshland birds, a demonstration of converting pants into a flotation device in case he was lost at sea. The others were too busy having fun.

Tonight, he was receiving a badge for having made it through a "survival campout." The boys had been taken to Death Valley. No tents or sleeping bags had been permitted. No backpacks or flashlights. For three nights they slept under crinkly emergency blankets; they built elaborate contraptions to collect condensation; they attempted to cook meals without utensils, skewering food with sticks and holding them over an open flame until it was cooked through enough to eat. As an ultimate lesson, the troop leaders released chickens that the boys had to catch and kill. The evening after the trip, Ben came into Manda's room and described the wooden board into which two nails had been hammered an inch apart, the way the chicken's neck was stretched for the axe. "They did it right in front of us," he whispered, his eyes still glazed from shock. "The chicken flapped its wings after. You have to hold on tight or it can still run away." Manda tried to find out how bothered he had been by it, but he only shook his head, less willing to confide in her than he used to be.

She was certain a new savagery had awoken in Ben after the camp-out. Maybe it was better for him, but she grieved his loss of innocence. He and Kamron had a heated argument upon Ben's return from the trip. He had found his father drunk, and he called Kamron pathetic. By the time Manda could reach them, they were both shouting at full volume, both on the verge of lunging at each other. She was relieved to have been able to send them back to their corners.

It would only be mother and son going to the ceremony tonight. Kamron had hurt himself at the factory earlier in the day, and he was recovering in bed. An arm injury, Siripon had said, though, out of propriety, Manda hadn't gone into their bedroom to see for herself. She asked Ben how his father was, and he shrugged.

In the guesthouse, the sound of the bubbling oil came to an end. Siripon rushed into the living room while untying her apron. She stooped in front of Ben and asked him to smell the top of her head.

"If not greasy, then I don't take shower."

"Shower, please, Mom. Everybody's going to shower."

"How do you know? Do they tell you?" She hurriedly washed and got dressed, briefly considering one of her Thai silk dresses before settling on a black business suit.

"We're going to be late. My patrol loses points if we're late," Ben whined.

"Okay, okay. Take wonton to the car, then. We going!" She called back to remind Kamron to take his pain medication. The door slammed. A moment later, Siripon's car scraped against the concrete as it bumped out of the driveway.

2

The weather report finally came on—the storm was expected to pass in the late evening. Manda assumed she would spend the time alone. She was startled when Kamron appeared in the doorway.

"Did she leave us any dinner?"

"Turkey," Manda replied. A plate of wontons—those that had accidentally bloomed open in the oil—sat cooling on the counter. Kamron dipped one into a bowl of chili sauce and fit it into his mouth. He took out a Michelob from the refrigerator.

"Should you be mixing alcohol with your medication?" Manda asked.

"Make us something else to eat, will you? I went to the hospital before our lunch break."

She took out some leftover rice, the egg carton, a half-empty container of chili paste. The two stood around the stove while the eggs fried in a pool of bubbling oil, their edges puffing and crisping. Manda's gaze fell on Kamron's arm. The bandages were taking on a faint color of rust. "How did it happen?" she asked.

"A clumsy fucker." The jagged edge of his anger sharpened. "He let go of a sheet, and it slid right through me. It should have been a lot worse. Of course, he won't admit he did anything wrong."

"No one here ever takes credit for their mistakes. They just blame others, find fault in the people or the process or the company. Next time, you let one of those sheets slip across his pecker. I mean it. You slice that thing right off."

"There's nothing we can do," Kamron said. "The whites try to control it all. The rest of us are invisible at the bottom. That's America. But, damn it, it was embarrassing to get hurt in front of the entire department. I dropped to my knees. I thought I was going to faint. Some of the other guys had to wipe up my blood."

Manda wanted to console him, but she didn't know what else to say. She brought the steaming food to the table and told him to eat, content with the act of service.

"Are you sorry you won't see Ben receive his award?" she asked.

"There will be other awards."

"Did you two get into another fight today?"

Kamron didn't answer. He scooped a bite of rice into his mouth.

"Nothing he does impresses you, does it?" Manda asked. "He works hard all the time, and you don't see it."

"You tell me, what does it say about a family when a son is constantly criticizing his father? What does it say when someone goes to the emergency room and everyone else carries on as if nothing happened? I get hurt, but we all have to celebrate Ben chopping the head off a chicken." He pushed his chair back and went outside. Under the narrow shelter of the awning, he smoked a cigarette as rain fell around him.

Left alone, Manda decided she would only wash her own dishes. She was irritated by Kamron's childishness, by his standoffs with the other members of the household. She tried to keep his upbringing in mind, the loss of his father, the moves from school to school. His suffering was often visible on his face, particularly during nights when he was drunk. There had been a time when she was first getting to know him that she thought he could shed away that pain. She remembered the way Kamron carried Ben around the house when he was a baby. That vigorous love was gone. And though she would not analyze it too closely, she suspected her own relationship with Ben was partially to blame.

She was lost in thought, her hands under the water, when Kamron came up behind her. She jumped at his touch. She started to laugh, but her voice caught. He was pressing down on her shoulders. His thumbs moved in circles at the base of her neck.

"Don't even try it," Manda said.

"I'm not trying anything."

She twisted away, but his hands found her again. They felt as if they were coated in oil and were leaving a residue on her skin. They slid down around her waist, pulled her into him. She could feel his hardness.

"Don't," she said. The timbre of her voice had changed. There was no confidence in it, no command. He led her out of the kitchen, and she remembered that this was not her house. Her room was not her room. Her bed was not her bed. She understood that she had a decision to make: She could refuse him, or she could surrender to him. She let her body soften, trusting him with her weight. He stepped out of his pants and then pushed hers down to her ankles.

This will fulfill something in me, she thought. *This will answer a question.* She eased herself down on the bed. In all these years, Manda had never had sex. The knowledge of it had fallen into place over time from movies and rumors, but she had never experienced it herself. Ever since Manda had met Kamron, she had tried to reconcile the different sides of his personality: his silence, his anger, his strength, his charm. They always arose unpredictably, a gamble with each glass of alcohol. But in bed, his different sides merged. The hands that had frightened her when she first saw them now guided her and opened her. She was angry, ashamed, but she felt pleasure too. He drew from her an unexpected need she hadn't been aware of. She felt accepted by Kamron in a way she never thought she would be. Her body felt attractive.

They were together for no more than a few minutes before Manda sat up, listening for the gate. She pushed Kamron away and stood, aware that blood was smeared along her thighs. She dabbed at it before putting her clothes back on. "Don't ever do that to me again. I don't need that sort of dirty business."

Kamron steadied himself as he sat up. The sex had unwound him. He grabbed at his arm as if the pain had suddenly come back. "You can't tell her," he said.

"I have no intention of telling her. I wouldn't do anything to imply that I want you for myself."

"Have you ever thought of it? You and me?"

"I'm not going to have this conversation. We barely tolerate each other as it is."

They emerged into the light of the hall. In the kitchen, Kamron offered to wash the rest of the dishes, but within a few moments, Manda realized they wouldn't be clean unless she did the job herself. She washed and stacked. She wiped down the counters and stove top. She went down on her hands and knees and scrubbed the kitchen floor. Her body was sore, and she suspected she might still be bleeding. The injury frightened her. But she was relieved too—maybe she had found another way to remain part of the household.

3

Westminster Presbyterian Church was three miles from the Chiwitchaiya house, only a ten-minute drive, even in the rain. It was a plain, pleasant building—tan and flat with manicured lawns and geranium borders, though the storm had muddied the landscaping. In the rain, the white cross that rose above the main hall took on a stoic quality, a desperate and sailless mast of a ship seeking shelter. Siripon turned in to a parking space, relieved to see other families still climbing out of their cars and opening their umbrellas. They drifted toward the double doors flanked by stained-glass windows, the blurred shapes of the other guests skipping behind the textured panes.

"Mom proud of you," she said, watching Ben prepare to step inside. The organization was good for him, especially after her classmates stopped coming over as often as they used to, their teens having grown too busy with their own school activities. The boys in the troop were welcoming, and the fathers were encouraging. Everyone folded Ben into their ceremonial choreography with its left-handed handshakes and three-fingered salutes, its motto and oath. Siripon could see that out of this silliness emerged values. The former Scout Master, Carl Glidden, was said to have thrown his body over a boy to protect him during a bison stampede on Catalina Island. Siripon liked that Ben was surrounded by these role models, so that he might take after them when he grew older.

In the bustling hall, the boys gathered in their patrols. The American flag and the state flag were posted on opposite ends of the stage while everyone stood for the Pledge of Allegiance. Siripon could recite the words if she needed to—she had memorized them for her citizenship exam—but tonight she stood with her hand over her heart and her mouth closed. The boundary between those in uniform and the civilians was clear. She didn't have to try so hard on her side. It was enough that the guests didn't ruin the facade; whether or not they thought it was silly had no bearing.

It began with an inspection. The boys jutted their elbows out to create the proper spacing. They held their hands up to show that their palms were clean, raised their pant legs to show their polished shoes. When Ben first joined, Siripon worried he would be uncomfortable here. He had been the only Asian in the troop, just as they had been the only Asian household on Caroline Street. But times changed. In the neighborhood, older residents passed away, and new families from all over the world were buying their houses. She didn't find it unusual anymore if, while taking a walk around the block, she caught the aroma of pickled bamboo or fish frying in someone else's home. The Salamacas had joined the troop too. They were a Filipino family with two sons. Mr. Salamaca brought balut to the potluck, and the boys dared each other to eat it, peering down into the gray craters of the eggshells before turning away in disgust. Siripon stuck to the favorites—it wasn't about shocking people. Despite her son's doubts, the other families seemed to appreciate Thai food. Twice, she brought curries that left people sucking air through their teeth, but they still went back for more. She glanced at her watch. She was tired, but there were still hours to go. One of the fathers summoned a group to receive their merit badges. Siripon watched Ben climb up onto the stage. There was something overly meticulous about the way he carried himself. He was too rigid, too uptight. She wondered if he stood out for the rest of the parents the way he stood out for her or if every parent saw something in their child that was quirky. It didn't matter. She was proud of her son. He took center stage, and she clapped.

That afternoon, she had woken up early enough to finish her cooking with plenty of time to spare. She hadn't anticipated the phone call telling her that Kamron had been taken to the emergency room. By the time she arrived, he was pacing in the hospital lobby. One of his forearms was bandaged almost entirely around, though at the sight of him she was relieved that it wasn't more serious. He noticed her approaching, shrugged, and balled his hand into a fist.

"Was it deep?" she asked. She wanted to know what had happened, but she saw that he was aggravated already and didn't want to provoke him further.

"Twenty-two stitches," Kamron said, using the English words but pronouncing the last as if it had no vowels.

"They didn't give me any details," she said.

"What is there to say?" He led them out to the parking lot, and because he wouldn't know where she parked, Siripon guided him in the right direction without taking the lead. At home, she unwrapped the dressing and inspected the injury herself. A deep gash ran from the crook of his elbow and into the wrinkles of his wrist, stopping just before it reached his palm. In places, the blood was still pushing up, and she was surprised his clothes hadn't been more stained. He swallowed two painkillers, not bothering with water, and told her he wanted to be left alone.

"We have Ben's ceremony tonight," she reminded him.

"It doesn't always have to be about the boy," he said.

She wasn't surprised by the remark. Lately, she often felt that Kamron was jealous of their son. The room seemed to overheat whenever they were together. Just this morning they had argued before Ben left for school, something about secondhand cigarette smoke causing cancer. Siripon assumed it was the typical teenage discord, but she saw that it went both ways. Kamron lost his temper too. "Can't you try a little harder?" she said.

"Let's not get into this now," he replied, waving his arm as if she might have forgotten what happened.

She quieted down. She had not been able to get through to either of them. She settled Kamron into bed and returned to her cooking, rushing to make up for lost time. When Ben came home, he noticed all the trays.

"How many are you making?" he asked. "You don't have to make them for everybody."

She guessed he was anxious about the ceremony. Attention always made him more likely to vomit. "Go and check in on your father," she said. "He got hurt today."

"What happened?" Ben's face sobered.

"See for yourself. He should be awake."

He crossed the patio and went into the main house. A few minutes later, he returned looking relieved. He poured a glass of water for his father. "Dad can't go tonight," he said. "He just wants to sleep."

Maybe Ben didn't like Kamron to be at the events—the thought had never occurred to her before. All of the other fathers attended and told their silly jokes and their exaggerated stories: fish stories, sports stories, gun stories. Kamron was one of the quieter ones. Of course, Ben could be upset over the argument they had had. Maybe he just needed a break from Kamron. She left the matter alone. As long as Ben wasn't disappointed by it, she was happy to let her husband rest.

Now, as the boys dragged the tables out into the center of the room and laid out the dinner, Siripon caught Ben watching their trays of wontons. He smiled as several of the parents remarked on how excited they were to taste them. Siripon had already known they would be. She sat among a group of mothers she had never spoken to before. As they chattered, she tried to pretend she was in the break room with the other nurses so she would be more herself. But the conversation moved quickly, and she couldn't come up with things to say. It was a mix of compliments and complaints, and everything seemed to be accompanied by laughter. She wished Kamron were beside her.

When it was over, Siripon was surprised to see Ben acting anxious again. She had guessed it would subside now that his time on stage was over, but she caught him pacing in the parking lot beside their car.

"Mom, can I go out with the rest of the patrol? They want to eat at Denny's." His voice was high, nervous.

Siripon would rather have had him home, but she was pleased to see him making more friends. "Not too late," she said in English.

"We're just going to—Mom, can I talk to you?"

"What now?"

He led her to the back of the lot, away from the crowd. The rain had lightened up, but it was still drizzling, the droplets carried by the wind so they swirled and eddied around them. There was a shack in the far corner of the parking lot where they stored the bundles of newspapers the Scouts collected. Ben pulled her into the shadow of the building.

"What wrong?" She was getting nervous, but she tried not to show it.

"Mom, I need to tell you a secret, but I'm scared you'll be disappointed in me."

She needed to know what he had to say. "Of course I not disappointed. Not if you tell the truth."

He crossed his arms and turned his face up toward the rain. She thought back to their visit to the psychologist all those years ago, the struggle he had opening up about what bothered him.

"I just want you to know who I am."

"Oh, I see. And you think I don't know my son?"

"I want you to know everything about me. All of it. I don't want anything to be hidden between us. Mom . . . I think I'm a homosexual."

For an instant, the word had no meaning. It was like the complicated instructions on a document that seemed to be nothing more than random combinations of letters. But she thought about it more patiently, thought about this word that she had heard in other places. The consequences of what Ben had said came to her. He was gay. She thought about how society would look at him if this secret came out. Ben was watching her, waiting for a response—she needed to say something. "You mom always love you," she said. "Okay? You know that?"

He nodded, obedient.

"Nothing you do make me stop loving you." She paused. She needed more. "What make you think you that way? Did someone do something to you?"

"I just know," he said. "It's just a feeling."

Siripon's tears were coming. She wouldn't be able to hold them back if she stayed here. Across the lot, families were walking to their cars. They were chatting and laughing. She tried to understand why Ben would choose this moment to tell her, here, of all places, where he should feel most like a man. "Go. Go with your friend. We talk more later."

"Okay, Mom."

"Be careful. Always be careful."

"Okay, Mom."

She rushed to her car and started the engine. On her way home, she pulled away from the lights of the main road and parked so that she could cry. Ben already had his vomiting. She couldn't imagine another thing wrong with him. Now he believed he was gay. How? How could it happen? Her intentions had always been pure; she had genuinely tried to raise a good boy. But his mind went to troubling places. Maybe it was the life of a son whose mother didn't spend enough nights at home. She let herself fall into despair, and there she wallowed as traffic passed ahead. By the time she moved again, her fingers had grown cold. She started her engine and pulled back out into the street.

At home, she found Kamron waiting in the kitchen.

"How did it go?" he asked, more gently than he normally would.

She only grunted. She had hoped to hide her emotions, but under the kitchen lights, she could feel her forehead wrinkling.

"What's wrong?" Kamron said.

"Your son."

"What about my son?"

"It's nothing. Just sit here. Be with me for a little while. How's your arm?"

He didn't answer. Beside them, a clock ticked. Siripon let herself imagine that she could tell Kamron what had happened, that the two of them could solve this problem together. But she didn't tell him anything.

4

Ben hid in the darkness of the shack as cars huffed to life and drove away. He could discern his mother's sedan among the others and was relieved when it was gone. The talk had been clumsy, caught at the boundary of his ability to speak Thai and her ability to understand English. All day he had gone back and forth on whether he should use the word "gay" or "homosexual," finally deciding on the latter because it seemed more medical. Now he wondered if it had been the wrong choice. They had been rushed, too, but Ben didn't feel like he'd had any other choice. For weeks he had been trying to tell Siripon, but they were never alone at home. Tonight had been his last chance. He wished he could repeat the conversation, go over it a hundred times to make sure they had understood each other. At least he had gotten it out—there was a lightness in that. He wanted her to know him for who he was. And she had said she loved him.

The rain stopped to reveal the slow, rhythmic dripping from rooftop corners. Dampness in the air revived the mildew from among the stacks of newspaper. It mixed with the oily odor of twine, a combination that had grown familiar to him. He was grateful for it.

When it was quiet outside, he turned the light on and scanned the pegboard wall. Tools hung within their painted outlines: a saw in a saw-shaped silhouette, a hammer in a hammer-shaped silhouette. He found some smooth white rope that seemed somehow gentler, more merciful than the others. He formed one end into a loose S and wrapped the triple-stranded bundle with tight coils. He threaded the tip through at the top and tested the knot to make sure it slid. All the boys had learned to tie a noose even though the fathers declared it forbidden. Even before the idea of killing himself had gotten into his head, Ben was drawn to the knot's neat repetition, its elegant mechanics. He tied the end of the rope to a horizontal beam and tossed the noose over the rafters. He hung on it to make sure the structure held his weight. He was crying. He was not crying. He was tired of being different from everyone else. The name-calling at school had become relentless. His classmates always found ways to announce that something was wrong with him. This week, there was a story spreading that Bonnie Stewart had been eating lunch beside a tree when her hand sank into a puddle of his throw-up. She had told Ben accusingly before one of their classes but not before she told her friends. The others were avoiding the corner of the field where it had supposedly happened. Someone wrapped caution tape around the area as if it were a crime scene. Then there was the secret, the dark weight of his desire that grew more desperate every day. He had begun to suspect that the older boys knew. They caught him staring, aware of his attraction the way they must be aware of the girls who were drawn in.

He began his work, grateful that the other Scouts were familiar with death from the survival campout. They would be able to handle discovering his body better than his family would. He built the stack of newspapers on which to stand. He used the rope to climb it, almost unaware of the tapping of a ring against the paper shack door. It was the same sharp tap his mother had made against the front window all those years ago when she came home from the hospital. But tonight it didn't penetrate his consciousness. He slipped the loop over his head. The door creaked open and let in the naked band of sky newly stripped of clouds. Mrs. Broge, one of the mothers, called in her bright voice, "Hello, hello! I saw a light left on." She smiled at Ben, but her eyes moved up, tracing the white rope suspended from beam to beam. "Oh, oh, oh," she said, and she raced to him, wrapped her arms around him. He tried to twist free, but she refused to let him go. "No, dear. No, never," she said, freeing him. "I will help you. Here, I will help you." In her voice Ben heard a tone he never heard before, one that he would remember for the rest of his life. It was a tone of universal love from a mother to a son not her own but whom she loved completely in the moment. His body struggled to free itself. He was still methodically following through with his plan, and Mrs. Broge's arms around him were nothing more than webs that he needed to push aside. He twisted away from her, but she enwrapped him again. She pressed him against her as if she could slow his heart rate. It was a long time before she let him go. He stared at the open doorway and the blue of night outside, thinking that it would be the last time he would see it; he did not realize that he had already been rescued. When Mrs. Broge let him go, he felt off-balance and took hold of the wall. She guided him outside, and he looked at the night, this time from within it. The sky was expansive like time; he could imagine letting it pass over him before he would try this again.

Outside, the church and the parking lot looked so ordinary. The white lines dividing each parking space appeared thin and fragile. He saw Mrs. Broge's Cadillac, and inside was Timothy Broge looking out at him. His mouth was slightly open, so that Ben could see the shadows and reflections of his braces.

"I'll take you home," Mrs. Broge said. She stepped into the shack for a moment, and when she came back, she had the rope in her hand. At the car, she opened the passenger door and spoke to Timothy, and he nodded in response.

"Hey, Ben." Timothy stepped aside and held the door open for Ben to climb in. He closed the door without getting in himself. Mrs. Broge handed her son her jacket and umbrella and told him that she would be right back.

It was perhaps the most comfortable car Ben had ever been in. Its engine hummed effortlessly, and it seemed to glide on a frictionless surface. He sat with his head back against the headrest, his eyes half closed, letting the traffic lights blur in his vision. The reflections elongated and sped by.

"You can come over to talk to me anytime," Mrs. Broge said as she followed his brief directions home. "You can call anytime. You can call Timothy. Do you know our number?" She made him repeat it until it was memorized. She made him promise that he would call her the next morning to let her know he was okay, that he had made it through the night. It was only a few minutes before they reached the house. The kitchen light was on, and Manda was sitting at the breakfast table with her head turned toward them. Ben thought about the church and its shack and the parking lot. He didn't know why Timothy had stayed there, and yet Ben was grateful to be alone with Mrs. Broge.

"Will you let me go in by myself?" he asked.

"I need to talk to your parents," Mrs. Broge said.

"Please don't tell them. I can't let them know." His voice was mousy, shaking. He thought maybe his pleading would make it seem as if his parents were the cause of his suicide attempt, and though he didn't want her to suspect them, he hoped that her fear of it would keep her from going in.

"They need to know, honey," she said. "They need to know so they can help you."

"I'll call you tomorrow. I promise I'll call you if you don't come in." And though he was scared before, his fear compounded. He felt that he would be exposed by her, until his family's love for him completely evaporated. Mrs. Broge sat still for a long time. She stared out of the windshield as if she was deciding where to drive next. Finally, she sighed and nodded, though she still looked uncertain. Ben slid out of the car so that she wouldn't have time to change her mind. He closed the door behind him. He wanted her to hurry back to the church and be with Timothy. He didn't want anybody to be alone that night.

5

Manda had been awake, staring into the darkness, when she heard the gate latch scrape its post and then clang shut. Siripon's heels clacked against the concrete walk, but Ben's footsteps didn't accompany them. She wanted her nephew home. She wanted him telling her about the evening as he changed out of his uniform, scattering the pieces carelessly around his room, a habit he had never outgrown.

She had turned the light off knowing that she wouldn't sleep. She wanted to try to force the evening to a close. But it lingered there still, maniacal, staring back at her. Kamron's footsteps came from the other end of the house. The groan of the floorboards reminded her of his weight pressing down against her body only a couple of hours ago. He had given her something. In a sense, he had freed her from some suspended curiosity. But he had vandalized her too. She heard him greet Siripon, his tone friendly. Then both of their voices dropped. Manda stood, uneasy, listening. She opened the door and stepped into the light.

They were sitting at the breakfast table like two people in prayer. Manda cleared her throat to announce herself before coming into the room. "Where's our troublemaker?"

Kamron glared at her, but, as if he couldn't maintain the expression, his face softened, his mouth fell slack. It was not clear what he had said already.

"Did something happen to Ben?" Manda asked.

"Nothing, nothing," Siripon said in English. "Everything fine." Manda often suspected her sister used English as a sign of surrender, an admission that the Outer Country had overtaken her. She watched Siripon carry her trays to the sink and turn on the faucet. Her eyes were red. She had been crying—she was crying still.

Water struck the aluminum bottoms of the trays. Siripon swiped the debris away and then scrubbed them with a sponge. Manda tried to sense if their tenuous bond as sisters had snapped. Siripon wasn't one for confrontation. If she knew what had happened, she would not bring it up here. It would come out in silence, death by starvation rather than a firing squad. Manda held her breath as her sister trudged to her bedroom without saying good night.

Kamron looked drowsy. Even if he wanted to keep the secret between them, he may not have been able to.

Manda put the kettle on to boil. "Tea?"

He didn't answer. He sat with his back to her so that she only saw his silhouette. The glow from the hanging kitchen light struck the top of his head and shoulders, creating a sharp outline of his muscled physique. He was examining the bandages on his arm.

"What did you tell her?" she asked.

"Leave us alone, will you?"

"She was crying—you might as well admit it if the truth came out. There's no point in keeping it from me now. I'll need to make arrangements, find somewhere else to live. I know I don't have a say in whether or not I'm welcome here."

"Who told you to come out of your room anyway?" Kamron's eyes remained down at his bandaged arm. Even with the injury he looked powerful, brutal. She wondered if he felt the way he looked, if he was aware of his power. The kettle whistled. Manda took down two mugs for tea, but Kamron stood and walked down the hall toward his bedroom. When she called his name, he acted as if he didn't hear her.

She sat with the tea hot in her hands. She sat with her legs folded beneath her, and though they were going numb, she did not move them. From the window, the cold air seeped in, a minor annoyance. She realized how grateful she was for this house, how much she had grown dependent on it. In moments like these when she was alone and comfortable, she had even tricked herself into thinking that comfort belonged to her.

A car pulled up to the house, and Ben was visible in the back seat. As the light inside the car came on, Manda saw a woman behind the wheel. She was white, someone Manda had never met. Her face was made up, and when she moved her mouth to speak, there was a sheen to her lips. The woman spoke to Ben for some time before letting him go. Manda watched her expression as Ben shook his head in response to something she said. She looked serious, even concerned, but not angry. An agreement was made. Then Ben walked up the driveway to the back door. His uniform was disheveled, and his face was pale.

"Did you go out with your friends?" Manda asked, curious what he would tell her without being prompted.

"Denny's. We went to eat."

"Why would you waste money going out like that? We have food here."

"They wanted pancakes, not rice." He pulled off his shoes and arranged them neatly on the shelf. Manda noticed how much his body had developed over the last year. As he bent down, his shirt pulled taut across his shoulder blades, and his sleeves cut into thick arms. Kamron's strength had been passed down to Ben, but it was translated differently in his body. While Kamron's face matched his musculature, Ben's face, wide-eyed and innocent, seemed threatened by the power beneath it, as if the child was unprepared for the man he was becoming.

"Leave your uniform in my room. I'll wash it and iron it myself. You know your mother isn't as careful—it's always rush, rush, rush with her."

"I won't need it for a while," Ben said.

"The week will come and go before you know it. Just do what I say. Come here, let me help you unbutton your shirt."

"I'll take care of it myself."

It nagged Manda that Ben didn't cooperate. She felt as if the entire household was turning against her. He headed down the hall, but he stopped halfway. One hand reached back to the light switch. "Did Mom say anything tonight?" he asked.

"What would she have said?" Manda replied.

"Do you think she's still awake? I need to see her."

"She's turned in for the night, ja. Your father too." She was coming to a different understanding. Maybe Siripon was crying for another reason, something that had to do with Ben. He was the age her students had been when she was teaching at Benjama School. He was the same age Jaroen had been when he decided pesticide was the only remedy for his pain.

"Remember that your mother is delicate," Manda warned him. "If you have anything to talk about, you should tell it to me. We can solve it without concerning her."

He looked over at her for a long moment before nodding complacently. Then he walked down the hall to his room. Manda thought of all the things she had done to make sure he was raised properly—all with that tentative hold of an aunt instead of a mother. In thirteen years, he still did not know everything she had done for him.

6

Siripon's sleep was troubled, her body tense in bed for hours after the news of her son's death. She saw it as death—Ben's body would be destroyed by the disease that was taking so many men away. She had watched the spread of AIDS in her hospital bulletins and on television, the rise in cases at White Memorial mirrored internationally. Scientists had yet to find a way to stop it.

She started her day with simple chores. She went to get the laundry hamper, which stood just outside Ben's room. He was sliding books into his backpack in preparation for school. He spoke when he saw her, a tentative greeting that Siripon couldn't respond to. She reached down into the dirty clothes. The material was soft from wear. It smelled of skin oil, the traces of her family's last few days. Twisted among them, Ben's uniform was still faintly damp. She bundled the load in her arms and attempted to walk on, but she couldn't pass his door without stopping.

"The thing you tell me yesterday," she said in English. "You do anything yet?" She had waited all night to ask this question, and as she stood listening for his response, she wondered if she would be able to bear the answer.

He looked uncertain. His hands moved cautiously, zipping his pack around the corners of his books.

"Sec," Siripon said, unable to properly pronounce the *x*. Then, in Thai, "Did you let anyone go inside of you?"

"No, Mom," Ben said, caught off guard by her bluntness.

"Are you sure?"

"How do I know for sure?" He came to her and let her embrace him, the clothes dropping around their feet. Her hand went to his bottom, to the spot where he was most vulnerable, as if she could hold it there and protect him from ever being penetrated.

"So, you have done something," she said.

"Sometimes on camping trips we all slept together in a row. Sometimes we all went swimming together naked." He nuzzled his head against her shoulder. He was trying to go back in time, she thought, to be a child again, but she couldn't see him as a child any longer. The wildness of teenage boys roared in her mind, boys alone in the California deserts, dusty troops scattered among the hot desolation. What happened out there? How far had it spread among them? She couldn't ask any more questions. What she had asked was too much already.

"If someone did that to you, it would hurt," she said, trying to convince herself that this was true. Kamron had never tried to have anal intercourse with her. She would not have been able to tolerate it if he had. But a few times, as they made love, his finger grazed her there, nudged in small circles as he tried to ease it in. She cried out, unable to ignore the feeling that it was dirty. Men needed to enter wherever they could; you couldn't keep them from their urges.

"Tell me before you do anything, okay? I don't want anything to happen to you." Her desperation threatened to overflow. She was relieved when Ben nodded. His cheek was still pressed against her. "Okay." She stepped away gently, picked up the laundry, and marched to the washing machine. She saw that his clothes held the pieces of him that soon would be gone from her. She wanted to collect that essence. She wanted to preserve this moment.

That afternoon, folding laundry in front of the television, she looked up when the news of a death was announced. On the screen came images of Freddie Mercury wearing tight white tank tops, tight jeans. She had thought he was handsome when she first saw him, but she didn't like the way he carried himself, the attention he craved. Only now did she realize that he had suffered from AIDS.

She rushed to the VCR, trying to remember how to record with it. She inserted the first tape she could find, not caring what she was recording over. The station played clips of Mercury's performances, celebrating his exuberance on the stage, his enormous voice. Siripon imagined his nights touring, the countless hotel rooms he would have stayed in and the strangers who would have sought him out. This was the threat that surrounded her son.

During Siripon's next call home, she didn't mention anything about Ben coming out, instead telling her mother and siblings that things were fine. At the hospital, she stopped seeing her old classmates during breaks. She drank her coffee alone, sitting in the break room with her back to the door so that the others wouldn't notice her crying. There were magazines and newspapers left on the table, and every night she sought out the stories about AIDS patients, photos of people who couldn't maintain their weight, people with sores that wouldn't heal, lists of those who had died. She clipped out each piece and slipped it into an envelope so that she could read through them more slowly at home, going over each sentence until she understood. She hoped for some detail revealing that doctors were close to a cure, that Ben might be saved when the worst befell him.

The week passed too quickly. When the next Thursday arrived, Ben didn't dress for his troop meeting. Siripon watched the clock, counting down until it was too late for him to make it to the church on time. She set a place for him at the dinner table. He appeared at the kitchen door just after seven.

"I'm going to have dinner with Mrs. Broge." He had changed out of his school clothes and was wearing a polo and a pair of khaki pants.

"Won't they be gone?" Siripon asked, surprised.

"It's just her. She said I could come. Is that okay?"

"I suppose you can, but why would you want to? What would the two of you talk about?"

"Just stuff," Ben said. "Normal things."

Ben stood at the curb while Siripon waited under their kumquat tree. Soon, a ruby-colored Cadillac pulled over, and Mrs. Broge waved without getting out of the car. Ben climbed in casually, as if he had done it many times before. In the moment when the door was open and the light was on, Siripon saw her son's smile. It was relieved, grateful, and she wondered again why he would want to spend time with another woman. Mrs. Broge tapped her horn and waved again. Then they were gone, and Siripon stared at the empty spot where the two had been.

"I bet it was the woman who was here before," Manda said when Siripon went back inside. "Last week, she dropped him off after his little pancake run. I don't know what her game is."

"Why would she be up to anything?" Siripon shrugged, not wanting to show her concern. Her sister's jealousy quietly pleased her. For once, Manda could know what it was like to feel another woman trying to steal her child away. She brought the food to the table and told the others to eat while everything was still hot. No one spoke. There was only the sound of utensils clinking, the sloshing of food in their mouths.

7

Mrs. Broge made it clear that Ben didn't need to talk if he didn't want to. He stepped inside, followed her to a seat at the dining table, where two place settings were arranged across from each other. Like his own parents, the Broges had only one child, so on nights when Timothy and Mr. Broge went to troop meetings, Mrs. Broge was left alone.

"I brought out the good silver for you," she said.

Ben glanced down at the gleaming utensils arranged neatly around him. He wondered if silver tasted different from the brass utensils he used at home. The entire house was beautifully decorated. It was more formal than Ben's, like houses he saw on television. As she finished the dinner preparations, Mrs. Broge filled the silence by describing her day. She talked about finding conjoined carrots at the grocery store that looked like a pair of orange pants, a giant head of cabbage that barely fit into a plastic bag. Her voice was cheerful when it reached him, loud while she worked in the kitchen and softer after she sat down. The meal of brisket, green beans, and mashed potatoes was arranged on their plates instead of served in the center of the table the way it was at home. There was no rice, no little bowl of fish sauce with chilis floating in it. Still, it was delicious. He wished his mother knew how to make the same kind of food.

Ben tried to come up with things to say, but most of the time he only listened. He sensed that Mrs. Broge was telling her stories to make things feel more normal between them. They didn't talk about the night she found him in the paper shack, but it was present, like a framed photograph in the corner of the room. Everything that occurred between them seemed to be focused on not having to look at it.

He went to Mrs. Broge's four weeks in a row. Each time, as she was on her way to pick him up, he grew nervous over how his mother would react. But Siripon never objected, never asked any other questions about it. She only said, "Be careful," as he went to wait at the curb. The phrase nagged at him. It was a reminder that he had frightened her simply by telling her who he was.

Spending time with Mrs. Broge, Ben felt as if he were borrowing someone else's life. He liked the neatly arranged table, the food served on his plate, the casual conversations. Slowly, he thought of things to say. He told her about his experiences at school, about being a teenager. They were conversations he wished he could have with Siripon, if only she could understand him the way Mrs. Broge could. Lying in bed, he imagined similar conversations, pretending that he and his mother could speak easily to each other, that Siripon was as fluent in English as Mrs. Broge was so that he didn't have to translate his thoughts, oversimplify them to suit his limited Thai vocabulary the way he did in reality. Sometimes, alone, he wrote dialogues down in tiny print that no one else could read. His voice and Siripon's voice responded to each other. They were back in the shadow of the church, his coming-out scripted more carefully, her response what he wished she had said.

Mother, I don't want to hurt you, but I'm gay. I'm attracted to boys.

That's okay, son. There is nothing wrong with you. It doesn't bother me at all. Why would it?

He hid these messages beneath his bottom dresser drawer so that when he opened and closed it, he could hear the pages scraping gently against the wood to let him know that they were still there, still safe.

Ben stopped going to his math club meetings and his yearbook group. He focused on his studies, no longer tolerating missed questions or unfinished math problems during exams. Perfection became his standard.

"Your parents must be so thrilled," Mrs. Broge said when he told her he earned the highest score possible on all of his tests that week.

"I didn't tell them," Ben said. "I just wanted you to know."

Mrs. Broge started to respond, but she stopped herself. She winked and told him that she was proud of him.

"I got a phone call from an old friend this afternoon," she said. "We've known each other since third grade—can you believe that? Her name is Amanda. She lives in Redding, where it snows all the time. They have these things called 'snow days,' when school gets canceled because no one can leave the house."

Mrs. Broge often talked about how important friends were. She seemed to have been popular when she was Ben's age. She brought out an old photo album and set it on the coffee table while they ate ice cream out of glass bowls. They flipped through images of her as a student. There she was on a stage, dressed as Glinda the Good Witch. There she was smiling proudly while working at a cinema concession stand. She posed with people who squeezed in beside her, people who made funny faces and threw their arms out at zany angles. A lot of images were like that: people laughing and hugging and toppling over one another. Ben never let his own friends get too close, preferring to spend most of his time alone. He avoided a lot of them now, embarrassed, as if they knew what he had done. Only Timothy made a point to ask how he was feeling.

"You don't have to check on me every day," Ben said once.

"You can feed my turtle on Thursdays if you want," Timothy replied. "Just let me know so we don't feed him twice."

"I don't have to go to your house. I know she's your mom and not mine."

"Go ahead. Just tell me if you end up feeding my turtle. Besides, we're going to move soon."

The news came unexpectedly. Mrs. Broge had never mentioned them leaving.

"We have to go to Arizona for my dad's work," Timothy explained. "Mom was probably going to tell you soon."

Ben decided not to bring it up unless Mrs. Broge did. He kept going to see her as if nothing had changed. Without his noticing, the details of the night at the paper shack were being lost, so that, though he wasn't completely aware of it, he forgot whether or not it was still raining when he tied the noose. He forgot the sense of comfort he felt surrounded by the odor of mildew and twine. Only the larger details remained—the white rope, the bare light bulb, the shack—and even those memories began to fade.

Bodies in the Light

1

We can't hide who we are. This was what Kamron concluded about his life. He had carried a stain in his youth. Maybe he had been born stained. Each new opportunity he had been given, each new person who came into his life revealed it, proved once again that he was not a good man. In Los Angeles, it emerged as guilt on his skin after being unfaithful. Here was a reminder that he did not deserve Siripon's love.

His days had become a string of performances. He was too kind to Siripon, and then, worried she would suspect something, he became too mean toward her. He ignored Manda and then worried he would upset her and cause her to reveal their secret. It was all an act; it was all deceit. And he could only blame himself. At night, he swallowed shots of Grey Goose to dull the pain. He locked the bathroom door and took a hot shower, staying under the water until his skin was red and tender.

Still, he and Manda didn't stop sleeping together. They looked at each other in the early evening and knew he would come into her room later that night. He maneuvered Manda's body in ways Siripon never permitted. He lay on his back and coaxed her into riding him, aroused by the mattress dipping as her body bounced above him. He took her standing up, parting her legs and entering her from behind. He could not say why he was more controlling with her except that afterward he felt powerful; he felt as if he had reclaimed something.

In January, his wedding anniversary arrived. He woke with a sense of invincibility: Another year had passed, and Siripon hadn't realized she should leave him. He whistled as he dressed for work. He carried the lightness with him around the factory. On his way home, he stopped for a card and a bouquet of carnations, offering them to Siripon as she prepared to leave for work.

"Happy anniversary," she said in a childish voice, as if she was embarrassed. He was always more excited for the occasion than she was. Perhaps she simply took it for granted that there was no threat to their relationship. But he sensed, too, that she had grown more distant. He feared she could tell that the forces of gravity in the house had shifted, pulling him in more than one direction.

"Why don't you call in sick?" he asked her.

She rolled her eyes. "Imagine how upset the others would be."

It was Manda, later, who complimented him on the flowers. "Look at you," she said, placing them in a vase and setting them in the middle of the dining table. "The romance hasn't died completely."

"Tell that to your sister," Kamron said. "She wouldn't look at them."

"What did you expect?"

The two often mocked Siripon, commenting on her lack of joy, her obsessions with healthy cooking and fastidious cleaning. They depended on her to keep the house, but her zeal amused them too. Life would go on without her constant tending, if only she would stop to realize it.

Evening came and Kamron thought about how much he loved Siripon. He thought how lucky he was to have found her, how wonderful and pretty and caring she was. His admiration swam in his mind, mixing with the liquor, and soon he was undressing Manda. They began as they always did. But in the middle of the sex, he turned on the lights, exposing Manda's body spread before him. Her limbs were contorted, and he couldn't help thinking she looked like an injured animal.

"You jerk. Turn it back off!" Her voice was angry and embarrassed. She rolled away, pulling at the sheets, but he eased her back to him.

"Let me watch you."

He began again, feeling the slip of skin, the friction that built into something more urgent. He took her with no need to impress her. No matter how many times they had sex, he would never fall in love with her.

When it was over, Kamron turned the lights off again. He grew quiet, listening to the silence in the rest of the house. Then he crept back to his room and fell into his own bed. He loved Siripon. There was no one else he would want as a wife.

2

Manda stripped her bed and replaced the sheets with a fresh set. She was having to do it once or twice a week, after each of her encounters with Kamron. Their furtive meetings had become so frequent that she kept her eye out for discounts during her shifts at JCPenney, buying new sheets and towels that she tucked in the back of her bedroom closet. Refreshing the linens became a way of resetting herself, erasing the traces of what had happened.

She became responsible for other practical matters. Their first night together was spontaneous, careless. For weeks afterward, Manda worried she might have gotten pregnant. Later, relieved when her period arrived, she bought condoms that she hid among her bras. She knotted them after sex, wrapped them in tissue, carried them in her purse until she could throw them away at the mall, not willing to risk her sister finding them in the trash at home. They reminded her of shed skin, as if Kamron was leaving her with only his decay.

Sex was meant to be slow and sensual, a tenderness between two people. At least that was what she believed. With Kamron everything was assertive and firm. She felt she was nothing more than a body for him, a thing he could manipulate and tease. And yet she invited the sex too. She craved it, though she didn't experience the feeling as passion. She craved being a woman on the other side, a woman who knew the body of a man. She craved the knowledge that she could satisfy a man.

She crept out into the hall and pressed her ear against Ben's bedroom door. He breathed heavily inside, settled. They had all eaten dinner together. Then, briefly, they watched television together before Manda sent Ben to his room to finish his homework. Here was another night when she had taken care of Ben and satisfied Kamron. She played a mother's role, a wife's role. It was what Siripon left to Manda on nights like this, when Siripon was busy at the hospital making money and taking care of other children, other families. She was the mother of many. She divided herself as part of her insatiable need to please everyone—she had not changed since she was a girl. Manda didn't spread herself so thin. That was just one of the many ways the sisters were different.

The next day, Manda was still preoccupied with this comparison when she met Aunt Seamstress to go shopping. In her friend's presence, Manda felt she was strong enough to never sleep with Kamron again; she could end the affair, bury it, so that normal life resumed.

"I've missed you, Sister," Manda said. "We must stop letting so much time pass between our dates."

"You know I never have too much going on. I'm around whenever you want to see me."

They rarely spoke of the children anymore. Manda imagined Jessica growing into a driven young woman, someone who had cut the ties to the past. The old days, the picnics, seemed so long ago. "Have you trimmed down?" she asked. In all the time they had known each other, Aunt Seamstress had been consistent to a fault. She spent her days patiently hunched at her sewing machine or meditating at the temple. The lifestyle cultivated a sense of wellness, something translucent in her. She was not beautiful, but she had taken care of herself.

"Tell me again how you found your husband," Manda said.

"That's an unexpected request! What is there to say that I haven't told you many times before?"

"Tell me why you were attracted to him, how he finally won you over."

"Those were different times, Sister. We didn't flirt like people do today. We were around each other, both of us working at the police station, and we realized we got along." Aunt Seamstress's voice grew soft, as it always did when she spoke about her husband. Manda could hear the devotion that her friend still felt for him.

"And what did you see in him?" Manda asked.

"He was simply a good man," Aunt Seamstress said. She had stopped walking and looked directly at Manda. "When you are finally ready for a man of your own, the only thing you need to know is whether or not he's good. Everything else can be navigated. But what brings this on? Do you have a man in mind for yourself?"

"Of course not! No, I was just curious about your life."

"There's more to it than that, isn't there? Someone has caught your eye."

"There's nobody, Sister. Honestly, I would tell you if I was falling for a man. No, it's nothing like that. I couldn't be further away from romance." Manda could feel that her face had flushed. Her entire body felt warm. She marched on ahead, pretending to be drawn to a coat displayed on a conspicuous mannequin. "The evenings are growing so cold," she complained.

At home, she refreshed the water in the vase of carnations and moved it to the shrine room, where she wouldn't have to look at it. In all her years of gardening, she had never tried to grow carnations; she had never tried to grow flowers of any kind. They had no purpose. They were nothing more than makeup and fancy dresses. She preferred the herbs and fruits and vegetables, the things that provided nutrition. They carried their own beauty, the beauty of purpose and need.

She spent the rest of the day in the garden. Over the years, she had come to understand it more deeply, so that she could work intuitively, fertilizing and pruning and transplanting and harvesting based on its subtle cues. This time of year, everything was lush and thriving, the entire plot radiating green and giving off sharp perfumes that changed from one bed to the next. There were many more plants than what she had carried over in the hem of her skirt. She had traded cuttings, split and shared some that were doing well. When she wrote home to her family and friends, they were amazed by what she had managed to grow in America. It had become a standing joke originated by Kiet: She didn't speak the language of the Outer Country, but she understood its dirt.

3

When high school began, Ben convinced himself he knew everyone he needed to know. Students from three middle schools came together, familiar faces mixing with new ones, but he still recognized a handful of people in each of his classes. He avoided the others, letting them drift by as if they were in a current of life he couldn't access. The approach worked well enough the first couple of years. Then, his junior year, a boy caught his attention. His name was Collin Brennan. For weeks, Ben tried to be in his presence whenever he could.

Collin didn't seem to be intimidated by anyone. He was one of the most talkative people in their classes, asking questions nobody else thought of or offering information that wasn't in their textbooks. Teachers didn't discuss homework and grades with him the way they did with other students. With Collin, they brought up current affairs—the appointment of a new Supreme Court judge or the new House Speaker. A few times, Ben even noticed them inviting Collin into the teachers' lounge, from where he would emerge a few minutes later holding a cup of coffee.

Ben's fascination with Collin came after the Broges moved away. That had happened much later than expected. For several months, Mr. Broge hadn't been able to find a house in Arizona that met their needs. His frustration was what prompted Mrs. Broge to tell Ben that they were leaving.

In the weeks leading up to their departure, Ben spent every other evening with them, helping them pack, looking through the objects of their lives one last time before they disappeared. The day the family was to leave, he asked Siripon to drive him over to say goodbye.

"Who will you spend time with after that woman is gone?" Siripon asked, her face stern as she watched the road.

"I don't know. Maybe no one."

"It will do you good to spend some time at home with your family."

The moving truck had already been loaded by the time he arrived. Mrs. Broge was just dropping her keys into a lockbox that hung from the porch railing. "My dear, we thought we missed you," she said. She wore a tattered pair of jeans and an old gray sweater, an outfit Ben never would have imagined her owning. She took him aside and looked into his eyes, and for a second Ben felt the weight of the night in the paper shack. He didn't like to think about that time. Whenever he did, a swell of pain, like a stomachache, came up.

"You'll keep in touch," she said. "I'm excited to see what you make of yourself this year."

"I don't think I'll do anything special," Ben replied, close to tears.

But Mrs. Broge shook her head. "Find something that excites you. And make new friends. Promise me."

He had moped for too long afterward, moving through his classes as if he were in a trance. Once in a while, he remembered the old photos Mrs. Broge had shown him of her friends surrounding her. Still, he was intimidated by all the other students speeding by in their own current.

Collin had a lean build and a smooth, clean-cut face that reminded Ben of actors from old black-and-white movies he sometimes watched while doing homework. When no one was paying attention, he stole glances at Collin, fascinated by his red hair, his freckled skin, his lean but muscular arms and legs. Collin's shirts were never tucked in, and occasionally when he stretched his arms, he revealed his stomach muscles and a line of wiry hair that grew up from beneath his waistline and circled his navel. Ben imagined this patch of hair brushing against his own skin, their two bodies pressed together.

"It's too early to say for sure, but I bet we're neck and neck for valedictorian," Collin said to Ben one day. They had just gotten through their second round of exams.

"I didn't realize," Ben said, surprised that Collin was talking to him. "No one mentioned anything to me about it."

"They're afraid to bring it up. They don't want to make you nervous."

"What do you mean?"

"Stress." Collin stretched out the word. "Everyone's, like, so careful not to stress you out."

Ben walked faster, realizing where the conversation was headed. He no longer had to warn his teachers at the beginning of each term about his throwing up—they already knew. The entire high school already knew. Whenever he ran out of the classroom, no one asked any questions or stood in his way. He turned invisible from the moment he left his chair until the moment he returned.

"They told me I should talk to you about it," Collin said. "You know, they assume we're friends because we're both nerds."

"I'm just trying to stay focused," Ben said grimly.

"Totally cool." Collin leaned in. "But there are counselors if you need to talk. I can introduce you, if you want."

"I don't need any counselors."

Ben couldn't sleep that night, his thoughts focused on what more he could do to keep people from paying attention to him. In class the next day, he didn't volunteer any answers during discussions. He kept to himself and slunk away at the end of each period. Before the week was over, though, he worried the change would attract even more attention. His teachers might decide he was withdrawn or even suicidal—a label that always felt too close, too immense. He circled the larger groups of classmates, eavesdropped on their conversations as if he could learn how to be more like them. He wanted to be normal, and normal meant making mistakes. When he was sure it wouldn't affect his final grades, he gave wrong answers for some of the test questions. For weeks, he didn't earn a perfect score, hoping the teachers would forget about him. He was startled when Collin approached him again.

"I know what you're doing."

"What do you mean?" Ben asked.

"Okay, fine. You just got an answer wrong. It was probably over your head."

"It wasn't over my head."

"Then you did it on purpose. Why would you do that? Are you stupid?"

"I'm not stupid."

"I know you're not stupid. That's my point, stupid."

Ben laughed. He realized how panicked he had been. "It's harder than you think," he said. "Do you know how much work it takes to calculate the consequences of a wrong answer?"

"One hundred divided by the number of questions."

"Right, like no one ever gives partial credit."

"Fine, but I bet it's, like, ten seconds of your time."

"Then *you* do it," Ben said. "Next pre-calc test, I dare you to get exactly ninety-seven percent."

The competition began. The two challenged each other to get impossible scores, sometimes even agreeing to miss the same question before ever seeing the test. Each week, they compared grades, closing their eyes before exchanging papers. Ben knew without knowing that they were becoming friends. They found each other every morning, even when they had nothing to talk about. He didn't want a new friend, someone who might see him too clearly, but he imagined one day having a photo album like Mrs. Broge's, something that would show he had lived. Collin invited Ben to a play, a retelling of *Romeo and Juliet* set in Creole country. There would be witch doctors and voodoo dolls, love potions and talismans. Ben started to decline the invitation, not yet ready to commit to something outside of school, but Collin told him they would be able to apply it toward extra credit in English class. He had already gotten permission from Mrs. Phelan.

When they came back to Collin's house after the play, he imitated the actors, and Mrs. and Mr. Brennan, meeting the boys in the kitchen, joined in on the scenes. A sword fight erupted with wooden spoons.

The defeated Mercutio, Collin's father, writhed in pain on the granite island. "A plague on both your houses! They have made worms' meat of me!"

In the glowing haze of the commotion, Ben compared the Brennan family to his own. His parents wouldn't have the lines of a Shakespeare play memorized. They wouldn't have banana cream pie waiting on the dining table for them the way Mrs. Brennan did. She brought over four plates and placed a slice on each. Mr. Brennan began to tell a joke about a house that was haunted by the ghost of a rosebush, but before he could finish, Collin insisted that they had to go study.

"Trust me, it's better this way," he whispered as they rushed down the hall. "Once you get Dad started, you can't get him to shut up."

Collin's shelves were lined with awards and photos. He posed next to people Ben didn't recognize, people in dark suits with American flags behind them. He cleared off his desk so they could put their plates down. Then he removed his shirt and jeans and tossed them into an open hamper before stepping to his closet. Ben was always shy about undressing in front of others, aware that his own lack of confidence only made him seem more awkward. But Collin apparently thought nothing of undressing in front of Ben. His body was pale and freckled at the shoulders. The same wiry red hair that grew around his belly button also circled his nipples. Ben didn't permit himself to stare for long before turning his gaze. But that night, alone, he tried to reconstruct what Collin looked like. The image only came back in fragments. The more Ben tried to fill in details, the more others slipped away.

The boys studied in Collin's room after school, and on nights before big tests, they often worked so late that Mr. and Mrs. Brennan insisted Ben stay over. Siripon never argued. She told Ben to be careful, and she would speak briefly with Mrs. Brennan to thank her for her hospitality. Sometimes, on the line, Ben heard his aunt's voice in the background. "Again?" or "Wouldn't it be better if he just came home?" she said. But it was never enough to change his plans. He had come to realize that, in the world of mothers and fathers, his aunt's words didn't carry much weight.

Ben liked spending time with Collin, but whenever they had plans to get together, he also felt a new sort of anticipation, a quiver in his solar plexus. Despite how fun it was to talk and joke around together, Ben longed for occasions like after the play, when Collin undressed in front of him. They were rare, occurring weeks apart, so that when it happened, Ben would try to commit to memory as much as he could. He paid attention to how the muscles in Collin's neck ran down to his shoulders, how the shadows of his abdominal muscles continued down behind the waistband of his underwear. Ben grew more courageous over time, daring to speak to Collin while he was undressed so that Collin would get distracted before stepping over to the closet. Once, Ben even made a joke as an excuse to punch Collin in the arm.

"Have you ever met a guy who was into other guys?" Ben asked one day.

"You mean like someone who's gay?" Collin said.

"Yeah, I mean, maybe."

"Of course I have. You have, too, haven't you?"

Ben crept closer. He had wanted to bring up the topic for a long time, and now that he'd started, he wouldn't let himself stop. "I know someone," he said. "But he told me I had to keep it a secret."

"There's nothing wrong with being gay," Collin said.

"You don't think so?"

"I don't think so."

"And you wouldn't think there was anything wrong with me if I told you *I* was gay?"

"I wouldn't." Collin approached Ben slowly, nervously. He took off his shirt slowly and nervously. He took Ben's hand and placed it on his chest. Ben felt his skin, felt his muscles tighten. He leaned forward and kissed Collin's sternum. The area turned white in the shape of his lips for a second and then returned to its normal color.

"I wasn't expecting that," Collin said.

Ben didn't have a response. He scooted back, but Collin stepped forward so that they were touching again. He tugged Ben's shirt up over his head.

"Should you lock the door?" Ben asked.

Collin stepped quietly to the door and locked it. When he returned, Ben could see that he was hard. They unbuttoned Collin's pants together, their hands getting in each other's way. Ben pulled the pants down, pulled down the waistband of Collin's boxer shorts. He took Collin in his mouth. It was the first time he had ever done that with anyone. After a while, Collin got down on his knees, unzipped Ben's jeans, and sucked him. They kissed afterward, and Ben smelled a scent like cedar around Collin's mouth. He knew that it was his own smell, and he wondered if Collin sensed it, too, or if he was also smelling himself on Ben's lips. He felt grateful that Collin didn't seem ashamed about any of it. He was tender and reassuring. They took turns. They lay down in bed together. Ben felt his orgasm approaching. He clenched his muscles for fear of what might happen. He tried to stop, but Collin's hands tightened around him, encouraging him to keep going. Collin himself was moving harder. The sensation became overwhelming. Ben felt as if their bodies were pools of water that were spilling into each other. When it was over, Ben lay shivering in bed. He felt sensitive to the touch and cold, but he didn't want to ruin the moment by slipping under the covers. He ran his hand over Collin's body, taking measure of his skin as it cooled so he would remember the feeling.

"Do you think your parents know?" he asked.

"I don't think so. I've never done anything like this before. I just imagined it. I imagined it so often," Collin said, laughing.

"I don't want to be valedictorian," Ben said.

"Yes, you do. We'll tie like we talked about. It will work." Collin's voice was relaxed and sleepy.

"I don't want to have to get up on stage. I don't want everyone looking at me. You do it. Do it for both of us."

The room was dark. Ben could just make out the features of Collin's face. His eyelashes caught the faint light from outside as he blinked. Light reflected against his lips, a streak of roughness on an otherwise smooth surface.

"Why do you throw up?" Collin asked. "Are you sick?"

"I don't know." Ben turned away, not wanting to talk about it and face Collin at the same time. "Does it gross you out?"

"No."

"Yes, it does."

"I mean, puke is gross in general. But it doesn't bother me when you, specifically, do it. You almost make puking seem normal."

"Don't use that word. I hate it."

"Okay, I didn't know."

"I know. I know you didn't know. I just don't like that word."

"Okay, I won't use it ever again. I promise."

Ben had believed that no one would ever like him if he was honest. But Collin seemed to like him. The two kissed even after they had been talking about Ben throwing up. Food was cooking in the kitchen. Soon Mrs. Brennan knocked on the door and called them to the table for dinner. Ben stood up and turned on the light. He was excited to go out to her. He wanted to be out among other people while the taste of Collin was still on his tongue.

4

A new counselor joined the high school. Her name—Marybeth Digby—made Ben think of people from an older generation, women who wore bonnets and built homes on new frontiers. But Marybeth was younger than any of his teachers. During her first semester there, the student body president announced that there would be a volleyball tournament that anyone could enter, and Marybeth teamed up with Nicholas Keough, the varsity quarterback. Ben watched all their games, fascinated by the two of them together. He had had sex with Collin enough times that he had stopped counting, and he was constantly watching others, wondering who else was doing the same.

Marybeth threatened him, too, though the feeling hid like an amorphous thing within him. He didn't like that she infiltrated the student body. He worried, vaguely, that she would see them in a way none of the other adults could.

An envelope from Marybeth was delivered to him during his precalculus class. He was to report for a meeting. It didn't say why. He slid the note back into its envelope, hoping no one would ask about it.

Her office was filled with prints from old horror movies: *King Kong* and *Godzilla* and *Dracula,* grainy images reproduced and framed. Monstera crept along her bright windows and spilled over her file cabinets. The place was nothing like the suffocating psychologist's office he had been to as a child.

"I want to talk about your vomiting," she said, smiling without showing any teeth. "I'm wondering if there's anything going on that's triggering these episodes."

"I get nervous," Ben said. He questioned whether the answer was true. He had used it as an explanation for so long that he couldn't remember who came up with it or when. He *did* get nervous, but he didn't know if he was nervous before throwing up or if it was the throwing up itself that made him nervous.

Marybeth moved on as if she hadn't expected the problem to be illuminated so easily. She slid over a sheet of paper with a list of calming techniques. It recommended slow breathing, counting backward from ten to one, closing his eyes and imagining himself on the shore of his favorite beach. Ben didn't bother to explain that he had tried all these techniques already. He simply nodded and thanked her. Then he picked up his backpack to leave.

"You're vomiting around campus, in the trash cans and on the blacktop where everyone can see," Marybeth said, gesturing for him to sit down again. "The smell bothers people, and the custodians have to come and clean up after you. That will need to stop. When you vomit, you have to go all the way to the bathroom and use the toilets so you can flush it down. Do you understand? We have to be considerate of the other people in our community."

Ben nodded again before leaving the office. His only concern was to get away from this person who saw too much. Returning to his class, he grew anxious at the thought of having to run across campus every time he felt sick. He wouldn't be able to hold it for that long. He still carried his Glad-Lock bags in his pocket, but he had learned years ago that the students only made fun of him more if they saw him use them, accusing him of saving the contents to eat again later.

A larger revelation occurred to him. He was humiliated at the thought that others were having to clean up after him, that he had become a burden to the school. He had never considered that before.

The rest of the week, whenever he threw up, he thought of the custodians, and he wondered if they hated him. He was worried that if he didn't stop quickly enough, he would get called back in to Marybeth's office, or maybe to the principal's. Maybe they would expel him. The next time he had to throw up, he stepped outside of the classroom and braced himself. When the acidic liquid filled his mouth, he clamped his lips and swallowed it back down. It had just come from him, but it felt like a foreign thing he swallowed, and all that day he felt it inside of him like a poison. He didn't give up. He repeated the process as the weeks passed. Sometimes it worked, burning his throat but settling inside again. Sometimes it made more of a mess, sputtering out on his hands and face, so that he had to run to the bathroom to clean up before anyone saw him. For so long throwing up had come quickly and easily. Now it disgusted him. The dread of having to swallow it made him do whatever he could to stop it from happening in the first place. He bit his thumbnail. He pinched his inner arms. He anticipated times when he might throw up so that he could prepare for them, breathing slowly, counting backward from ten to one. His only comfort was the idea that he could still throw up, he only had to swallow it afterward. His body could hold it so that no one would know. Eventually, the right muscles grew stronger to help him. He didn't get called to the counselor again.

The realization of what had happened came to the rest of the family over the next several weeks. Siripon suspected it when the ziplock bags no longer disappeared as quickly as they had before. Several days in a row, she opened the drawer where they were kept and found the little box still heavy in her hand.

But though she was relieved and grateful, she was still concerned for her son. He stayed out with Collin until late into the evenings, sometimes spending the night at the Brennan house, never telling Siripon what he did while he was away—he would say only that he had been studying. Maybe Collin or his parents were responsible for him stopping. And because she was suspicious of them, she was suspicious of why and how he'd stopped. She walked around the house with her brow furrowed, her lips pressed together. She couldn't help wondering if Ben could be using drugs that were changing him. After all, his father drank as soon as he came home from work. He stored bottles of whiskey in the storage shed beside the garden, where he would sneak off in the evenings to refill his tumbler, pretending that it was still three-quarters full from his original pour. Ben wouldn't drink. He hated his father's alcoholism too much. But there were other substances out there, delivered in the form of pills and powders and needles.

Siripon was burdened with these questions. But she didn't ask Ben about them. She had come to think she didn't have the strength to dig into everything. The vomiting, the homosexuality, the late evenings out with Collin—when would it end? She wouldn't be able to get on with her day. She paid the bills. She prepared lunch and dinner for the following day. She washed the dishes and stacked them neatly in their cupboards. She did the laundry, methodically ironing her uniform and Ben's shirts, folding the rest into perfect stacks. These were things she could do.

Manda was working in the garden when she realized that Ben had stopped vomiting. She had been thinking of him as she often did—he still occupied her mind, though he no longer spent as much time with her as he used to. Their love had become one-sided, flowing from aunt to nephew but not the other way.

When had he vomited last? A week ago? Two weeks? She couldn't remember. Over the last few days, she couldn't recall a single occasion when he threw up, though she may simply have not noticed. Still, the thought that Ben might have stopped gave Manda a tentative sense of buoyancy. Maybe the effects of the ceremony had finally come to an end. Maybe the girl's spirit had left his body after so many years. Was it possible after all this time? After so much hope was lost?

She found Siripon in the kitchen and leaned in close. "Do you suppose—" she said in a conspiring tone. "Do you suppose our boy could have stopped his little habit?"

Siripon grunted and nodded her head once. "Four or five weeks already," she said.

"I only hope it lasts," Manda said. "That night—" She stopped herself. She had almost told Siripon what she had done, wanting to be thanked for making the right decision. But she was being too optimistic. Siripon would still be angry, even now that the problem was resolved.

Kamron came home from work. He walked stiffly through the gate and sat on the step to untie his boots. He set them on the rack, but he didn't get up right away. Watching him, Manda felt a new sense of sympathy for her brother-in-law. In many ways, he had become the outsider in the family instead of her.

"And have you noticed? Our investment has paid off after all," she said to him later. Siripon had left for her shift, and they lay in bed together, though they were no longer touching.

"What are you talking about?" Kamron asked.

"Your son," Manda said. "Have you noticed anything different about him?"

Kamron didn't respond. He sat up and reached for his clothes.

"He stopped," Manda said, shaking him. "Your son has stopped vomiting. I bet you didn't even notice."

He lay back down and sighed slowly. The room was dark, but she could tell by the pronunciation of his words that he was smiling. "He told you this?"

"No one had to tell me. I can see it for myself. Siripon noticed it too."

"Almost ten years," Kamron said. "I didn't think it was possible."

"All you had to do was trust me," Manda said.

They got dressed and walked out of her room together, made their way to the kitchen together. They brought out bottles of beer cold from the refrigerator. That evening they stayed up for hours. Their conversation grew more animated as it got later. They exchanged stories about their jobs and all the ways in which they were unhappy with them. Kamron still complained about being powerless at the factory. Manda was constantly annoyed by the careless customers who tromped through the aisles of her department. Suddenly, she was amused by having these little irritations in her life. They all seemed silly, tolerable, now that the bigger problem of her nephew's sickness was resolved.

She decided to celebrate. She prepared Ben's favorite meal, boiling a whole chicken, mixing chicken fat with shavings of toasted garlic and ginger and using it to cook a pot of fragrant rice. She made a sauce of fermented soybeans and ginger and chilis. When the time came, she called Ben and Kamron down for dinner. Her nephew was suspicious when he sat at the table and noticed the others in high spirits.

"Eat more," Manda said, spooning a second serving of rice onto his plate, sliding him another piece of chicken. "My nephew is all grown up," Manda sang. "He doesn't have to *uok, uok, uok* anymore."

Ben nodded, but he didn't look up.

"You thought no one would notice, but we see you. From now on, you're the man of the house," Manda said.

Ben nodded.

Eventually, Siripon brought it up with Ben as well. On her next day off, she announced that she was going to the grocery store.

"What about the bags?" she asked. "Do you need me to get you any more of those?"

"I don't think so," Ben said. He looked up from where he had been lying in front of the television. He had a strangely glum expression, a look as if something had gone wrong. Her fears returned. She wondered why being a mother was so difficult, why she could never just have a day when she didn't worry.

"No?" she asked one more time.

He shook his head.

"Okay," she said as she grabbed her list of groceries and reached for her keys on the hook. "Be careful," she said, but she thought she had said "I love you."

Departure

1

Wintry's Coin-Op Laundromat had stood in the shadow of a twelve-story medical and dental building for as long as Siripon could remember. She passed the squat, humming business on her way to visit Dr. Kavita Anand, a periodontist who had patiently repaired her mouth since she turned forty and began waking up to green and swollen gums. She hadn't gone inside Wintry's for almost two decades, since she bought a washing machine of her own, grateful not to have needed the place all these years. It was dull and gray, with rows of machines that churned monotonously in their metallic cells. Washing clothes there was nothing like doing laundry in Phuket, the fields of white bedclothes and uniforms that fluttered beside the ocean. Still, she was drawn to the shared vision, the patrons with their singular goal of cleaning.

She carried the laundry toward the oversized washers that lined the back wall, hesitating only to gather her strength. Her grief was heavy. Since Ben had announced that he was going to Stanford—358 miles away—she had withered, no longer boasting to her family back home about Ben's ambitions to become a chemical engineer. She spoke less to Ben himself, going to her son only when she had questions relevant to his move. She was confronting the limit of what she could bear, her inability to save him from the dangers that threatened to take him from her.

For three days, she and Manda had been busy making the final preparations for Ben's departure. They cooked wokfuls of kaprow fried rice and pots of green and massaman curry that they packed into Tupperware containers and stacked in the freezer. Manda painted Ben's name in white nail polish onto lamps and pencil holders, tubs and trunks. She stitched it with thread into the corners of his sheets and pillowcases. Siripon opened a checking account for Ben and deposited five thousand dollars into it. She helped him apply for his first credit card, a Visa with a two-thousand-dollar limit. All that was left was the laundry: three baskets' worth, along with two comforters and several towels.

She went to exchange her dollar bills for quarters. She had sacrificed her old coins prematurely, shimmying them into paper sleeves so that Ben would have change for his own laundry trips up north. Through the windows of Wintry's, the medical-dental building seemed more imposing than it usually did. The high wall facing the laundromat had no windows, only staggered red brick that reached from the parking lot to the sky. Siripon examined the caduceus that clung to the building's facade. It was such a strange collection of objects: the winged staff and the two snakes that wrapped around it. With Ben gone, there would be no more barrier separating Siripon, Kamron, and Manda. They would be three snakes with no staff between them.

Of course, no one had seen much of Ben in the last year. His disappearance had started with Mrs. Broge—Siripon never could come up with a good explanation for why Ben would want to spend time with her, except that he was unhappy with the mothering he got at home. Then his focus had turned to Collin, a boy who seemed to be successful in everything he tried. He and Ben had nearly identical schedules, a full day of Advanced Placement courses they so coveted. They only diverged because Ben chose robotics for his single elective while Collin competed on the Constitution team.

Now they were both going to Stanford. Siripon was suspicious that Ben had chosen to go only to follow Collin. She would struggle to cover her son's tuition along with everything else she still paid for at home. But she would not stand in his way.

Her son's decision to leave hadn't been obvious in the beginning. Last year, when his winter break arrived, he took over the dining table with his college applications. Glossy brochures from all over the country were fanned out according to Ben's mysterious organizational system. They included several that were close to home, but now Siripon wondered if those were just decoys to keep her from getting upset.

For a week, he looked through his lists of pros and cons, flipped through thick catalogs. After everyone else in the household settled into their bedrooms, he got to work filling out forms on his electric typewriter. The keys clacked steadily until one or two in the morning, when she would finally climb out of bed and tell him to stop. On nights when she worked, she suspected he went to sleep just before she came home.

Kamron didn't get involved. Siripon guessed he was pleased by the prospect of Ben moving out of the house. The last time they had argued, Kamron had swiped the wall clear of all its photos, and Ben had screamed so loudly his hands turned pale from lack of circulation.

In the beginning, Siripon was quiet herself as Ben worked through his applications. She left the guesthouse to him, serving dinners on the coffee table in the living room of the main house, where the family sat on pillows on the floor. When the meals were over, she let Ben go back to his work as she carried the dishes back to the kitchen and washed them. Then one day, she had enough. The sun was setting, and they were preparing to eat. "The rest of your family members live here too," she said, gathering up Ben's neatly ordered piles into a heap before he could protest. Ben was outraged over the shuffled information, the wrinkled forms. "I guess I should just give up on college altogether," he said. "I'll just go be a tube bender like Dad!" Unfazed, Siripon arranged the place mats and utensils on the table. She carried over a bowl of tofu soup, not flinching when it splashed and scalded the webbing between her fingers. Ben didn't eat. He spent hours re-creating his arrangement on the floor of his bedroom, exaggerating the effort it required. That night, the typewriter clacked on until sunrise, and only after everyone else got up did he draw the curtains closed and fall asleep.

On the morning of their departure, Collin arrived early, placing his hands together and carefully saying "Sawadeekrup." Siripon acknowledged him, but she didn't like him. She was torn between wanting to enlist him to protect Ben and wanting to cast him away as Ben's biggest threat.

Everyone grew quiet when the time came to load the car. Siripon thought back to the day she'd left Thailand for the first time and the loneliness that hit her at the airport. She understood what her mother must have felt, that mix of sorrow and hope, betrayal and pride. She wished she could impart to Ben the wisdom that would keep him safe, but the challenge was too immense. She didn't even know enough about the American university system to give him useful advice on school. She would have to count on Collin to help her son navigate these things, certain that his parents had received extensive educations.

The last things to be brought out from the house were the frozen containers of food they prepared earlier in the week. A coating of needled frost clung to their corners as Siripon stacked them into a cooler. Ben protested the idea of taking the food up, particularly since Collin was with him. But she knew he would be grateful later, just as she had appreciated the sweets her family tucked into her suitcase. The loneliness would make him yearn for home, even if he couldn't imagine it now. She kissed him and gave him a long hug, letting go before she started to cry. The others said their goodbyes, and soon the car was out of sight. Siripon turned back toward the house. It was nothing more than an empty shell.

2

The jagged crowns of palm trees passed overhead as Ben and Collin entered the Stanford campus. Ben wondered if he had moved far enough away from his family. He could have chosen the Ivy League schools instead, or one of the smaller liberal arts schools—Bennington or Amherst. Yet here he was, far away, but not too far away. He had not been able to cut his tethers completely. Something kept him close.

The memorial church came into view with its stained-glass windows. Hoover Tower and the amphitheater loomed a short distance away. It was all so intimidating—the historic buildings, the stadium, the legacy. He and Collin were two of sixteen hundred people in the class of 2000, nobodies who somehow needed to differentiate themselves from the others. They were lucky to have ended up in the same residence hall, even if they couldn't be roommates.

Ben entered his dorm to find half of it already moved in. His roommate's bed had been made with stiff-looking sheets, and one side of the closet was lined with suits. On the desk were well-worn finance books, the stack topped with a tear-off calendar three-quarters of the way through that featured Ansel Adams images paired with inspirational quotes. There was a framed photo of a tall but baby-faced boy in a life jacket and shorts, somewhere by a river, a paddle propped beside him, his nose shielded behind a streak of zinc. According to his bio, Eric Tolman was from Florida; he was a business major who had already done some internship at a company Ben figured he should recognize. Ben wished they were already friends so that he could avoid the awkward introduction. He quickly slid his things in and pushed them against one wall so they would be out of the way. Then he escaped the building.

Cars were backed up along the road leading to the residences. There were students with their parents, back seats loaded with cardboard boxes and suitcases as Collin's had been earlier that day. It never felt like an option for Ben to be delivered by his family. He didn't want his new classmates to see how his parents behaved in public, their inability to blend in after all these years. He didn't want the students to know how his aunt orbited around him, the way she still tried to define him, as if he belonged to her rather than to himself. He found the Science and Engineering Quad. It was where most of his classes would be. The thought of exams and labs triggered a pang of nausea that pushed up toward his throat. It was a common enough reaction for anyone, he told himself. People threw up when they got nervous. But Ben knew it was different for him. He had gotten better at stopping himself, but the need was still there. Maybe, like a scar, it would never go away.

He wandered north to the biology buildings, these more populated than the SEQ. They emptied out to Roth Way, and across the road, he saw a sculpture garden—the Rodins. They were impressive figures. Some of them were recognizable from his art history text: *The Martyr, The Three Shades* with their straining necks, the too-big head of *Pierre de Wissant*. It was the first time he had seen any of them in person. They were exquisite, but they were frustrating too—characters unable to live beyond the moment in which they were captured. Another wave of nausea came, this one cold and dense. He walked deeper into the garden, grateful that some of the other visitors had gotten their fill and made their way toward the exit. In front of him, a looming rectangle emerged. It was the famed *Gates of Hell,* teeming with suffering. There were the figures he could easily recognize and the others forced into the background to perish in obscurity. Standing in front of it, Ben felt a pull, as if the gates might open for him, transport him to another existence. Or perhaps he was already on the other side.

More than two hours passed before he returned to the dorms. Still avoiding Eric Tolman, Ben went to Collin's room, where Collin was just finishing a phone call. He rolled onto his mattress and sprawled his thin arms and legs. "We have to get ready for Recruitment," he said. "I'm going to pull together a list of fraternities we should go after."

"Wouldn't that mean we'd have to live in a house?"

"Who wouldn't want that? We need to start building our networks."

"No, I wouldn't like it in a frat house. Don't you have to be, like, straight?"

"So act straight. Act fucking straight! I've heard you use your deep voice!" Collin lunged forward and pulled Ben into him, contorting the inadequate mattress so that their elbows and knees struck the wooden baseboard beneath. A knock came from the unit below, unfamiliar classmates already annoyed with them. Ben sat up, nervous. He moved to the opposite end of the room.

"I didn't know you were going to abandon Crothers to join a fraternity."

"It's just an idea," Collin replied. "But I think we should look into it."

"It's bad enough we can't be roommates here. I got paired up with some business major. I've seen his closet—he dresses like he's going to a job interview."

"You're letting yourself get intimidated."

"I just know my limitations." Ever since Ben turned down being the valedictorian at their high school, the two of them often argued about missed opportunities. Collin's stance was that they should be proud of everything they accomplished. But Ben didn't want to be the center of attention. He made a decision. If Collin was going to join a fraternity, Ben wouldn't follow him. He would join a research lab as he had planned, find a faculty member who was developing something practical. He would focus on classes and research and hope that this first year went smoothly.

"Have you talked to anyone yet?" Collin asked.

"Just statues," Ben said.

"We should go to the dining hall before it closes." Without waiting for a rebuttal, Collin took Ben's arm and pulled him out the door.

The place was crowded with new students and their families shuffling from counter to counter. Everyone else seemed excited and happy to be there, as if only Ben had any sense of foreboding. He followed Collin through the line, mindlessly placing food into his takeout box and hoping he didn't do anything to embarrass himself. They found a small table and sat watching the activity around them.

"This is going to be good for us," Collin said. "We'll expand our horizons. And if anything goes wrong, we'll help each other get through it. But there's nothing to stress about, okay? Cool? We're all the same here. We just have to get out there and do our best."

"This is worse than a homecoming rally," Ben said, looking down into his box, a sloppy mingling of lasagna and chow mein he regretted placing side by side. He was losing hope. Tomorrow, they would have to go through the new-student orientation, with its embarrassing icebreakers and ridiculous scavenger hunts. In only a few days, he would be going to classes and taking tests and making presentations. He wanted to be back home. Soon his family would settle in for the night without him. The dishes would be washed and set on the rack to dry. His aunt would be watching soap operas on the old television she still kept in her room. His father would be drunk and wandering around the house with that maddening tumbler in his hand. His mother would be sleeping in her fragile way, always ready to rise at a moment's notice. Ben knew she felt abandoned by him. He hadn't been able to explain that he wasn't trying to get away from *her.* He was trying to get away from *them,* the family, the complicated web they formed when they were together. He had figured out that his dad and aunt were having an affair. Several nights he had heard Kamron creep down the hall and enter Manda's bedroom. There would be quiet talking that lasted for only a few seconds before the sound of bedsprings came. Ben was used to accusing his father of being an immoral man, but he realized it wasn't so one-sided. He wished he could separate his mom from the others, free her as he was freeing himself. But she didn't want to escape the way he did. She just didn't want to suffer alone.

Across the table, Collin brought up the fraternities again. He rattled off Greek letters while Ben considered throwing his meal away. The tables around them grew quiet, several people looking up at something that was happening behind them. A tall young man in a suit rose and made his way toward them. He stopped in front of Ben with robotic enthusiasm. "You're Rattawut, right?" he asked. "I'm Eric. I think we're going to be living together." His voice was kind, and his smile was warm. Ben stood and offered his hand—it had begun.

3

Manda's sadness over Ben leaving was tempered by memories of her own time at university. She cherished the intimate friendships she developed with her dormitory roommates at Phet Buri College. The group kept in touch still, exchanging airmail letters to share their whereabouts. She had told them excitedly about Ben's acceptance to Stanford, a university that was respected, even in Phet Buri.

With Ben gone, Manda spent more time in the garden. She had come to accept that her work would never be finished. The garden evolved as more Thai markets popped up nearby. It was easy to buy bitter melon and chayote now; she felt no need to grow them herself. Instead, what she raised was precious, coveted by anyone who heard about it. She had a row of pea eggplants and a robust thumleung vine with tender leaves that reached up over her head. She had coaxed a nam wa banana tree to bear fruit by secretly urinating on it every other day. Beside it grew a tall makrut tree with so many leaves she regularly sold them to Thai Delicious, the local restaurant they ordered from when they were too lazy to cook. She didn't know how long she would be able to keep it up. Sometimes she wanted nothing more than the freedom to forget about the garden, maybe even to move back to Thailand.

The holidays came, and everyone was relieved to have Ben back home, first for the long Thanksgiving weekend and then over the winter break. Siripon returned to her normal self, fussing over him and making sure he had everything he needed for the coming term.

Ben didn't divulge much about his first few weeks away. He simply said he was earning good grades and making friends. But he dressed differently, wearing heavy cable sweaters and a gray scarf circled loosely around his neck, even when he was inside. In the mornings, he vacuumed and mopped and swept around the house. After meals, he helped to wash the dishes. Manda was amused by the transformation, curious if he would slip back into his childish ways after the newness of college faded away.

The time passed too quickly. On the day Ben was to leave, Manda had an early shift. She embraced him tightly, knowing he would be gone by the time she returned. As the first customers arrived in her department, she was in a good mood. "You want me help you, just let me know, okay?" she said in a tone that was pleasant and bright. She had come to rely on a few practiced phrases to get her through her shifts. This could be her new routine, she thought, a simpler life focused on her garden, Ben visiting when he could. But by the afternoon, she was irritable. "It there," she said, pointing instead of escorting a pair of women who had asked her where the linens were. She missed seeing her nephew every day. She wanted to be beside him as he discovered the world. She wanted to see how his mind developed and who he was going to become.

A short while after Ben returned to college, a man showed up at the house. An architect. He carried a metallic storage clipboard that creaked when he opened it for a notepad and pencil. Siripon led him through the house, describing all the changes she wanted. Windows would be sealed, and new ones would be cut out. Doors would shift. The flow of the house would go in a different direction, like a river that had been rerouted. Manda called Ben and told him what she could.

"I don't know what's gotten into your mother," she said. "Has she ever complained about the layout of this place before?"

"Well, it's her house, after all," Ben replied. Though Manda couldn't be sure, she suspected his voice had grown deeper.

"It's as if she's lost her mind, don't you think? Moving the windows. Why do the windows have to be moved?"

For weeks Siripon went back and forth with the Department of Building and Safety. Whenever she had another appointment, she woke up early, put on a neat business suit, and gathered her binder of documents. The plans were sometimes left out on the breakfast table, but Manda couldn't tell what was going on just by inspecting the blue lines and dimensions that had been written on them. As she understood it, the point of contention was the patio. Siripon wanted to close it up, turn it into a game room that connected the main house with the guesthouse. But the proposed remodel didn't meet code. There wouldn't be enough exit routes out of the guesthouse once the changes were complete. If she wanted to move forward with the rest of the work, she would have to give up the idea.

Negotiations for the construction schedule were also tricky. The workers couldn't come on days Siripon needed to sleep. That stretched out the duration of the work, but they didn't see any way around it. Siripon considered switching to the day shift. With Ben gone, it wasn't such an inconvenience if all three of them worked at the same time. But she decided against it. She was too used to her nocturnal routine.

The contractors trudged in with their boots and equipment and Igloo coolers. From the garden, Manda listened to the banging and buzzing, worried about the fate of her room in the back of the house. Each day the workers came, Siripon prepared food for them. She served fried rice, noodles and duck, Thai iced tea sweetened with condensed milk. They were appreciative, though it seemed to lengthen the lunch breaks and make the project drag on even more.

The entire effort took just over two months. When the workers finally announced that they were finished, Manda was relieved to find that her room was mostly untouched. Still, she felt that the remodeling was done in part to exclude her. Her door had been moved from one wall to the other. She had to walk farther to get to the living room, around the back of Ben's old room, where a new, narrow hallway had been constructed. And though she despised herself for counting, she was aware that there were now five doors instead of three separating her room from Siripon and Kamron's.

Manda expected the household to settle down again afterward. Siripon took care to clean the dust out and vacuum the carpet as soon as the workers were gone. She tested each of the new windows and doors to make sure they opened and closed smoothly. Then she carried some belongings from her bedroom to Ben's.

They were just a few things—a pillow, a lap blanket, a stack of magazines, and her reading glasses—but they were enough to let her spend the afternoon there without having to come out. Manda didn't mention it. She cleared out the rotting fruit that had collected under the trees, staying outside until late in the afternoon, when Siripon rushed to her car and left for the hospital. Then Manda came in to see if she would have to prepare dinner. She never knew. Sometimes she found leftovers: curries simmering in a pot or fried fish crisping in the oven—Siripon's commitment to turkey had been eroded by Kamron's steady complaining. Other times, Manda had to assemble meals. She kept them simple, stir-fries and soups, just enough to show that she wasn't neglecting her responsibilities. There was food tonight—Siripon had been in a good mood. Manda and Kamron ate at the counter. She waited for him to bring up his wife moving into the new room, but he said nothing. He ate and drank and watched television. Occasionally, he glanced over at her. She had been anxious about their encounters in the early days, nervous they would get caught, that he would confess to Siripon on some drunken night. But he was good at keeping secrets—they both were. Siripon never seemed to suspect. Still, Manda wished they were not alone. The guilt of their sneaking around had come to outweigh her sexual curiosity.

Manda felt Kamron's hands on her shoulders. She felt his stubbled chin brushing against her neck. He led her to his room, to his bed—to his and Siripon's bed. Manda avoided looking at the only object that contradicted her sister's austere aesthetic: the framed photo of their wedding night centered on the bureau. It was a copy of the image Siripon had mailed home all those years ago—the couple in a gown and tuxedo, standing in front of gold curtains. Manda had been jealous when she first saw it, and she was jealous still. She wanted the other parts of Siripon's life that she couldn't have.

She and Kamron agreed to skip dinner the following night. It was warm and clear, and Manda didn't want to be cooped up in the kitchen. They sat on the porch drinking Michelobs and snacking on peanuts that had been roasted in their shells. The sky had taken on the color of flesh, pockmarked by the occasional parrots or crows that flew by. The perfume of jasmine growing on a wooden trellis mixed with the smell of peanuts and Kamron's cigarettes, recalling for Manda her life in Phet Buri, a sense memory that rarely came to her these days. She thought of what her life would be like if she had never left her hometown. Generations of children would know her by now, lineages spread across the country, maybe around the globe. But then she wouldn't have known the comforts of America—the luxurious houses, the many shops, the ease of life. She wouldn't have known Ben.

"Do you still love your wife?" Manda asked.

"What kind of question is that?" Kamron stretched his arm out in front of him and examined the scar running down from his elbow. The years of healing had given it a waxy surface that contrasted with the skin around it.

"I'm asking you seriously. Do you love Siripon?"

"For fuck's sake." He stood and walked down the steps into the darkness of the front yard. Manda could make out his angry movements as he took a last drag of his cigarette and flicked it into the street. A spray of orange embers erupted and faded. She followed him down. She cast a bottle of beer out into the street, where it shattered with surprising volume.

"What's gotten into you?" Kamron demanded.

"I'm trying to ask you a simple question, and you can't even answer. You can't even say whether or not you love your wife."

"Of course I can. I love her. She's my life. She's my entire world.

But you don't want to hear that. You want to hear that I prefer you. You want to believe that you are part of this family. But you aren't—you're just taking advantage of us while you tend to your garden. You don't help with the bills. You don't cook or clean. And now that Ben is gone, you have no purpose here anymore."

She cuffed his mouth. She would have struck him again, but he caught her by the wrist and forced her back.

"Now everyone knows how ludicrous we are," he said, gesticulating at the neighboring houses. He walked back inside. Manda followed, flinging a fistful of peanuts at him as she stepped over the threshold. He was on her quickly, pinning her against the wall.

"Go for it! Try to hurt me. I'll show you exactly what I can do back," Manda said. It was an empty threat, like the ones she had made as a child. She decided she would show no pain, no matter what he did to her. But that was as far as it went. He backed off, walked away and into his bedroom. The door slammed.

Alone, Manda hauled her suitcases down from the closet shelf where they had lain untouched for years. She filled the cases with clothes and tucked her more precious items among them. Even as she worked, she knew she had nowhere to go. In all this time, her job never provided enough for her to save beyond the purchase of some government bonds and the few hundred dollars she tucked into the pockets of old jackets for emergencies. Leaving the bags behind, she drove to Aunt Seamstress, checking to see if the light was still on in her bedroom and then tapping on her door. Her friend appeared, clasping her nightgown at the throat. She looked at Manda with a sideways glance. The two had not seen each other for almost six months.

"The time has finally come," Manda said, forcing out laughter. "I knew I wouldn't be welcome there forever."

"Thuy, thuy! What happened?"

"I don't want to trouble you with this, ja. But I can't live with them anymore. They are selfish people, only looking after themselves. I've been an unwanted appendage for too long. Nothing more than an extra toe. And now—" She grew quiet. Aunt Seamstress was not inviting her in. She stood in the doorway, still clutching her gown as if the night air chilled her.

"Sister," Manda said. "I hate to beg, but I would be so grateful for a minute to collect my thoughts."

"Come in, come in," Aunt Seamstress said, finally stepping aside.

Her room in the evening had a feminine quality Manda never noticed on her afternoon visits. Lotions and creams were laid out on Aunt Seamstress's nightstand, a faint rosy perfume arising from at least one of the containers. In a corner by the foot of her bed, a vaporizer softly hissed as it sent up plumes of eucalyptus. Aunt Seamstress poured Manda a glass of water from a gallon jug. She brought over a box of tissues and a little tin of butter cookies like the ones she used to store her sewing supplies.

"I'm embarrassed," Manda said.

"Nonsense! Hardships can befall anyone, even the best of us." Aunt Seamstress sat with her back perfectly straight. She wasn't seeking out more details. Manda considered asking if she could spend the night. The room was still and peaceful; it felt hidden from the chaos of the Chiwitchaiya home. But she sensed that she wasn't welcome. Aunt Seamstress had not moved from where she sat. Her hands were folded in her lap, waiting. Manda lifted the glass of water to her lips and drank.

"That's all I needed, Sister. Just a chance to catch my breath."

"Of course, Sister. You know you are always welcome here." Aunt Seamstress squeezed Manda's hand and rose. After hesitating a moment, she walked over to the bureau and slid open the top drawer. She found a green satin pouch and produced from it a Buddhist amulet on a thin gold chain. It was triangular, no larger than a dime. The gilt edges surrounded a piece of dark stone from which the figure had been carved. Aunt Seamstress unclasped it and put it around Manda's neck. She placed her hands together and whispered a chant.

"Satu. I'm grateful to you," Manda said. The object would not solve anything for her tonight, but still she felt calmed by its weight against her breastbone.

"Will you be all right, Sister?"

"Ja," Manda said. "Of course."

She drove home, dreading her steps through the door and the walk from the entrance to her room—no, it wasn't her room but the room she was permitted to occupy. She imagined Kamron mocking her or, worse, standing in her way, refusing to let her in just as Aunt Seamstress had done. But the house was dark when she arrived. Only the porch light had been left on, its solitary glow illuminating the front door and the concrete steps leading down to the walkway. Manda quietly fished out her keys and entered. She made her way through the dark. Down the hall, Kamron snored in his room. The sound was earnest and vulnerable, and she almost felt sorry for him. No—she shook her head, irritated with herself. She closed the bedroom door behind her and stepped over to the mirror. She did not look so different from Aunt Seamstress. She was not pretty, but she had been well preserved, despite her hours in the sun. The new amulet hung just above the point where the plumpness of her breasts developed. She lifted the chain, held the small weight of the Buddha between her hands and chanted until she lost track of the Sanskrit words. She would sleep deeply tonight, and neither she nor Kamron would speak of this incident tomorrow.

4

Ben didn't worry about his winter finals. His grades placed him near the top of his science classes and rivaled some of the liberal arts majors in his one and only literature class. It was easy when he spent his evenings alone, tackling his stacks of books. A few people on his floor and in his smaller classes still smiled at him when they passed, but Ben didn't socialize with anyone beyond exchanging pleasantries. Only Collin convinced him to leave campus for the occasional dinner out, and even then, Ben was unwilling to travel far.

But he unintentionally found a new distraction. It came in the form of flyers around campus, bright green sheets advertising some sort of seminar. *Register for the Nenantis Journey,* they read. *Free yourself from the past. Reinvent your future.* The mysteriousness lured him, the sense that it would fill something in him that was missing.

Ben couldn't say when this feeling first arose. He suspected it had been with him for much of his life, and he had managed to ignore it. It lay in him like a hollow that sent out a dull pain whenever he moved, but until recently the pain was never severe enough to warrant a reaction.

Collin rolled his eyes at the mention of the seminar. "That's one hundred percent a cult recruitment," he said. "If you have to do it, make sure I know exactly where you are at all times. No blindfolds allowed. No bus rides. And if they offer you Kool-Aid, do not drink it."

The claims were ridiculous—even Ben could see that. *Free yourself from the past. Reinvent your future.* But he was willing to risk the cost of registration to see for himself. He would never try to explain it to Collin, but he didn't choose not to have friends or go to parties. He didn't choose not to play beer pong or smoke weed. He didn't choose not to reach out to any of the faculty to ask about open research positions. These things were beyond him. The idea of life—a vivid and liberated life—frightened him.

Spring break arrived, and Ben told his family he would be a couple days late coming home because of an unexpected assignment. He made his way to the Palo Alto Hilton and checked in at a small registration table. In the hotel ballroom, an audience of four hundred arranged themselves in stiff-backed chairs and watched a man confidently climb onto the stage. He spoke calmly at first, introducing himself as Randy and telling a story about how he had been a competitive baseball player in college. He explained how he had been injured and how that had destroyed his chances of getting recruited by a professional team. As he spoke, his voice became more compelling. He explained how the injury had not only ruined his athletic career, but kept him from wanting to pursue anything in life. "Why do we carry these injuries with us everywhere we go?" he pleaded. "Why do we let them weigh us down?" His tailored suit stretched as his movements grew more passionate. His crimson tie swayed like the pendulum of a clock.

The other participants nodded as Randy told his story. They seemed to sympathize with him as if they had all been exceptional baseball players. Ben thought of high school and how he could have competed to be the valedictorian. He thought of the fear he felt at the prospect of being the center of attention.

As the day went on, the group was coached through exercises meant to remind them of the dreams they had given up. They were offered large pads of paper and bold-colored markers. They were to imagine their childhood homes, their schoolyards, their families and friends and lovers and enemies. The room transformed into a playground of expression, people on their hands and knees coloring and talking to themselves. Randy told them to prepare for long sessions. He told them not to expect to get home before midnight. They were told to engage their senses, to write about smells and tastes. They had permission to cry whenever they needed to.

There were breaks to get to know one another. Most of the attendees were techies—PhDs and MBAs in the throes of start-up companies. But others had been drawn in too. Ben spent a coffee break eavesdropping on an anxious librarian and a former member of the Hells Angels who now spent his time customizing car stereos. They had all seen the green flyers and the promises they made. They all felt that something was missing from their lives.

The afternoon session came, and participants were asked to arrange their chairs into a large circle. One by one, they revealed their heartaches, their anger, their years of addiction and abuse. A crying young man blamed himself for his brother's suicide, the horrible scene where the body was found hanging in a hall closet. Another person admitted to hoarding food after growing up poor and hungry. The problem had gotten so severe that the neighbors called the Department of Mental Health to come and check on him. Ben's turn approached. He didn't know what to say. He bit his thumbnail, disappointed when a trail of spit ran down his finger. The remnants of *that* problem never went away completely. He could talk about it, the years of throwing up. He could talk about his suicide attempt, something that he could look at more cooly through the distance of time. But those things felt like consequences, not causes. There was no cause. Any attempt to distill it left him empty-handed.

"I just don't know if I'm a bad person," he said to the crowd. They had clapped for others, but for him, they were silent, unimpressed. He nodded for the next person to share, aware of his irrelevance to the group.

The following day, he felt no closer to any resolution. He arrived at the Hilton more determined. There was a new, electric tentativeness among the others. They had relived their trauma. They had touched and seen and smelled it. They were frightened.

On the stage, Randy urged everyone to confront their tormentors. He gave a long lecture about being fearless, about the catharsis that came from confrontation. They would not be eating lunch today, Randy announced. They would not get the satisfaction of satiation. They could write letters or make phone calls, saying what had gone unspoken for too long. They could pair up and role-play, having a stranger take the place of someone who was no longer around. Ben thought of Bonnie Stewart, the girl in his fifth-grade class who had come up with the name "Puke Boy." He imagined being in the school auditorium with her again, asking her while surrounded by the smell of canned green beans and Wonder Bread why she had been so cruel. The details of the scene took on a vivid, dreamlike quality. He wrote to her and to the children who had stuck their fingers down their throats to mock him, the ones who had put up police tape to mark off the desiccated mess he had supposedly left on the field. But he had no desire to look up any of these people. It wouldn't make any difference. His pain went deeper. It reached to the hopelessness he confronted at the Westminster Presbyterian Church, when death was the only solution he could come up with. Something within him was still drawn to that nothingness.

The session became blurry. Even as Randy spoke with more passion, as his tie swung and sweat beaded at his temples, Ben was lost in his own thoughts. The idea that he had so many unresolved issues embarrassed him. He had worked so hard to control his image and his grades—even his body's response to things that made him nervous. He hated the idea that none of it mattered.

When the last afternoon session arrived, he questioned if any of the work he was doing would make a difference. He felt no better than he did on that first day. In some ways, he felt worse. But the tone in the room was different. As the exhausted participants trudged in, Randy seemed happy for the first time since the seminar began. Cheery staff members had been posted at various stations around the perimeter of the room; they handed out what looked like party favors, little plastic wands, to each participant. "Prepare to free yourself. Prepare to free yourself," they chanted.

Randy told everyone to trace the wands over themselves and focus their consciousness on any repressed memories that might be trapped in their bodies. He called a volunteer up onto the stage to demonstrate, the woman's movements akin to inspecting herself at airport security. "This is the last reservoir," Randy declared. "If the mind wants to let go of the past, the body must also agree to it." The lights were turned down. They were told to close their eyes. As Randy guided them, Ben half-heartedly waved the wand over his feet and legs. He felt nothing. He moved the wand upward, pointing it around his midsection, his arms. He was embarrassed now that he had thrown so much money away. He shifted his attention to his throat. There, too, he felt nothing until the familiar constriction returned. He had to control himself to keep from throwing up in front of everyone. He tried to open his eyes, but his vision was obscured. Gravity was shifting. He was on his back. He was lying on the floor with a cloth draped over him. A voice came through, a man speaking in Thai. "Lie still." It was a monk in an orange robe. He had been let into the house by Manda and Kamron on a night when Siripon was at work. Ben felt them crouched around him in the shrine room of the house on Caroline Street. Candlelight flickered on the other side of the cloth and shadows shifted and stretched.

"Whatever happens, let it happen!" Randy's garbled voice said.

Ben looked out from beneath the cloth. The monk's hands were working. He had long, bony fingers. He folded and twisted a sheet of paper until a form emerged. Tiny white arms. Tiny white legs. A twisted foot poking up. It was a paper girl, rigid and small in the monk's hand. In the flickering light of the candles, Ben thought he could see her burdened face.

The monk placed the girl into a paper box the size of a bird's nest. He placed the box on Ben's chest, where it rose and fell with his nervous breathing. Ben slipped a hand out and touched his aunt's leg. She clicked her tongue and moved out of reach. Frightened, he told himself to think about dinner. Manda had used his special plate with the different compartments. She made him hot dogs that she cut to look like four-armed octopuses—but his mind drifted further. He saw in tiny detail the girl in her box, the walls containing her. She waited, pinned to one side. She was frightened like he was.

The grown-ups whispered. They had a way of using big words he didn't understand. The monk's brown hands pulled out a bundle of sticks from a satchel. They lifted a metallic bowl with pictures of lotus flowers etched into its side. The sticks dipped in. They rattled above him, and Ben felt the water coming down like a sprinkling of rain. The monk chanted louder. Ben wanted morning, when his mother would come home wearing her uniform covered with rainbows or colored fish. Manda and Kamron touched him on the shoulder while they chanted together. Then it was just the monk again. He said something that Ben finally understood: "Burn it."

The monk lifted the paper girl's box as if it were an ashtray. He handed her to his father, who carried her outside. Ben saw the darkness that the girl must have seen, the moths fluttering in the swell of light by the door, white specks of life so small and frantic. Maybe his dad would burn her beside the makrut tree, with its thick and waxy leaves, its wrinkled and oily fruit. Maybe she'd escape, jump out of her paper box, down into a pool of water collected in one of the flowerpots while fire rained down around her.

Inside, his aunt asked if the monk wanted a glass of water.

The monk's voice was soft. "Yes, yom."

Then Ben was alone with him. He sat up. He called out to Manda, finally. He had been obedient long enough. "Auntie!"

"I'm right here. I didn't go anywhere. I'm getting water for the ajan." Something in her voice was softer too.

"It may take a few days for the spirit of the girl to leave his body," the monk said. "Watch for signs of its departure as things progress."

Ben didn't know how much time had passed when he felt a soft rocking. He opened his eyes to his aunt and his dad on either side of him. They carried him to the bathroom, stood him on the toilet seat, and slipped his pajama bottoms down to his ankles. They waited while he peed, talking to each other on either side of his naked legs. His aunt looked up at him, expectant.

"If you want to let it out, you can. The monk said it will all come out."

Ben shook his head.

"Are you sure?" she asked.

He nodded. His dad carried him to the hall toward his bedroom, but his aunt stopped them. "We should try one more time."

They went back to the bathroom. This time his aunt lifted the toilet seat and helped him kneel in front of the bowl with his head stooped down over it. "Do you want to let it out? Do you feel like throwing up?" She rubbed circles on his back—slow, steady, soft. His eyes adjusted to the whiteness of the porcelain and the clear water waiting. "Do you want to let it out?" she asked.

He nodded.

He opened his throat.

5

Ben tried to follow the instructions not to look at the other participants, but he was awed at the thought that they were experiencing similar revelations, that four hundred people were having epiphanies like he was. Sounds erupted: crying, laughing, moaning, groaning. A man let out a clenched growl as if he were trying to shatter his teeth.

"You've held it in for too long! Don't hold it in anymore!" Randy shouted.

What had been a quiet, obedient audience turned into a raucous, emotional mob. Ben let his eyes adjust to the orange light spilling down from the chandeliers. Beside him, someone gripped the back of a chair and shook it frantically.

The chaos lasted for what seemed like an hour. The bodily noises built up and then slowly subsided as Randy's words became more soothing. "How do you feel?" he asked. "Are you better?" The brighter lights turned on and the place emerged as just the ordinary thing it had always been. But there was a newfound calm present. People breathed more easily. They laughed. They applauded, grateful. When Randy encouraged them to sign up for the next retreat, Ben was one of the few to refuse, a promise he had made to Collin. Still, he couldn't deny that something had happened. The years of throwing up, the trauma, the alienation—all of it had a source. *How ridiculous,* he thought.

Later, as the others filtered out of the Hilton, Ben wasn't ready to go back to the dorms. He slipped into a diner a couple blocks away and took a seat at the counter. He ordered a slice of pie and a cup of coffee, aware that he didn't want either. Nodding to the waitress to hold his seat, he made his way to the restroom.

The motion detector clicked faintly and signaled the lights to flicker on. He was relieved to have the place to himself. His perspective had shifted. He had become a believer. And with it came the nagging feeling that he had disrupted his recovery in the hotel ballroom by holding himself back. His body had wanted to throw up, but he hadn't let it.

He locked himself in a stall and looked down into the darkened toilet bowl. There had been a time when the view had been soothing for him. Now it was only filth. *Like riding a bike,* he thought. He stooped his head down. His throat opened. What had he eaten today? A bowl of cereal before he raced for the bus stop. He could still predict the texture and taste of what would come out. The bolus crept upward, stopping for an instant in his throat. Then the food and the emotions roared into the water. It was messy, hitting the rim of the bowl, splattering against his clothes. When it was over, he sat back, eyes closed, catching his breath. He felt a profound sense of lightness, an amplified version of what he had experienced countless times before. But this time was different. His body understood that it was done. He laughed—the power that one evening had on him, one ceremony by some man in an orange robe. He considered throwing up again, this time as a celebration. He only stopped because he heard the restroom door swing open. A group of young men entered, perhaps three. They spoke in that laconic style of people who were familiar with one another. There was a quick scratching sound. The smell of pot drifted toward him. Ben flushed the toilet and washed his hands at the sink. The others were around his age, probably Stanford students. They had dyed black hair and eyeliner. They seemed to be complaining about a professor, but Ben didn't recognize the name.

"Sorry to interrupt," he said, trying to suppress his joy.

He returned to the dorms, happy to find Collin waiting in the lounge. Seeing him lit by the ceiling lights overhead, Ben felt a surge of pleasure. He was comforted by something in Collin that was almost angelic.

"That was a weird experience," Ben said, still buoyed by the headiness of his revelation.

Collin stood and opened his arms, not knowing whether to smile or console.

"I remembered something," Ben explained. He described what happened, the resurfacing of the ceremony. As he spoke, more details emerged. He remembered being barefoot. His feet had been cold because the material had not covered them completely. He remembered wishing his mother was home, wishing she would put a stop to it.

"My dad was there, but it was all my aunt's idea," he said. "All of it was her, I'm sure of it."

Collin was sitting beside him now, his hands tensed, grasping his knees. "You have to confront her," he said. "We'll go back down to see them tomorrow."

"Stop—no. We aren't like your family; we don't just talk things out. My family couldn't take it."

"You can't just ignore these problems all the time."

"How could I tell them they ruined my life? We wouldn't ever get past that."

What Ben didn't explain—what he knew intuitively but not yet consciously—was that he and his family didn't have the language for the confrontation, even if he wanted one. Any attempt to discuss it would hit that barrier, all of them incapable of exchanging their deeper thoughts. He felt but did not know all that had been lost between them because of this. Telling a story in a different language meant telling a different story.

By the time he got up the next morning, his mother had called several times. Her voice sounded more irritated with each message, so that he could imagine her wrinkled brow and the muscles of her jaw clenching. He called back, apologized, made an excuse about having caught a bad cold and not being able to come down after all. He spent the rest of the break around the Quad as the other stragglers passed by, lost in their own thoughts. The days blurred together: drowsy mornings, vacuous afternoons, nights that slipped by too quickly. The buoyancy he experienced when he left Nenantis was weighed down by the thought of eventually having to be around his family again.

But the new quarter began. Ben threw himself into another demanding schedule. He had grown to like his physics classes and was better at spreading out his labs so that he didn't have to finish all his reports on the same night. His elective was a figure-drawing class. When he registered for it, he thought it would be a nice change of pace, an easy A. Now he was afraid the hours of silent drawing would give him too much time to think. Home and family lay coiled in the back of his mind, a thorny vine he didn't want to untangle. His past would have to be reconstructed to discern the lies of his childhood from what had actually happened. He sat on his hands while the tiger-eyed professor named Edmund Holliday stood in front of the class in paint-spattered overalls. He gave the impression of being ancient, though Ben guessed he was no older than sixty. The professor's own self-portrait was projected onto the studio wall. It was a younger version of himself, from his art school days. He explained that he fell in love with painting when he captured a raised vein on the back of his hand, when he felt that he had created something three-dimensional on the flat canvas.

Off to one side, a man stood waiting in a white robe. He was medium height, dark-haired, scruffy, and calm, Ben thought, for someone who was about to stand naked in front of twenty strangers. Holliday told them that the session was beginning, and the model disrobed and climbed onto the small pedestal. Illuminated by bright lights overhead, he got into his first pose, one leg forward, arms up over his head. Ben tentatively touched his charcoal to paper. He followed the curving line of the model's torso, traced it up to the arm and hand, where he clumsily sketched five outstretched fingers. He glanced around the studio, noticing the variations among the other students' work. It was different from his science classes, where everything felt so systematic, so rigid. When he met Collin for dinner, Ben raved about the class. They walked back to the art studios, where Ben pointed out his sketch among several that Holliday had pinned to a wall ahead of the critiques that would take place at the next session.

There were a handful of models who rotated through the class. As each session started, Ben felt a thrill watching them step onto the pedestal, their body exposed and illuminated. He tried to guess what they thought about as the students worked, each one scrutinizing a different part of the model's body. There must be a sense of resignation, he concluded, as the model came to realize there was no point in trying to hide anything. He admired the self-confidence that must come from that.

Ben began to notice the models outside of the studio. One in particular, Owen, was always walking alone. He had been the first model for the class. His body was toned but not overly muscular, covered in a thin layer of dark hair. He eased gracefully in and out of the different poses, not self-conscious but not showy either. Around campus, he wore thrift store clothes: old gas station attendant uniforms or vintage shirts and slacks. He often carried his own art supplies and canvasses, his hands smudged with color. Ben dared to speak with him once when they were both entering a café at the same time. The days were getting warm, and Owen sighed as he stepped into the air-conditioned space.

"What kind of art do you do?" Ben asked, suddenly aware that Owen might not even know who he was. But there was a hint of recognition.

"Painting," Owen said, smiling. "Mostly portraits, if you want to see them."

"Oh, that's not what I meant."

"Why? Aren't you into art?"

"Of course I am. Well, it's an elective. But I'd love to see your work. That's just not why I spoke to you."

"Then you probably spoke to me because you like how I look naked."

They made plans to meet at Owen's studio. Ben didn't tell Collin about it in the beginning. He convinced himself that it was nothing more than two art students discussing work. But he recalled the nights he lay in bed listening to his father creeping across the house. He thought of the muffled voices in his aunt's room, the creaking of the bedsprings. He worried that he had inherited the same tendency for secrets, for deeds that hurt loved ones.

"I'm meeting a guy," he said. "There was this hot model in one of the classes, and I talked to him. He invited me to his studio to look at his paintings. I'm sorry. I don't know what I was thinking."

Collin laughed about it coolly. "You're allowed to talk to other guys," he said.

"I'm imagining more than talking. I've been having all these fantasies of him. I have fantasies about a lot of guys around here."

"God, well, I don't necessarily want to hear about it," Collin said. "Look, we can't control our fantasies. Just don't take it any further."

"No," Ben said. "No, I won't."

On the day he and Owen were to meet, Ben ironed his shirt and shaved. He arrived early to the art building and paced the halls, startled when Owen poked his head out of his studio door and waved for him to come in. Inside, two easels had been set up on either side of a pedestal.

"I thought we could do a trade," Owen said. "You can draw me, and I'll draw you."

"But I came to see your paintings." Ben glanced back at the closed door, not sure if he should leave.

Owen undressed. "Go ahead. You've got fifteen minutes."

They had done this before. Ben had become familiar with Owen's body. But here, alone, the experience of looking at him felt like a secret. His hand moved nervously over the sketch pad as he rendered a figure as well as he could. It seemed like not much time had passed when Owen began to relax in his graceful, controlled way. He put his clothes back on and went to sit down as he waited for Ben to take his turn. "Don't be afraid," he urged. "It's actually fun."

"I never thought I'd be a model." Ben removed his shirt, embarrassed when goosebumps rose on his arms from the cool air coming in from the vents. Soon he was undressed and glancing at himself in a mirror that leaned against the wall. Owen was unperturbed. He positioned Ben's limbs into a more interesting pose. He sat down and worked, his pencil gently scratching against the tooth of the paper. When it was over, he offered his hand to help Ben down. Before Ben could get his clothes back on, Owen gave him a kiss on the cheek. "You should sketch yourself next," he said. "But don't do it like an exercise for Holliday. Do it for real, like if you were an actual artist making stuff for a show." Without waiting, he rearranged the space so that Ben was able to look at himself in the mirror and sketch at the same time. Then he left the studio and locked the door behind him.

Ben glanced around, trying to decide if he should get dressed. He turned and inspected his body again. He hadn't done anything wrong with Owen, but perhaps he would have—he didn't know what he was capable of. Here, shed of his past identity, shed of the boy he'd been, he imagined himself as one of Rodin's sculptures, caught in an instant, the possibilities before him infinite. He began to draw, letting his hand move to the curves and angles of his body. He did not think of representing anything other than himself in this moment. He was someone with no past and no future.

6

An envelope arrived from Stanford. Manda watched as Siripon snipped the short edge with a pair of scissors and pinched out the contents. It had been three weeks since they heard anything from Ben, whether by phone or mail.

But the letter wasn't from him. It was a newspaper clipping from the Arts & Life section of *The Stanford Daily*. A message from Collin was scrawled along the top margin: *Sawadee. Since your son was too shy to tell you . . .*

"Okay," Siripon said. She made her way through the article and then read it again more carefully. When she was through, she lay the page down and turned back to the kitchen counter, where she had been preparing dinner. Manda read it over for herself. Apparently, Ben was involved in some sort of art show. There were photos of paintings, including one of a naked man standing several feet tall. She recognized the shape of Ben's face, the proportions of his body.

"Did he tell you he was taking art classes?" she asked, too embarrassed to bring up her more serious concern.

"Of course. Why not?" Siripon said in English.

Manda suspected it was a lie. Whenever she talked to Ben, all he did was complain about science tests, laboratory experiments, reports.

Later, she mentioned it to Kamron, who only seemed annoyed by the question. He brushed the page aside and stooped down to untie his boots. Workdays had become more of a struggle for him. The job was taking its toll. He pressed his knuckles into his lower back, working out a knot as he straightened up.

Manda poured herself a bowl of Corn Pops and carried it to her room. For years she avoided the processed American products, but lately she found the sweetness comforting, just as she found Korean dramas comforting. She slid in a video cassette with the next episodes of *The King and the Queen* into her VCR. It was a series the owner of the Thai bookstore in Hollywood had recommended. There weren't any subtitles—those were only available on DVD—but Manda was able to piece together the plot if she paid close attention.

The show was comical and cathartic. People clawing for love and power. She thought of Ben exposing himself. Somehow he had crossed over into this world of drama. He didn't want a quiet life like she did, a life where they could be left alone, nibbling at the feast instead of trying to swallow it whole. He was from the next generation. He existed in a different age.

Across the patio, in the guesthouse, she glimpsed Siripon and Kamron eating dinner. They didn't speak to each other, simply moved their utensils back and forth from the dishes to their mouths. Afterward, Kamron helped to clear the table while Siripon put the leftovers away, washed the dishes, and left for work.

Manda was surprised, later, while washing her bowl, to find that Ben's article was missing. Siripon must have taken it to share with the other nurses. When she returned the next morning, she had no glow of pride like she did when she shared report cards or A papers. She laid the envelope on the table and went to wash out her lunch container.

"Why would you show that outside of the family?" Manda demanded.

"I'm proud of my son," Siripon said.

"Are you? You like that he's taken his clothes off for his entire university? It's an embarrassment." Manda braced herself for retaliation, but Siripon only nodded.

"Why do you think he did something like this?" she asked, her voice high like a child's.

"Why don't you ask him?" Manda said. "Maybe we've let him be too independent."

Nobody spoke about Ben's exhibit for the rest of the week. The article ended up on the refrigerator door, but it went unacknowledged. Manda assumed it would be slowly obscured by photos. Tassanee regularly sent family pictures over from Thailand. Niran had gotten married out of high school, and he and his wife recently had a baby, a plump little girl. Tassanee's youngest, Paitoon, was excelling in school.

We await anxiously for Ben to get married. We will all come to America for the wedding, Tassanee wrote at the end of her recent letters. It was only natural she should bring it up. Ben was healthy, handsome, and educated. He would find a good job after he graduated. It was strange for him to still be single.

His nose is always in his books. We tell him to focus on college for a little longer, Manda wrote in response. This is the young man they had created, she admitted to herself. Ben was the perfect student. The driven scientist. The boy who didn't care for romance.

He called later in the week, a surprise after days of silence. Siripon's first question, even before asking about his health, was about the show.

"Of course we care. We *care,*" she replied to whatever Ben said on the other end of the line. There was an injured tone in her voice. "We could have driven up to see it. Maybe we still can if it's going to stay up. Hmm? Okay, okay."

"He's too busy to host us," she said after hanging up. "Tests again."

"Always testing," Manda said. Her sister had been weary lately. Siripon didn't bother to put on makeup like she used to. And instead of wearing her neatly ironed pastel uniforms, she wore hospital scrubs to work.

"This is how everybody does it now," Siripon said. "Nobody makes a fuss anymore."

Some of the other nurses had gone part-time. Classmates from her school in Phuket were buying property back in their hometowns so they could return for six months out of the year. Their kids were grown. Their kids were finding jobs. It was time for the older generation to go back to the familiar. Manda sympathized. The other week, her supervisor called her into his office and offered her a promotion. He wanted her to be a department manager overseeing the other associates. It meant a pay increase, predictable shifts, better benefits. But she turned it down. Her job was easy now. She only had to keep the aisles clean, change the displays according to the seasons, and make sure the money in the till could be accounted for at the end of her shift. It was brainless, which meant she could save her thoughts for other things. And Siripon still never brought up the idea of her paying rent. She didn't need the money. She had enough to take care of the mortgage on her own.

No more news came from Collin or Ben to let them know how the show was going. Maybe the painting was only a phase and would amount to nothing in the end. Manda still worried, though, that she had lost touch with her nephew, that he had changed without her knowing. They had barely spoken to each other when he was home for the holidays. He stayed in his room, busy with his reading or working at his computer. At least, that was the impression he gave. They had drifted apart, but she couldn't pinpoint why or when it had happened. In bed, drifting to sleep, she saw the younger version of Ben floating before her, the boy who had been so happy with her in the garden, the one who had leapt into the air.

7

"I didn't think anyone would care about the painting," Ben had said when Siripon asked him about the exhibit. The words had hurt. He was always the first thing on her mind, and yet somehow he didn't realize it. She stopped to fill her gas tank before returning home from her shift. She had the next three days off, enough time to drive to Stanford and back. When she told Kamron she was going, his voice grew harsh. "Why must you get involved in his business?" he said.

"It will be a good opportunity to make sure he's doing all right up there," she replied calmly. Her decision was made.

"I suppose you'll want me to go with you."

"You're tired. I don't mind going alone."

She took a nap, packed, and left without any fuss, pulling over every fifty miles to consult her Thomas Guide and make sure she was traveling in the right direction. The route was filled with stretches of farmland, shifting rows of citrus trees and strawberries, so that Siripon's mind wandered with their rhythmic passing. She was so far away from her childhood home. It was distance, certainly, but it was time too. She often went for days without thinking of Phet Buri, without thinking of her mother and her siblings. The last time she had spoken to them, Tassanee complained again about Gimjaa's favoritism, how their mother treated Kiet so kindly while being so demanding of her. These arguments that had once bothered Siripon so deeply now felt insignificant.

But life in America had its problems too. Money and comfort gave rise to new complications. Maybe she admired that—she wasn't sure.

She liked that Ben's mind was nimble, but she wished he'd chosen a smoother course. He should be looking for love with a woman. He should be trying to find a reliable job that gave him time to raise a family. Instead, he had become a gay artist.

The sky had taken on an anxious red by the time she made it to the campus. She asked her way to Crothers and then followed a group of students in through the security door. Then she braced for Ben's reaction. It had become a common fear for her, the expectation of his disapproval, his insistence that she did everything the wrong way.

"Mrs. Chiwitchaiya! I didn't know you were coming for a visit." Collin had rushed into the lobby with an armload of books he let topple into a nearby chair.

"I come to see my son," Siripon said.

"He's at the gallery. It's the closing reception. I'll take you there. Just let me—" He gathered his things and ran down the hall. A few minutes later, he appeared again with a crate of refreshments. "I'm late getting there too," he said.

They walked through campus, Collin using his chin to point out landmarks and buildings with names Siripon didn't bother to remember. She still resented him for luring Ben here. But she liked knowing more about where her son was living. The campus was more imposing than any school she had seen in Thailand. She had a sense of how elite it must be, how far her son had come.

"What was I thinking? You must be starving," Collin said. He dropped his crate and rummaged through it for something he could offer her.

"First I go to see my son."

"Sure. Of course. I hope you don't mind that I sent you that newspaper clipping. He was just so proud—I don't know why he didn't tell you himself. Oh, God, he might kill me." He laughed nervously.

They arrived at a group of brick buildings, people still visible inside despite the late hour. She followed Collin down some stairs to a small, inconspicuous space. A handful of people stood inside. *Children trying to act like adults,* Siripon thought. They stood with practiced poise, but they had an air of self-consciousness. She spotted Ben in the center of a crowd. He wore what looked like a secondhand gas station attendant's shirt, jeans that had frayed along the cuffs. He was smiling and animated, waving a plastic cup of some liquid that could have been wine, obviously pleased by the attention he was getting. He only noticed her when she touched his elbow.

"Mom."

His face grew tense upon seeing her. It was the reaction she had been bracing for, but she would not apologize for coming. He excused himself from the others and led her back toward the entrance, where he looked to Collin for some explanation. "Mom, what are you doing here?"

"I want to see your show. Mom proud of you," she said.

He gave her an awkward hug, aware of his friends watching them. A few stood with their cups half-raised in their direction, as if they were waiting for a toast.

"Let me see what you paint," she said.

"I said you didn't need to come."

"Well, don't you know I want to see what you do? So let me see." The weight of motherhood pressed down on her. It was love through force.

Ben passed Collin his cup and put his arm around her shoulders. He steered her along a tight orbit, quickly passing each of the paintings, ready to turn her back toward the door after only a few moments. It would not do. She slipped out of his grip and went back to his painting.

"I told you it's nothing," he said, tugging at her. "You shouldn't have driven all this way."

"This nothing?" She stretched her arms to take in the borders of the painting. "This?"

One of the other students passed by. A young woman in black, her hair and eyebrows dyed. She walked her fingers up Ben's shoulder and tugged on his earlobe. "It's incredible," she said. Siripon could sense that he was still aware of her, but he couldn't resist talking about his work. "It's a study on exhibitionism," he said, his voice low at first but building in enthusiasm. "It's a declaration that I want to be seen." Siripon inspected the painting again. The figure had a sense of heft to it, a sense of heat. She examined the body, wondering how accurate it was. Did he really have a scar below his ribs? If it was true, she didn't know when or where he got it. While Ben turned back to try to pull her away again, his body tense, almost jumpy, his image on the canvas stared out with patient confidence.

"Mom, what's wrong? Are you crying?"

"I'm okay, I'm okay." She fumbled in her purse for Kleenex. When she couldn't find any, she pushed out the gallery door, turning down the hall in search for a restroom.

"Let me get you out of here," Ben said.

"I go, you stay. Stay with your friend."

Ben led her to the slanted cubby beneath the staircase. She finished her cry and slowly composed herself. As unhappy as she was that Ben would keep so much from her, she was relieved to be beside her son, to stop constantly worrying about his whereabouts and know what he was doing in the moment.

"You don't want Mom to see this, okay," Siripon said. "You don't want me to know, okay."

Ben looked down at his hands. She was aware she was squeezing him. She had held things in for too long, telling herself that she didn't need to pry. Now she was prying. She wanted her son back.

"I just don't know how to explain it all to you," he said.

"You can't just try?" She thought she had taken care of everything that mattered. She had given him food, safety, a clean house, clothing, an education. But Ben needed more. He needed something she had never wanted. "Okay," she said. "So I go."

"What are you talking about—where would you go? Did you get a hotel room?"

"I find one. I don't bother you."

"You're not bothering me. I just didn't know you were coming."

"But you know something else, don't you? You know I love you, even if I don't understand this thing. I always try my best for you."

"Mom." He placed his hand on her shoulder, lightly, surrendered. Maybe he was going to say more, but the gallery door swung open, and Collin appeared. He matched their somber expressions as he approached.

"Ben, I'm sorry, but Holliday showed up. He's excited to talk to you about your painting."

"Mom, I need to do this. It's my professor."

"Go," Siripon said. "We talk later."

Her yearning feeling returned, but she would not get in the way of her son's success. She nodded when Collin offered to take her back to the dorm. Tonight, they were the same, the ones left behind. He made her a cup of coffee while he searched for a hotel. Watching him at his computer, she tried to see the situation for what it was. He was not a bad young man.

"You his boyfriend, right?"

Collin's fingers paused above the keyboard. He thought for a moment. "Yes," he said.

"I just want him to be okay."

"Me too."

"And you help take care of him?"

"Of course." His eyes grew more excited. "Yeah, Ben and I are a great team. We have these plans—I've been telling him he should share them with you."

"Plan like what?"

But Collin caught himself, unwilling to reveal even more of Ben's life without permission. For a moment, Siripon felt like she could see his true personality. Collin was enthusiastic. He had a good spirit. She sighed—an acceptance. He had come to sit beside her; his hand fell to cover hers. If this was what it meant for Ben to be gay, maybe she didn't need to worry. If the two of them stayed together—if it was only them—Ben would stay safe.

When her son finally returned, they all went out to a nearby restaurant. Then the boys took Siripon to the hotel. The need for sleep was taking over despite the recent caffeine. She hugged each of them and told them goodbye. "I go early tomorrow. I no take time off."

"Mom, you're going to be exhausted," Ben said.

"So? I just want to see you. That's it."

"I could skip my classes. Maybe I could drive you back down and fly up here again."

"I see you for summer," she said. She hugged them each again. She followed the signs to her room, not permitting herself to look back. The visit had soothed her. Ben's new life was at least tangible, even if it wasn't what she had hoped for. He would never return to her, not in the way she wanted. But children had to leave, didn't they? *She* had left, and now it was Ben's turn.

Burning Girl

1

Monsoonal rains fell across southern Thailand. Rivers swelled. Officials in Kaeng Krachan opened the spillways to prevent the reservoirs from bursting. The water came down to Phet Buri. It flooded the streets, washing away shoes, leaving catfish twisting in gutters, dinner at the doorstep. It poured into Gimjaa's courtyard and lapped at the entrance of the house. She waited as her children rode out to see if anyone was crossing the bridge to town. They returned hours later to report that no vehicles were getting through. Only a few people desperate for supplies were daring to wade into the muddy torrents, and Gimjaa would not allow her family to do that.

The house was full of movement and noise. Everyone had congregated there before the rain began. The men rolled up their pant legs and stepped out into the courtyard to arrange sandbags along the gate entrance. They were singing a love song as they worked, their exaggerated voices pushing back the gloom.

"Remember, now, you boys can't gorge yourselves, or there won't be enough food left for the rest of us," Tassanee called out to them. "Who knows when I'll get to the market again."

"And even if you do cross the bridge, there may not be anything left to buy," Gimjaa added. She sat on the linoleum floor with her back to the windows, where the rain drummed heavily against the glass. A short distance away, her great-granddaughter rolled the stone pestle in its mortar, her tiny fingers close to being smashed before she was rescued by her mother. "Almost," Gimjaa said, laughing. Childhood still made her happy. And all of life was childhood, wasn't it? Her feelings were still childish, even after seven decades. She glanced over at her daughter. Earlier that morning, she'd wounded Tassanee with a careless complaint that her youngest daughter had not grown up to be as useful as the other children. Gimjaa never could explain why there was a hierarchy to her love, why she valued Tassanee less than the others. Nor was she tormented by the disparity. It was simply, childishly, how she felt.

"Maybe we'll starve to death," Tassanee said. Her tone was bitter. Gimjaa knew that her daughter was devoted to her with no expectation of anything in return. While Siripon and Manda had established their lives in the Outer Country and Kiet had found a lucrative job farther south, Tassanee was the only one who stayed to take care of their mother. But everything she did was clumsy. She had not been born with the same gifts the others received.

Dinnertime approached, and Tassanee set a pot of rice to cook. She searched through the pantry, deciding what else she would prepare. From the way she mumbled to herself and slammed the cupboards, it was obvious that she was frustrated. Gimjaa knew she was to blame. She was the cause of her daughter's worry. Everybody else was healthy and strong. Everybody else could escape to higher ground.

Gimjaa made her way to the kitchen, scooting herself along on her bottom. She couldn't manage walking anymore. "Boil some chayote until they're soft so that I can feed them to the baby," she said. She wondered if there would be favorites among the great-grandchildren as others came along. She loved her grandsons Niran and Paitoon equally, but she had not thought much of Ben until he volunteered to serve as a monk's apprentice. That had raised his status for her. *So, my mind can change after all,* she thought, surprised. She glanced again at her daughter, who was cutting the chayote into irregular lumps. When Tassanee had overheard Gimjaa saying that morning that she wasn't useful, she had made a crude joke in response. "I might as well hang myself," she said. "Then my ghost will have the pleasure of watching you grieve for me. I'll see that you really did love me after all. I'll know by your tears."

The memory struck Gimjaa oddly as she heaved herself up onto a counter stool and cracked some eggs into a bowl for frying. She couldn't know if her other children got worked up over such matters, if Manda or Siripon worried about not being loved as much as Kiet was. And then there were the dead sons. What did the living think of them? These questions preoccupied her mind during dinner, as she ate surrounded by the rhythm of the rain. They lingered as she tried to sleep that night. Annoyed, she sat up and looked out the window at the reflection of the courtyard walls on the water. *How deep they go,* she thought.

The following day, the rain still came down in curtains. Tassanee was preparing to check the bridge again when a neighbor arrived and told her that no one had been able to get through yet. She fried the leftover rice and served it with bowls of pickled mustard greens. Gimjaa prepared to lift herself up to join the family at the table, but Tassanee told her not to bother. She settled Gimjaa on the floor with a pillow and placed a bowl of rice on the linoleum in front of her.

"Tell me you love me," Tassanee said suddenly. "Just tell me so that I know you appreciate all these things I do for you every day." She spoke playfully but loudly, letting the entire household overhear.

Gimjaa laughed, but her gray eyes glinted sadly.

"Really, just once, Mother. Let us all hear it, even if it isn't true."

"I'm sorry I can't control my heart," Gimjaa said.

"One of these days you'll change your mind," Tassanee said. "You're going to love me the most—I can predict it." She grew quiet, and her husband coaxed her to the table, where she finally began to eat.

Gimjaa felt bad for Tassanee. She felt bad for all her children and grandchildren, and perhaps soon, she would feel bad for her great-grandchildren. How could she ever communicate to them that her unfair love was the only type of love she could offer? They would never fully know her. There were walls and floods everywhere. They separated the mortal realm from Sawan, America from Thailand, and one room of the house from another.

2

Manda remembered the tactless way Siripon had shared the news of their father's death, blurting it out first thing in the morning as Manda came out of her bedroom. She was grateful the information about their mother flowed in the opposite direction. She had been the one to answer the telephone, static filling the line, when Tassanee called to say that Gimjaa had not been able to sleep for several nights. Her hands and feet had become swollen. The family had taken her to the hospital.

Manda had been expecting her mother to fall ill ever since their father's death, but there was a sense of surprise too. Gimjaa's body had endured so much, yet she had clung on. Still, Manda had not received the news of death—she reminded herself of that.

She woke the others and explained. While Siripon called the airport to book flights, Manda rooted through the pockets of her coats to find the loose cash she had tucked away for emergencies. They would fly out the next afternoon—these days direct flights from Los Angeles to Bangkok departed every few hours. Siripon called Ben and left a message, telling him not to worry, that everything would be all right. Two days later, weary and unclear of the time of day, they entered Petcharat Hospital. In her room, Gimjaa lay sleeping under a thin blanket. One exposed hand was mummified in medical tape that secured her IV line. A bright bruise was visible underneath, where she had been poked too many times.

"I'm here. I've come home, na?" Manda said, cradling her mother's head in her arms.

Gimjaa squeezed her eyes shut. Yellow, viscous tears formed and dispersed among the wrinkles of her face.

"Mother, I'm here," Manda tried again. "I am here. You are not alone."

"She barely speaks," Tassanee whispered. "If she says anything, it's about the dead boys. She doesn't love the living anymore. Not even Kiet."

It seemed to be true. Gimjaa didn't acknowledge that her family was around her. When she finally spoke that evening, it was only to ask for her lost babies. "Children! Children! I've been searching all over for you," Gimjaa called out. "Where are you hiding? Where did you go?"

Siripon met with the doctors to learn more about their mother's condition. They suspected the swelling was a complication brought on by her diabetes. Her kidneys were failing.

The siblings took turns spending the night with her. The staff wheeled in a second bed, but on nights Manda was to stay, she couldn't fall asleep among the sick. She chanted for her mother and the other patients on the floor. Each night, as the hour grew late, her thoughts turned to the ugliness of death. She saw the pain on her mother's face, the wretchedness of her circumstances. Gimjaa had gained several pounds since Manda last saw her. Her hair had grown thin and white. The dentures she had worn for decades had been removed, leaving her cheeks sunken, her face nothing more than skin draped over bone.

"Where are you, children?" Gimjaa cried out. Her face twisted sourly. She was irritated by the oxygen line that ran under her nose and the IV tube taped to her hand. She tried feebly to pull them away, but her hands had been restrained. Manda tried to calm her. She told her that the boys were in Sawan, that they were happy. Out in the hall, the nurses passed by without looking in. One of them laughed over a comment another of them had made.

On alternating nights, Manda went home with Tassanee. The neighbors had heard of the sisters' arrival. They stopped by with the latest news, telling her of a child's burst appendix, a bad crop of oranges in the orchard, the damages from the floods. Manda was sympathetic, but she no longer related to their struggles. She only thought about her mother and her own hardships; each day now, she felt that she might be asked to leave her sister's house. She was angry at herself for not being more ambitious, not saving more money. She regretted that she had not done more to prepare for the future.

Moving back to Phet Buri was a possibility. Tassanee had mentioned it in passing, telling her that it would be nice to have someone around the house to help take care of the baby. Manda considered it, but she had grown too comfortable in America. The air-conditioned supermarkets. The garden store. The wide roads. She had been spoiled.

She heard from Tassanee that Ben had been calling long-distance from Stanford. He wanted to come to Thailand and be with the family, but Siripon convinced him to stay in California and focus on his studies. The summer term had just begun, and he had decided to take extra courses.

Manda wished she had the chance to speak to him herself. The two had exchanged hardly any words for several months now. But only she knew what Ben needed to hear. He would want to know how Gimjaa was doing so he could decide for himself whether it was time to come.

For eight days, the family held their vigil. On the ninth day, Gimjaa opened her eyes and sat up in bed so that Tassanee could feed her porridge. The entire family was called to the hospital, and they took turns visiting her. They were all relieved. They felt a sense of incredulity.

"Thuy, thuy, thuy, you've come back from the brink," Manda said. "You needed to scare all of us so that we would come and visit you."

Gimjaa laughed. She pushed away the bowl of porridge and raised her arms to hug her American daughters. Her eyes were bright. The swelling in her hands had gone down. The doctor said that she was stabilized. She might even be able to go home in a few days.

"But no more sugar," Siripon insisted. "From now on you're going to eat salads and protein. And you don't need rice with every meal."

"Then I might as well have died," Gimjaa said. "I'd happily go if I didn't need to look after my great-granddaughter."

Everyone fussed over her. They made sure that her feet were warm, that she didn't have any bedsores, that she could go to the bathroom. Soon, however, a tender sadness came over them. Kiet was returning to work in Ranong. Siripon and Kamron would travel back to the US the following day to save what little was left of Kamron's sick time.

Manda stayed at the hospital while the others drove to the airport. Gimjaa was more energetic. The nurses had put her on a diet, and she was picking at a tray of boiled chicken and bitter melon soup. Mother and daughter spent the afternoon reminiscing about the feasts they had cobbled together when Manda was a child, when they would scour the beach for crabs or cast their nets for catfish whenever one of the children's birthdays arrived.

That night, Gimjaa's skin turned red and swollen again. She itched all over, and when she scratched herself, her skin broke and bled. She begged for her dead sons to come home. Manda held her and told her to pray. She chanted to bring her mother peace. Gimjaa closed her eyes and didn't open them again. Her heart rate increased. Her breathing grew faster.

When Tassanee arrived, the sisters wept together. They sat in the room on either side of Gimjaa until they were nearly asleep, and then Tassanee went home, and Manda left a message for Siripon so that she would receive it as soon as she arrived in Los Angeles. Though Manda had not called him in weeks, she left a message for Ben and told him the name of the hospital where they were staying.

Gimjaa defecated, but what came out was undigested—her organs had stopped functioning. Three days passed. Her heart rate continued to increase, and her breathing grew faster. On the fourth day, she gasped for breath, as if she were choking on water.

"Let go of everything that troubles you. Bu-toh, bu-toh," Manda chanted. She held her mother until she died.

Siripon had not been home for two days before she returned to Phet Buri, this time alone. Ben arrived and took a bus and then a taxi to join them. The family cremated Gimjaa less than a week after her death. A dozen people were present. Her body twitched in the intense heat of the flame. She seemed almost to sit up, and she had to be pushed back down again.

In the days after the passing, Manda was grateful to have Ben with her. She sat quietly with him, cried with his hand held in hers. She talked about both of her parents, recounting all the things she remembered, good and bad. In her mind, their image as old people was replaced by their younger selves, when they would run the house and raise the children in their stern and loving way.

Ben was patient with her sadness. He urged her to eat even though she had no appetite. When she wouldn't come down to join the others, he brought her meals up to her bedroom. "Try and get a little bit down," he said.

Manda put her arms around him. She pressed her face into his chest. "I'll eat later, ja," she said, so as not to worry him. "I'm glad you could be here with me."

Ben sat still beside her. She noticed his gaze move up to a pale gecko that waited patiently above them. Remembering all of his questions when Pradit had died, Manda told him about Gimjaa calling to her two sons in her delirium. She told him about the food that Gimjaa's body could no longer digest, and how she gasped for breath twice, as if she were choking on water, just before she died. Ben listened attentively. He took it all in.

3

Having already lost her father, Siripon knew that the raw surface pain of her mother's death would fade. Even the deeper ache that would not go away, like hollows in her bones, was countered by the understanding that Gimjaa had suffered so much while she was alive. Siripon hoped Sawan healed her mother, restored her to a perfect form.

She didn't cry during the final meal before Ben returned to college. He would take a flight from Bangkok to San Francisco, where Collin would pick him up and drive him back to campus.

"I won't be able to come home before the new school year starts," he said as Siripon began sorting through her mother's things. They would donate what they could to the needy, but most of her clothes were too old to salvage.

She questioned her son, hurt. "How do you already know your schedule so far ahead of time?"

"My classes are getting so hard. I'm studying all night long. It would be easier if I stayed there."

She resigned herself to his decision, and she refrained from telling him to be careful. Ever since she had the opportunity to spend time alone with Collin, her mind had been more at ease anyway. Letting him go was another form of love, she told herself. She thought of how her own mother and father had let her go.

After Ben left, Siripon scrubbed the house for hours, not bothering to turn the lights on as the shadows elongated around her. Tassanee offered to flip the light switch on, but Siripon told her not to bother.

She worked in the dark on her hands and knees, enjoying the catharsis that came from hard work.

The house was full, almost crowded. Her nephews and the baby filled the place with much needed life. Still, the specter of her parents lingered. Siripon could even smell, faintly, her mother's betel paste in the air. Though she would not admit it to anyone, she thought back to the things she had written in her diary all those years ago. She had never known how to begin her apology to her parents. Now she would never have the opportunity.

Alone in her old room that evening, she wondered what had become of her diary after she moved away. So much time had passed since she confided in it, since the pages had been cut out and replaced by an amulet. She had worked harder than ever after the incident, dedicating all her energy to taking care of her family. Her attention had only been divided when she had a baby of her own, someone she loved even more than she loved her parents. From her bed, she could make out the frames of the open windows. Moonlight poured in, bringing with it the scent of the dying fires. Any moment now, as it had the previous mornings, a rooster would crow. Siripon slipped out of the covers and knelt beside her bed. She reached into the gap beneath the bottom drawer of her bureau. The diary was there; as soon as her hand ran across the leather binding, she remembered the lightness that had caught her off guard after it had been hollowed out. The book seemed to float in her hand. She opened the cover and touched the sharp edges of the cut pages.

Rising, she went to slip the book into her suitcase. She would take it home, bury it among her own things. As she lifted it, she heard the soft rattle and the thump of the amulet hitting the ground. She quickly brushed it off and asked for forgiveness. It still had a power over her.

"I'm sorry," she whispered, crossing the distance between worlds to speak to her parents. Somewhere beyond the courtyard walls, the rooster crowed.

4

It was five o'clock in Los Angeles. From the green liquid shade of the patio, Kamron looked out past the guesthouse, toward the garden drenched in sunlight and the bright shack beside it. This was his seventh day alone, his seventh day getting drunk just to pass the time. He clung unsteadily to the gate. Around him, the walls of the house were two shades of yellow, some untouched from years ago, others newly painted to accompany the remodeling. Kamron hadn't thought the house needed work, but it had been refreshing to have a change, the sense of something gained rather than something lost. Ever since Ben moved away, the threads that held the household together clung tenuously. The sisters hardly spoke to each other, even on the rare occasions when they sat at the same table to share a meal. Kamron had been lodged between them, forced to convey messages from one to the other when they wanted to communicate. Then, a few weeks ago, Siripon abandoned him too. She climbed out of bed and told him she was going to sleep in Ben's old room. At that late hour, she muttered something about Kamron snoring too loudly, but the next morning, when he found her working in the kitchen, she blamed hot flashes brought on by menopause. She said she couldn't even be under the covers anymore, let alone lie beside him. It seemed like nothing more than a simple adjustment for her, like trying a new brand of dish soap that was on sale.

While the others were away, he was relieved not to have to hide his glass behind a potted plant. He took another drink, letting it calm the insecurities that would otherwise be overshadowing his thoughts. That was all he needed every day to soothe him. He was careful not to drop the glass. He had become sensitive to cold against his fingers. The acid baths at the factory were to blame, the green pools he had dipped his hands into every day as part of the metal-cleaning protocol. Others complained about the same problem, but no one would report it to their supervisors for fear of being let go. They needed to get to retirement. They needed their measly pensions.

He returned his gaze to the shack, unsure if he could make it over there without stumbling. The little structure was one of the few areas of the house that still belonged to him. He had watched, passive, as Siripon steadily took over the house with her spartan aesthetic, emptying it of anything unnecessary. Last week, she began rummaging through the garage, finally getting rid of old furniture they hadn't been willing to part with when they were younger. Kamron had watched her swivel a writing desk onto a dolly and roll it to the open face of the dumpster she had rented, refusing his offers to help. The dumpster still loomed in the driveway, the work unexpectedly halted when Gimjaa got sick. Kamron was grateful that his own mother was still alive and sharp. He had only seen her briefly on this last visit, the trip so lacking in preparation. It had only been enough time for the two of them to eat together and sit for a while before he had to go to Phet Buri.

Dinnertime approached, and he let himself go dry for a couple of hours before driving to a Mexican food stand. He ignored the disapproving look from the cashier as he paid and made his way back to his car with some tacos and rice. At home, it was hard to get any of it down. He didn't like to eat alone. He thought of Siripon and how her skin had glistened as she worked in the garage. She had pushed her dress up to her thighs to cool down, revealing just for an instant that she wasn't wearing any underwear. Knowing that nothing lay between the air and the hair between her legs, Kamron had felt lust he hadn't acknowledged in years. He had wanted to take her in the garage, among the dusty and abandoned things. But with her resurgence of energy, he was anxious too.

Maybe she was like an exotic flower that spent the last of its resources for a brief, final effulgence before withering away.

Abandoning his food, he paused beside the door to let his eyes adjust to the darkness outside. *Night is a solid thing,* he thought. *More solid than day.* He walked toward the garden, to the shack he had stared at all afternoon. In front of him, the lawns floated like supernatural planes in the ether of space. All those years ago, he was supposed to have started a fire here, but he had not been able to do it.

The stone path shone pale through the darkness. Beyond, the silhouettes of Manda's plants overlapped one another like dark webs. He balanced his cigarette on top of a cinder block column and placed his glass beside it. He opened the door of the shack and fumbled for the flashlight he kept on one of the support beams. The place smelled of mildew and the leaked fumes from leftover paint and turpentine. He would clean it out someday, perhaps, but he felt no rush—no one came in here other than him, not yet, at least. Everything was hidden away: things wrapped in bags wrapped in other bags, boxes tucked in cupboards behind other boxes. He lifted a violin case out from behind a row of old suitcases. Strumming his fingers over the still-taut strings of the instrument, he let the notes resonate. Ben had played with the beginner orchestra for a year and a half before giving it up. Toward the end, he had managed to produce some graceful passages—tender, melodic lines rising out of the screeching that made up the bulk of his performances. Kamron wondered how these moments emerged, if the boy occasionally touched on something in his heart that was otherwise inaccessible. He had encouraged Ben to keep practicing, but the act of pushing only made his son resist. Ben did this with all things that came from Kamron, who represented the opposite of his plans and desires. The boy had shaped his life by filling the spaces that Kamron left empty.

He reached into a cupboard, snaked his hand under the lid of a cardboard box and down into the softness of the worn green blanket that Ben had clung to as a child. After the incident when the boy wrapped it around himself like a dress, Kamron and Manda convinced him that it disappeared. But Kamron never lost track of it. He had kept it a secret among secrets. All around him were these pieces of Ben's past, from a time when Kamron thought he could surround himself with his boy's innocence and be saved by it.

He emptied his glass. He set the flashlight top down so that the light was eclipsed. Reaching into an old shoebox he'd stowed on the top shelf of the back wall, he found the familiar figure he had come to know without sight. His fingers ran over the little head, the little arms, the little dress. The paper girl grew more brittle every year, this solitary figure that carried such a burden. He had lacked the courage to destroy it back then. He had not dared to burn it because he had not dared to burn his son. And now he had picked up the habit of visiting it only in the dark after the rest of his family abandoned him to his evenings alone.

Tonight, there was no fear of getting caught. He cast his light over the figure's creases and shadows. It was such a simple thing. Nothing more than clever craftwork. Yet he was afraid to treat it as only paper. Examining it, he thought he could see faintly a face there, the tiny rise and fall of her chest. He took her out into the night. Facing her toward the moon, he wished he could set her free. Yet he kept her in a coffin all these years. Someday the others would find her. Perhaps after he was dead. That was how they would find all these things that were so precious to him. Maybe then they would know that he cared for his son, that he loved him, though he had no ability to convey those feelings, that attempting to convey them made him too vulnerable because it reminded him that everything he had ever hoped for had been lost. He fumbled for his cigarette that still sat smoking on top of the wall. He pressed the tip against the doll, watching the embers crawl from the stub to the figure like glowing mites.

"We try to be good, and nothing comes of it. We do good a hundred times and they only see the one time we're bad," he said. He blew gently to stoke the flame. "Maybe if I'm bad a hundred times, they'll see the one time I'm good." The fire expanded, sweeping up her body until she was too hot to hold. She fell into a tangle of weeds and continued to burn for a moment longer. He was drowsy by the time he trudged back to the house. His meal was left half eaten in the guesthouse. He reached forward clumsily, pulled his chair out at the head of the table. He took another few bites, enough to stave off the hunger until the next day.

In the night, Kamron smelled smoke. Thinking Siripon had left something on the stove, he reached over to wake her, only then remembering he was alone. He rose in the dark, groping and stumbling. The source was not in the house, not in either of the kitchens. He rushed out to the yard to find that the shed had caught fire. The blaze was already above his head. It had consumed the door and the latticework along the front. He turned on the hose, spraying the flames and watching to see if they died down. They seemed to breathe, drawing in a patient inhalation and then exhaling quickly. The flames spread to the garden; they charred the delicate plants, the intricate networks of stems and leaves. Embers jumped from shed to tree, tree to rooftop, and now they were burning the houses. He shouted at them. He shouted for anyone to hear. He dashed inside, trying to think of what to rescue, but the smoke was building, the walls were growing hot. Blaring, flashing fire trucks took over the driveway, and he went out to them, shouting, waving his arms above his head. The water came with a burst of noise that for a moment seemed to make the fire larger before subsiding. They worked back toward where the fire started, barging into the house before heading to the blaze in the yard. More blaring trucks came. Neighbors gathered on the curb in pajamas. Kamron stood among the commotion in the driveway until finally someone ushered him farther back. The battle took hours. What had been all movement and noise coiled down with a hiss. The fire chief asked Kamron if he knew how it started. No, Kamron said. No, he had been asleep. Unless someone had broken in. Perhaps someone had broken in. There were many questions. Enough questions that he couldn't distinguish when he was lying and when he was telling the truth. The sun was rising by the time it was over. The walls of the houses were wounded. The garden was gone. The shed gone. He had let it all slip away.

The Empty House

1

From the street, the house looked like it always did, a neat yellow box, austere but familiar. Only when Ben walked through the gate did he see the devoured rooms, the burnt and crumbling structures of the kitchen, the shrine room, and the guesthouse, each destroyed layer by layer and coated in soot.

He found Kamron in the backyard, sorting through the debris. Ben's voice startled his father, drawing him away from his weary searching.

"It's all gone. All gone." Kamron looked back down into the ash. He still wore his bathrobe. His eyes were somber and apologetic.

"Have you eaten?" Ben asked.

"Yes . . . No . . . Not yet."

"I picked up some food for you. Why don't you get something in your stomach?"

"Yes, fine. Later." Kamron looked up again, suddenly focused on Ben. "Are you okay, son? What happened to you?"

Ben's hand was covered in a neat dressing, the result of Collin's over-protection and a comprehensive first aid book they had bought together. "It's just a burn," Ben said to Kamron. "Coffee spill."

"Last night? What time?"

"It was late. I should have been more careful."

"No, it wasn't your fault."

His father's voice had sounded tense earlier that morning. It had been strange that he should call and be so attentive. He asked how Ben was doing, how school was, even how his art show had gone. Several moments passed before he revealed that there had been a fire. He used the same words then: "It's all gone."

Ben helped Kamron inside, to his old bedroom. It was one of the areas that had been relatively undamaged. He laid out some breakfast burritos he had picked up at the airport, hefty bundles still faintly warm. Kamron stared vacantly at them for a moment. Then he ate ravenously, finishing his meal and rooting through the bag to see if there was more.

"I'm sorry. I should have gotten something else," Ben said.

Kamron shook his head and rose as if he was going back out to the yard. "Your mother is still in the air," he said. "She's going to be furious with me."

Ben wished he could say something comforting, but he blamed Kamron too. The story his father had given him over the telephone was disorganized, vague, something about losing his cigarette in the yard. Ben had thought briefly about ignoring it, but Collin convinced him to come down. After all, he hadn't really signed up for a summer term. That had only been an excuse to stay away.

He walked through the house, taking note of the alien transformations the fire had created. A boundary had been broken. Debris from outside had come in, and the guts of the house had spilled out. As he entered the shrine room, he confronted the strangeness of being able to see through it to what used to be the kitchen, and then through that to the entirety of the patio. It mirrored his mind, his knowledge of all the secrets that had taken place here. Only recently, Ben had explained to Collin that the Thai word for "family" translated to "around the kitchen." The two were linked: the structure and the people inside it.

They sorted through their belongings all afternoon, their survey interrupted once by a phone call from the insurance company. Kamron insisted he couldn't provide any information—they would have to wait for his wife to come home. The Minnuchs next door brought over a lasagna, which they ended up leaving on Ben's old desk, since the refrigerator was no longer working. In the afternoon, Ben borrowed his dad's car for a run to the grocery store and tried to remember what his family usually kept in the kitchen. He found their preferred brand of coffee and bread, a bunch of bananas to replace the fruit that always sat on the counter. He guessed on the snacks they might eat, chips and nuts and a family-sized box of Chicken in a Biskit. When he returned, Kamron was pacing in the driveway.

"You must be exhausted, Dad. Do you want to try and take a nap?"

"I'm all right," Kamron said. "I can't sit still." His face was drawn and pale. He inhaled hollowly and coughed.

"Did the paramedics examine you? Are you sure you're okay?"

"I'm always the bad guy," Kamron said. "Now everyone knows that's true. Now they all see it." He pulled out a pack of cigarettes from his pocket, inspected it, and then tucked it away again. "This family doesn't understand everything about me. I want you to know that. I know I'm not a good father—you don't have to tell me. But I try to do the right things for you. You don't always see the things I do."

"I'm not blaming you."

"Of course you are. Everyone does. I'm always the one who gets blamed."

Ben placed his hand on his father's shoulder, the admission lowering his defenses. He was grateful that their inability to connect was laid bare. His anger was no longer hot and aggressive; he accepted some things. The sun was setting. Above them, the streetlights flickered on down the line. The lights of the nearby houses appeared. They were bright on the porches and warmly filling the windows inside. The two of them carried the groceries into the house. Kamron looked through them, commenting on which items were correct and which he did not care for.

"There are some things you've forgotten," Kamron said. "I'll need to go back out myself."

"You're not too tired to drive?"

He nodded, deflated. "I am, I am. But I'll need to get some things."

A moment passed before Ben realized what his father was saying. He drove them to the liquor store and sat in the car while Kamron went inside. When he appeared again, he held a vodka bottle by the throat. They returned home, and Ben didn't see it again. He assumed it was tucked away somewhere deep in the house. As the night progressed, his father grew more incoherent. He walked in and out of his bedroom, opening and closing the door. He examined the lasagna and ate it directly out of the pan. By ten, he was snoring, and Ben found a place in the hall where he could sit and wait. It would be easier for everyone this way. He would have a chance to explain it all to his mother as best he could. Only a few feet away were the tarnished Buddha statues that survived in the shrine room. When he was a child, there had only been one little statue, but the collection had grown to include the Buddha in different poses and incarnations. They wore brass smiles, and they rested peacefully, maintaining their contentedness even among the damage. They had witnessed all the secrets too, watched without interfering. Ben nodded at the irony. He didn't place any value on Buddhism or on any religion, the concept of rules and gods too fantastical to him. A cold gust swept through the house, and he tried to shield himself. He went to his bedroom. He flipped the light switch, not surprised when it didn't turn on. His parents' bedroom door opened, and Kamron came out again. "It's all gone," he said, as if he was in a trance.

Ben directed him back into his room. "It's all gone," he agreed.

2

Siripon combed through the debris of the fire in search of anything that could be saved. The corner of the roof had come down after the walls crumbled, so she had to push the graveled panels aside to see beneath them. She felt strong as she worked, anger still coursing through her.

The shock of what happened had come gradually. Climbing out of the taxi, half asleep, Siripon was surprised to find Ben in the driveway. Her first concern had been that something happened to Kamron, that he had been injured. It was several moments before she understood that he was fine, that only the house had been damaged.

Nearly everything was ruined, but a few things remained untouched. Gathered in the old hall closet were some old coats and the silk dresses Siripon had brought with her from Thailand, the ones she had worn to parties when she first arrived in the country. All these things had been protected in their storage bags and looked oddly new amid the skeletal remains of the house. Her house. The house she had found with its clean, tiled kitchen and its brightly lit bedrooms. She could rebuild it if she wanted to, come up with the money on her own just as she had done the first time. But in the moment, she felt that she would rather surrender it to someone else. She no longer loved this place. She had stopped loving it years ago, even before Ben moved away. The yellow walls. The red concrete. The sickly green light of the patio. Even the new rooms that had still carried the faint smell of paint—she did not love them.

She almost laughed at the timing of the tragedy. Only the other day, Jerlie asked if Siripon wanted to join her on a cruise. It would be eight days around the Caribbean, a girls' trip with the nurses and Jerlie's cousins from the Philippines. Siripon had said yes without asking Kamron. She ordered new outfits for the trip that would arrive any day now—some floral-print dresses and a floppy wide-brimmed hat. She even found a bathing suit, a dark one-piece with a long wrap that would cover her varicose veins. The trip was only a few weeks away.

The plans had been prompted by a rumor, a joke, that the nurses were spreading about her. Siripon and a man named Manuel Huerta spent several evenings talking together as his daughter recovered from meningitis. The nurses called it "Siripon's affair." They clicked their tongues and stroked their pointer fingers in her direction. Then, when they learned the truth, it became an even bigger scandal. Siripon admitted that Manuel was a divorce lawyer. She had asked him for details about how much it would cost to leave Kamron and whether she would have to pay alimony. After many conversations, Manuel had prepared the paperwork for a divorce—he would proceed with the filing whenever she asked him to. When the others realized how close she was to going forward with it, they encouraged her to take a break from the marriage, clear her mind. The cruise would be a trial run, they said, a chance to experience life without Kamron for a few days. Jerlie printed out itineraries to peruse. She brought in her photo albums from previous cruises. "Afterward, you can decide if you like it," she said. "We will support you either way."

Was it reasonable to go now? Could she leave the others behind? From beyond what remained of the guesthouse, she heard Manda asking Kamron for help in the garden, apparently still trying to recover what she could. It seemed unfair that he would be helping Manda, but Siripon knew he was still avoiding her. When she confronted him earlier, he had been tender. It had only made her more furious. She demanded that he explain what happened, but all he did was apologize. Ben had stepped in to fill in the gaps of the story.

She returned to her searching, uncovering the artifacts from her wedding, her gown spilling out like ocean foam, the garment bag in which it had been sealed split open. She lifted it up, finding it heavier than she expected, the fabric weighing down her arms. She remembered what it had been like to wear that dress as Kamron embraced her. He had felt solid and protective then.

She carried the gown to the bathroom and locked the door behind her. Waiting silently, she listened to make sure no one approached. The dress brought back memories of the reception, the table of nurses who had come to support her, the evening in bed with Kamron, when she lost her virginity. He had been tender that first night as well, though it hadn't been due to drinking. He had not even used his tongue when they first kissed, not until she tentatively offered hers. Then he had opened her body slowly, using his fingers before climbing on top of her. It was over years that their lovemaking evolved, first with his playful side coming out, then his aggression. When they were together last, she felt like nothing more than a body that he used for his own pleasure.

She tried to slip the dress on, but after getting it over her head and shoulders, it refused to slip past her hips. Instead, she had to be content with holding it in front of her as she turned to face the mirror. The satin panels on the bodice shimmered under the light. The fabric exaggerated how much her skin had aged. She dropped her hands, embarrassed by how things had turned out. She had been so satisfied with herself on her wedding day; she had believed that her happiness had arrived. Now she understood how wrong she was. She knew that Kamron and Manda had slept together. Sometime over the last few months, she realized how familiar they had become with each other—how intimate their conversations were and how comfortable they were sitting closely together. It was not evidence, but she knew she was right.

She took the dress and pushed it to the bottom of her hamper. She couldn't decide if she would keep it or donate it to Goodwill. Even without considering Kamron, the dress represented something to her. It marked her survival in the Outer Country, her ability to establish things on her own. She still had that, even after everything.

3

They caravanned to a nearby Motel 6, Manda trailing behind alone in her car. The manager greeted them from behind the front desk. She was a gray-haired Indian woman in a sari who wore a dozen gold bangles on each wrist. Behind her, in the back office, a man was crouched beside a vacuum cleaner, apparently attempting to repair it. The two bickered, even as she was helping the family. They weren't speaking English, but it was clear that the woman was being critical of her husband, and her husband, lowered as he was, made no attempt to defend himself. He simply took the criticism and offered soft, apologetic phrases in return.

Manda would have said Siripon and Kamron's relationship was different, that Siripon chose to be more subservient. But when the couple had argued earlier, Manda heard the same anger from her sister and the same apologetic tone coming from Kamron. Manda had hidden away in her bedroom during the commotion. Eventually, Ben came to her door and offered to carry some of her things to the car. When she asked him what had happened, he only shrugged.

In her motel room, she was grateful to have a moment alone. She began to unpack her clothes and arrange them in the dresser drawers. Her bedroom at the house had gone untouched by the fire, and she was grateful to have recovered most of her belongings. But that had come with a sense of guilt too.

There was a knock on the door. She opened it expecting to find Ben; perhaps he was already saying goodbye. Instead, Kamron walked in, still with a soft, forlorn expression on his face. He wore a gray sweater smudged with soot. "This is bigger than your room back home," he said vacantly.

"It's heaven," Manda replied. "You did us a favor by burning your house down." Sex hadn't been mentioned between them since the night they argued. Instead, they bantered now, cutting each other lightly like siblings. She returned to putting her clothes away.

"I doubt we'll be here that long," he said, gesturing at her work.

"Your wife wants to buy a new house. Don't you think that will take some time?"

"Well, we don't have to stay here. We can find somewhere nicer. Or go back and sleep at the house."

"You can go back and sleep in that wreck if you want. Let's see if anyone goes with you."

Kamron grew quiet for a moment, seemingly annoyed. He paced around the room and confronted the unremarkable wall painting of a little thatch-roof cottage in a field.

"Were they right?" Manda asked. "Were you drunk when it happened?"

"Would you believe me if I said I wasn't?"

"I'm guessing it if happened at night, then you were drunk."

"But I drink every night, don't I? I've never burned the house down before." He stepped to the window, peeked through a gap in the curtain.

"Did the others go out?" Manda asked.

"To the market."

"So how did the fire start?"

Kamron shook his head, lost. He let go of the curtain, and the light in the room wavered. "A lot of time has passed since you and I have spoken about her. I bet you thought we'd never bring her up again."

"You're giving me a headache, Yai. How is anyone supposed to make sense of what you're saying?"

"It was the girl," he said. "The girl—the little paper girl."

"What are you talking about?"

"You know, don't you? I hardly need to describe it and you know exactly what I mean. We both still remember her after all this time. I kept her in the shed by the garden, in a little box, like a bed."

"What are you saying?"

"You didn't come out with me that night the monk told me to burn her," he said. "You didn't feel what I felt. It was like I held a living being—like I was being asked to burn my own child. How could I do that?"

"How dare you play with such a thing? And how many years did we wait for Ben to get better? How many years did he suffer? Huh? Now you tell me it was all for nothing, that there was never any hope of him changing because you couldn't follow instructions!"

"Don't you hear a thing I say? Do you know what it feels like to have death on your hands? I couldn't do it."

"We were trying to help him. We did it all for him."

"How can you be so sure? Tell me that." He paused. He looked down at his hands. "But whatever the problem was, it's done now—it's done. I finally burned her. She's gone."

Manda sat down on the bed. A sweater she had been holding fell to the floor. "Doing it now is the same as doing nothing at all," she said. But as the words came out, another feeling arose within her. She thought of the paper girl lying safe all these years, and a sense of yearning came over her. Knowing that only a couple days ago it would have been possible to take back what she had done, she ached to hold the doll in her hands, to protect it. "And why now?" she demanded.

"Maybe I was drunk and didn't know what I was doing."

"You finally did it because you stopped caring for your son. You've always been afraid to care for him. You're afraid if you care too much, he's going to hurt you. So you let go. You're a coward. You have a coward's heart."

"And what kind of heart do you have?"

Manda's face was still, stolid. She was anxious for Ben to return from wherever he had gone. "I thought it would be a simple ceremony," she whispered. "I thought we could fix things early."

Kamron sat beside her on the bed. Any tension she sensed from him earlier was gone. His arm rose as if he was going to wrap it around her, but he didn't touch her; he let it drift over to the bedpost. "I don't want to live in a new house," he said.

"You and I don't get to choose where we live," Manda said. "You know as well as I do."

Kamron didn't move for a long while. Finally, he rose and walked back to his room. Alone, Manda searched through the pockets of her purse, hoping to find a piece of candy, something sweet to soothe her. She unwrapped a cough drop and slipped it into her mouth, letting the syrup ease down her throat. Some time passed before she heard the distant sound of car doors slamming. Down below, Siripon and Ben lifted grocery bags out from the trunk of her car and carried them up the pebbled stairway. He moved with a certain grace, almost as if he were floating upward. Manda watched him until he reached the landing and slipped out of view.

4

Ben wouldn't have answered the phone if he had paused long enough to guess who it was. Three weeks had passed since the fire; his mother and Manda were calling him daily, their need to keep tabs on him more intense. Tonight, it was Manda, calling on the motel's rotary phone. He still had a hard time talking to her without getting angry, but he tried not to show it. She kept her voice low to keep the others from overhearing. "Your mother—sometimes I just don't know what gets into her head."

"What happened now?" Ben pressed his thumb against the teeth of his keys, the soft pain relieving some tension. He only had a few minutes before he needed to meet Collin at the Quad.

"I don't even know where to begin. The ridiculousness." Manda sighed, exasperated. "She said there won't be room for me in the new house, that it's time I got out of her hair. Is that the language she uses with me now? 'Get out of my hair'—like I'm some nit. My own little sister. I suppose blood doesn't mean anything anymore."

Ben wasn't sure if he should act surprised. His mother had shared her decision with him while he was still down south. They had been on their way back from the grocery store. She had asked him his opinion, whether it was fair of her. But he had said it wasn't up to him. It had come after a long conversation in which Siripon asked Ben if he knew the reason why Manda had come to the US in the first place.

"She came to help raise me," Ben had said.

"No," Siripon replied firmly. "Someone died back home. A student of hers. Your aunt left to get away from the tragedy. Never forget that. You don't owe her anything."

Ben had never heard that story before. He asked his mother for more details, but she replied that she hadn't ever asked. "You were going to arrive soon. I had too much on my mind as it was."

Now, in his room, he decided to play dumb with his aunt. "Do you think she was serious?" he asked.

"Something's not right with her head—believe me or don't. She says she wants to be alone with your father. You tell me, have you ever seen the two of them enjoy being together? You can barely call them friends, let alone husband and wife."

Time seemed to be catching up with the family. When Ben first moved out of the house, he had expected this split to happen. For months, he listened to stories about the sisters arguing with each other. But more than a year had passed—he was a sophomore now—and the household had held together, at least until today.

A familiar fantasy played out in his mind. He imagined an alternate universe where his father had married Manda instead of his mother. He often thought that, if the three of them had only gotten the pairing right, everyone could be happy. But he knew this was impossible. Manda would never put up with his father's demands. And his father would lose his temper over her refusal to let him have the last word. Neither couple was viable because the individuals weren't viable; no one was equipped to get along with anyone else. He reached under his bed for the signs he painted the night before. He was going to be late.

"I'll talk to her," he offered.

"You won't be able to change her mind now. Besides, she'll be off on her little trip soon—something else that doesn't make any sense."

"Oh, the cruise." Ben tried to hide the giddiness in his voice. For so long, he had wanted his mother to take a break from the burdens of the family. The others would be okay, he had told her. The inspection of the new condominium was complete, he could help with any issues that came up with escrow, and Kamron could sign any additional paperwork.

He asked Manda gently, "Do you know where you're going to go?"

"I'm still figuring that out. This country doesn't give a woman like me many options." She paused, leaving him the opening to offer to let her stay with him. Ben reminded himself of his sessions with the student counselor, his six weeks with Dr. Jennice Tomkins, whose repeated advice had been to set boundaries with his family.

"My other roommates would never agree to it," he lied. He and Collin had found their own apartment in August. It was a chance to try living together and deepening their relationship. "You'd be lonely here with me anyway. I'm always—"

"So busy," Manda said, finishing for him. "I know."

He refrained from apologizing. His aunt wasn't his responsibility, according to Dr. Tomkins. It had taken Ben several sessions to tell the counselor about the Buddhist ceremony, the throwing up. He still felt shame over it, even after Tomkins tried to convince him that it wasn't his fault.

"Your mom says I can stay in the new condominium until I find somewhere else to go. But I should just pack up and leave the motel tonight. If she wants to be alone with your father so badly, then let her."

"Don't be a hothead. Please. Find a good place first, somewhere you can be safe and comfortable." He could tell his face was turning red. He was getting pulled back into it.

"Anyway," Manda said. "I wouldn't even have a cardboard box to sleep in if I left tonight."

"I have to go. I'm still finishing up work at the lab."

"I knew I shouldn't have called. I don't want to be a burden."

"You're not a burden," he said. "But right now, I have to go."

"Yes, ja, yes. Don't worry about me." She stayed on the line, and he was the one who hung up.

A group was already gathered in the Quad with signs and rainbow flags and a pent-up, expectant energy. The students had set up a platform to overlook the George Segal sculpture, the same one that had been vandalized twice with homophobic slurs. It was a reminder to anyone who would pay attention that the hate had penetrated campus.

"Equality now! Equality now!" The chanting was picked up here and there, but it didn't gain momentum yet.

"They're being ambitious," Collin said. He came up behind Ben and bit him, vampire-like, on the neck. All month he had complained that the statewide civil unions they were fighting for weren't the same as marriages, that equality wasn't even on the table yet. Ben hadn't quibbled over the terminology. He only wanted to ensure they could visit each other in the hospital if one of them should get sick—that was the scenario people were using to highlight what was at stake. They created commercials with AIDS victims sick in bed as lovers watched helplessly on the other side of the glass. Besides, Manda had been right when she said his parents never seemed to be romantic with each other. Their marriage was not something he wanted to emulate.

He and Collin made their way into the mass of people. It was Owen on the stage. His body, even dressed, still radiated the same magnetic charm Ben had been attracted to in his art classes. Owen waved, a break in his focus that flattered Ben.

"Is he the reason you wanted to come?" Collin asked.

"This was your idea," Ben said. But they were on the same page. Ever since he started taking the art classes, Ben had become more aware of social issues, the importance of taking sides, of being seen. In his science classes, the goal seemed to be to strip away human interpretation. But art was just the opposite. Art required humanity, with all of its emotions and desires.

The crowd looked to be a few hundred strong. Ben was proud to be among them, to feel as if he was a part of something bigger than himself. He raised his sign into the air, his simple message of partnership directed at the counterprotesters a short distance away. Unlike the people around him, this other crowd seemed to be made up of outsiders. They stood in T-shirts with angry messages scrawled on their chests. They had banners with crosses and Bible verses and flames, declarations that a marriage must be between a man and a woman.

"Equality now!" The chanting was building. Around him, the voices moved in unison as Owen invited a new speaker onto the stage. It was the city supervisor from San Francisco. He was a tall, commanding figure. He spoke about Harvey Milk and George Moscone, the wave of registries created in cities like West Hollywood and Palo Alto and how they were not enough. He urged everyone to demand more, to make their voices heard. The group was getting rowdier. Beside Ben, three women took off their shirts before engaging in a demonstrative triple kiss. It inspired new cheers, louder chanting, fists thrusting into the air. Ben could feel his own excitement building. He raised his voice. "Equality now!" This was what life was about. Not meticulous measurements and repeated experiments, but the emotional and chaotic fight for justice.

"Glad there's security," Collin shouted. He looked over at the other group, which had gotten rowdier too. Ben was grateful to have Collin beside him. Somehow, despite their different majors and interests, they had grown closer these last few months. Their new apartment had two bedrooms, but they slept together almost every night. Ben didn't know if he was in love, but the feeling was akin to love. He stopped what he was doing and gave Collin a kiss. They became a moment of stillness in the frenzy.

But an object came into view. It was green, reflective—a bottle that shattered at their feet. Before Ben could decide if it was an accident, other objects came, pelting the crowd. A young man was struck in the head and fell. A crush followed. People were pushing in every direction, not yet sure how to escape. Ben scrambled to keep his footing. He leaned against others, sometimes unintentionally pushing them down as he tried to keep his own balance. As a child, Ben's mother and Manda had recounted for him a schoolyard fight they had been involved in, when Siripon had been bullied and Manda had defended her against a pair of older boys. It was a story that stood out in his mind because the sisters had agreed on almost every detail, from the way Manda had pushed the boy back to how she had protected his mother from the others who came to join the fight. He thought of this as he kept himself between Collin and the mob. As people charged at him, he did what he could to fight back, holding his own until police officers in riot gear finally dispersed the crowd.

He and Collin fell behind a hedge and inspected the scrapes on their arms. Ben thought it surreal that they should find themselves so disheveled in the middle of campus, a place where he had been careful to manage his image in case faculty should notice him as they walked by. Others were recovering along the paths. A group of medics in red jackets came along to administer first aid.

"My uncle always said everyone should get arrested at least once," Collin said, laughing uneasily.

"We're not going to get arrested, are we?" Ben asked.

"They might take our names down. You can lie if you want."

"No, I'll give them my name," Ben said. He wanted to be on record. He could feel himself solidifying, taking up more space in the world than he did before.

5

The *Tropical Princess* was a city floating on the ocean. Siripon followed her friends as Jerlie described the buffet, the water park, the casino, the bar. An enormous fountain appeared. Jets of water arced down and then seemingly leapt up again like living things. The spectacle stretched to the top of the room, meeting an oval skylight and a patch of perfect cerulean that felt almost artificial. It was all too much. Siripon had never been someone who needed a lot. She had the strength to give—to give and give and give. She had given lives away, she felt. And now she did not know how to take.

A young man in a white uniform offered to escort each of them to their rooms. He spoke with that lovely clipped Filipino accent that put Siripon at ease. He was perhaps Ben's age or just a little older. Angelo. A messenger of God.

"Ring me for anything you need," he said as he finished hanging Siripon's coat in the tiny closet of her cabin. He offered to unwrap the basket of fruit and open the sparkling wine that had been set into a nest of pillows on the bed.

"No, no," Siripon said. "I'm fine. I can do it."

"But you don't have to lift a finger here," Angelo said. With a flick of his hand he untied the bow and slipped the ribbon off in one elegant swoop.

"I don't drink," Siripon said, startled that he was already uncorking the bottle and pouring her a glass.

"I'll place it here," he said sweetly. "If you want it, fine. If you don't want it, I will take it away."

Alone, Siripon unwound the towels that had been arranged to look like swans. She took the shrink-wrap off the soaps. She got rid of the little tucks and folds of the blankets that made the bed feel untouchable. It was all on a different scale, but at the same time it was just like being in the motel. She wished she could fall back into a bed she had already slept in a hundred times, in a room that had her things arranged exactly the way she liked them. On her table, little trails of bubbles still floated up from the bottom of the champagne flute. Siripon couldn't say why she had never chosen to drink, except that it had not seemed proper. She had spent so much of her life trying to act how she was expected to act. Even now, she felt as if she were watched by her parents, like they would know when she did something wrong. She imagined other gazes too. She had to be a prim and proper wife; she had to set a respectable example for Ben; she had to control her anger and be kind to her sister. Every day she made a thousand choices that helped other people know that she was a good person, and she was tired of it.

From Angelo, Siripon learned about the nomadic life of cruise-ship workers. "We're homeless!" he shouted as he drew open her curtains. He wore a pretty pair of earrings, little opals that caught the light. He explained that the staff lived mostly on the ship and didn't have to pay for housing on land.

"Sound good," Siripon said, imagining the job for herself, an existence of transient homes and people. She could have liked it when she was younger. But she had made different choices. She showed Angelo the photos she kept in her wallet, two pictures of Ben and the photo from her wedding.

"You have a beautiful family," he said, sighing. "Your son is a little prince."

Siripon had been proud of Ben all his life—she understood this now.

She was proud even when he came out to her. "He like you," she said. "He have boyfriend."

"He's not like me, then!" Angelo shouted. "I'm not stable enough to have a boyfriend. When would we see each other? Never. Except when I fall in love with someone on the ship. That's a different story. I fall in love here all the time. I fall in love and get my heart broken."

"If you happy, just stay alone by yourself," Siripon said, thinking of the divorce papers waiting on Manuel Huerta's computer. "Trust me."

"No, no, no, my lady. I will find love. I know I will find love."

The group made their stops at Half Moon Cay, then St. Thomas, where the beaches reminded Siripon of Phuket. She stepped out into the cool water with her friends and posed for pictures. She mailed postcards to Ben and Kamron, short messages to let them know she was all right.

In the evenings, as the others got drunk, she ordered Shirley Temples and nursed them at the table amid chairs that held her friends' purses. On the dance floor, the others had such a wonderful sense of rhythm. When they sang karaoke, their voices were beautiful. They had a joy, too, Siripon realized, a thrill that came from being the center of attention. Had she ever had the same confidence? Had it been taken away from her? She thought of Manda mocking her as a child, the clever impressions that got the boys laughing so hard. But that had been Siripon's fault too. She had to have given in to it somehow to be so bruised.

When she told Manda that she would not be invited to live in the new house, it had hurt them both. Siripon could imagine her parents' disapproval, their scolding her for not keeping the family together. She imagined what Tassanee and Kiet would think when they found out, and how Manda would spin the story to appear as if she had been a victim. Maybe she was. Siripon worried that her decision was based on some unconscious need to retaliate, a pronouncement that she had finally won whatever it was they were competing for their entire lives. She had believed it was her parents' approval, but it went deeper than that; it was her sense of justice, of karma, of being rewarded for doing all the right things her entire life, even if she was rewarding herself.

She sat beside the pool while her friends lingered at the bar. The other women were nice enough, similar to Jerlie in some ways. But they were not content looking out at the ocean or enjoying the sea air. They needed more fun.

From a cabin room, Siripon heard Angelo's muffled voice. He was laughing absurdly—no, he was shrill from anger. There was a fragment of a sentence, a curse word. A door clapped open, and he stomped out.

"What happen?" Siripon asked.

"Can I get anything for you, my lady?" He quickly composed himself.

"You find boyfriend?"

"Love quick; hate quicker." He sat beside her, letting his shoulders slump. Siripon could smell on him a stale cologne that she didn't think was his. She wished she could reveal to him what she knew about love, that it tired everybody out, that it wasn't necessary to make people whole. The morning she left for the airport, Kamron had refused to speak to her. He was silent during the entire drive, only softening as she climbed out of the car, when he had told her weakly to have fun. The affair between him and Manda was his fault too. She did not ignore that. Kamron should be held accountable just as her sister was. And yet Siripon realized she would never leave him. Their history held them together. He had helped her during the hardest time in her life, when she had no family in the Outer Country. She could not forget that.

"Are you having fun?" Angelo asked. "At least more fun than I'm having?"

"Don't you see me?"

"You're not having as much fun as your friends." The others had taken their cocktails to the dance floor. Liquid splashed out of their shallow glasses, morphing blobs that caught the neon lights before splattering down.

"You don't mean it when you say you're happy by yourself, do you?" Angelo asked.

"Sometime I just tire," Siripon said, surprised by how easily she could talk to him. She didn't feel him judging her the way she was judged at home.

"Love is exhausting," Angelo said. Then, shouting over his shoulder toward the open cabin door, "Love is fucking exhausting!"

"You don't worry they fire you?"

"Let them write me up if they want to. I can't stop being me. Now, come on, our turn." He rose and took hold of her hand. "I'm going to show you a good time."

Siripon dropped her weight down, refusing to budge.

"You need the full experience!" Angelo said. "Just try it tonight. For me and my broken heart!"

"No dance, no dance," Siripon said.

Jerlie and the others had caught sight of the struggle. They surrounded Siripon and clumsily, laughingly, lifted her to her feet. She tried to twist free. She took hold of the chair on which she had been sitting, a recliner that weighed nothing and swung about awkwardly so that people turned to watch the commotion. Her friends were relentless. They forced her to the dance floor and its dark fog of bass beats and swirling lights. *This is what support feels like,* Siripon thought to herself, finally giggling. *This is how people cheer you up instead of bringing you down.* She shook herself free from their grips and shuffled to the center of the circle they had formed. Her elbows found the rhythm first. Then her knees, which alternated in and out. She could feel her mouth pucker, her shoulders shrugging. She stopped caring how silly she looked.

6

On the day Siripon was to return, Kamron was at the airport three hours early. He circled the terminals, trying to linger in the slower lanes, before turning in to the parking lot and taking a ticket from the machine. His days without Siripon had dragged. Mornings when he didn't have to go to the factory, he stayed in bed until Manda began moving around in the adjoining room. Listening for the sound of the water to stop running through the pipes, he would knock on her door and ask if she was ready for breakfast. They walked down the street to a diner, where he paid for pancakes and eggs. Neither of them spoke very much. They had run out of things to say. He didn't know how often they would see each other once they lived apart. Not many days remained before escrow closed on the condominium.

In the afternoons, he kept to himself, fighting the urge to drink before dinner. He drove back to the house and searched through the rubble. That first day after the fire, he had been looking for remnants of the paper girl when Ben had caught him off guard. Kamron searched for her still. He wished he could collect her ashes as if she had been properly cremated. But as he stared at the ground, all he saw was the desolation. Nothing had survived around the garden and the shed.

In the airport, he carefully navigated signs to the baggage claim area where he would wait. After all this time in America, he still felt awkward alone in unfamiliar places. Whatever grasp he had of the English language left him in these moments. He sat down at a bench, hoping to stay unnoticed. He wondered if Siripon had missed him while she was away. Perhaps she had met other men on the trip—they could have tried to seduce her. He had always been afraid of losing her.

Passengers from other flights made their way through the area. Happy reunions erupted around him. Other people were waiting expectantly with signs, with balloons, with flowers. He opened his wallet and checked to see how much cash he had. Approaching a kiosk, he inspected the buckets of flowers and a table full of stuffed animals.

"How much?" he asked.

"What you want, boss? Something for your wife? We have this for only twenty dollars. Very cute. She'll love it." The man held out a teddy bear with a carnation in its grip.

Kamron nodded. He slipped out a twenty, hoping he would still have enough to pay for parking.

"She'll be excited," the worker said. "She'll know how much you love her."

Walking back with the present, Kamron became aware of people looking at him. A few of them smiled to acknowledge that he was waiting for someone like they were. But the attention embarrassed him. He considered abandoning his purchase, waiting empty-handed as Siripon would be expecting him to. He kept himself closed and protected—he realized this. He had done so all his life. He assumed it was what everyone had to do, though sometimes he looked at Siripon or Ben or even Manda and admired their willingness to be more vulnerable. When Manda accused him of having a cowardly heart, the words had hurt. But maybe she was right.

On the screen, he saw that Siripon's flight had landed. A short while later, a line of tanned travelers in leis and straw hats overwhelmed the escalators. They were all still having fun, not yet ready to let go of the vacation. Kamron stood, his heart beginning to race. He scanned the faces, but he couldn't find her. It was possible she would not return with the others—this was a fear he often had too. He imagined her taking detours on her way home from work, meeting a man she respected more than him and leaving for a new life. He would not blame her. He never blamed anyone for giving up on him. That was the heart of it. That's what he had known all his life. But he heard Jerlie, spotted her in oversized sunglasses, her lips nothing but a little smudge of color underneath the big black lenses. She was surrounded by others her size, a squad of happy women. They were laughing and singing, all of them but one. A quiet woman stood patiently behind the others. A shy one. Siripon had returned.

7

Manda parked her car along a stretch of road overshadowed by a heavy, drooping network of power lines. She guessed why the other residents of Avedon Terrace Apartments avoided it—a long row of pigeons the color of dirty laundry roosted above her, and below them, like spattered paint, lay a line of droppings, coarse and white.

The apartment building itself was four blocks away, its dingy gables rising above the magnolia trees. The structure was mostly crumbling pink stucco, one corner of the little lawn sacrificed for a fountain that had run dry. Up along the front, columns of windows revealed dim interiors webbed with dull curtains, some of them scantily decorated for the approaching holidays.

This was her second day at Avedon Terrace. She had spent her first week back in America with Siripon and Kamron, their condominium a barrage of ivory tones that felt uptight and lifeless. Still, Manda was grateful they had welcomed her in. And yesterday, her move-in day, Siripon swept the floors and dusted the shelves of the new place. She didn't say more than a few words during the visit, though. When they were preparing to leave, Kamron was the one who made sure Manda locked the door behind them. Siripon simply waved goodbye.

Manda loaded her luggage cart and wheeled it along the wide gutter as cars raced by. Her movements were slow, her body tired from so much change in such a short amount of time. "Here we are. Just us now," she said to herself. "No point being in a bad mood about it."

Months ago, when she had returned to Phet Buri, she had suspected she wouldn't be happy there. Going back to the old house, she couldn't even settle on which room to sleep in, whether she would choose her childhood bed or take over the downstairs space where her parents had been. The entire house felt unlivable. The lights were harsh. The linoleum floors were hard against her joints. The darkness that slipped in through the open windows felt vacuous and eerie.

Still, Manda had tried to settle in. She took charge of a stand that Tassanee had set up outside the courtyard. Throughout the day children came to purchase sweets and soda. Manda collected their coins and empty bottles, packing the bottles away into crates so that they could be redeemed for a few more baht.

In the late afternoons, she got together with her old friends from high school, the men she had kept in touch with all these years. They sat in dim cafés, under churning ceiling fans, drinking iced coffee and oliang. They exhausted their conversations about the past and attempted feebly to talk about the present. But their adult lives had drifted too far apart from one another. She did not relate to their career ambitions, their family struggles, their diets and exercise routines. In turn, they were annoyed with her stories about Ben and got to teasing her whenever she brought him up.

Some of them mentioned finding Manda a husband. She was still young enough to enjoy romance, they insisted. They pointed out the single men in the neighborhood, early widowers or those who had focused on their careers for too long. Manda wanted nothing to do with them. She wouldn't go out of her way to please anyone. As for sex, she had come to understand that it was not something she needed more of. She no longer wanted to be naked with a man, to be entered by one.

Through those monotonous days, she grew more convinced that she shouldn't have left America. She couldn't stand to be far away from Ben, even if they didn't talk much anymore. Once, she cried after calling his dorm room and getting a message that he wasn't in. She understood a mother's love, the hopeless devotion that couldn't be surrendered.

She made her tentative inquiries, asking her siblings if they would forgive her for changing her mind. She called Ben and told him how much she missed him. She hoped to hear that he missed her in return, but he was quiet, ambiguous. "You have to do what's best for you," he said. It was enough that he didn't refuse her. She returned, embarrassed. She had become the type of person she always despised, someone fussy, someone who was never content.

Sighing, she slumped on the floor of her new apartment. The room was filled with plastic bags, each bundle hastily thrown together as she was loading her car. A coat hanger was within reach, and she used it as a hook; she would sort through whatever she could reach, and once that was done, she would give herself a break. Looking over the clutter, she entertained the idea of giving up, just keeping everything exactly where it was. What had she done with herself? She wasn't a teacher. She wasn't a wife or a mother. She was a spinster, an old maid lost between countries. But Manda believed that she was entering a new stage in her life, a new incarnation. She had enjoyed her youth, and she had made the best of her years in the Chiwitchaiya household. Now she was to live alone and fend for herself. It was another temporary situation in the eternity of her existence, and somehow she would make it through.

Then Ben's call came. He said that he was waiting downstairs. She found him pacing on the other side of the security gate; he examined his watch and then squinted up at the sky, impatient. For a second, she wasn't sure if it was him. His shoulders were broader, and his hair was styled differently. But there was something about the way he carried himself that was different too. Looking at him, Manda was reminded of her garden one spring following a particularly rainy winter. That year there had been a tremendous storm that lasted for several days. She thought the garden had been ruined, but when the seasons grew warmer, something beyond her took over. The plants had grown with unbridled vitality, the leaves broad and thick, the fruit vibrant and rich with perfume.

8

Ben had pulled in later than expected to the guest parking lot of Avedon Terrace. He had been dreading the visit, not yet ready to see his aunt after her return. Taking in the building, he was overcome by a sense of familiar disappointment, as if he had seen this place before on some television show or in some photo. A year and a half had passed since he and Manda were last together, when he had said goodbye to her before she boarded her flight to Phet Buri. Now, when she answered the intercom, her voice was bright on the other end. She said she would be right down.

He hadn't been surprised when Manda announced that she would be returning to Thailand. Considering everything, the decision made the most sense to him too. He guessed she'd expected him to be heartbroken, but he had been relieved. Living on different continents felt easier, even if they would never see each other again. Then Manda changed her mind. She didn't want to stay in Thailand after all. She kept him updated on every step of the moving process: her tentative internet searches from overseas, the gathering of references, the waiting lists, the submission of her financial statements. She warned him it could take months before any of the subsidized buildings would have room for her. But here she was, back in Los Angeles and alone for the first time in her life.

A glass door flashed as it swung out on the other side of the gate. Manda appeared in oversized jeans, cuffs folded at the ankles, and a ratty striped shirt Ben could remember her wearing when he was a child.

"Home sweet home," she called over in her exaggerated, accented English.

"I'm glad it's secure," Ben said in Thai. Not long ago, the language flowed easily for him, but after three years away from home, the vowels and intonations came out more clumsily. They hugged, Manda's embrace desperate, but she didn't hold him for long.

"You can help me take another load up from the car," she said. "Na? Just another load up before I give you the tour."

Her car was parked blocks away, beyond the one-hour parking zones that surrounded the complex. Manda wouldn't get her own space inside the gate until one of the other tenants moved away—someone whose driver's license hadn't been revoked.

Linens and bathroom decor filled the seats. In the trunk were a dozen bath towels, old clothes, and cartons of Miracle-Gro.

"I was smart to keep everything in storage while I was gone," she said. "Imagine if I had to start from nothing." She turned to him, embarrassed. Then she laughed self-consciously. "I'm so relieved to be back. You wouldn't believe the time I had over there."

"Did something go wrong?"

"All of it. All of it."

The two walked back toward the building still in view behind the rows of trees. Ben carried an armload of sheet sets, surprised she had accumulated so many. Manda's pace was slow and careful. Her legs bowed outward at the knees, making her body list from side to side. He had seen the movement before. It was how his grandmother had walked. But Gimjaa had shattered her pelvis giving birth. Manda never went through anything like that.

"Is there room for a garden here?" he asked.

"No more garden. I can finally stop worrying about the garden," Manda answered.

Past the gate, through the scratched glass door, they stepped into the lobby. The draft that followed behind them rattled flyers posted on the windows, warnings about rodents, insects, and thieves. The dim room lay in a rusty patina, the colors blending like a photograph taken decades ago.

Manda lived on the third floor, at the end of a hall that felt too long and too narrow. They stepped in among plastic bags scattered throughout the living room. Ben saw that they were full of scented candles, soap dishes, incense, figurines. There were no pots and pans, no dinner plates, no table or chairs, no bed. This had been her life for as long as he could remember. She only ever had to worry about the accessories.

"We could go furniture shopping," he suggested, although he already felt the itch to leave. He associated this place with a discarded life, one he thought he would never have to deal with. In high school, when the Asian population had ballooned, he always heard classmates complain about being tied to their families, about the younger generations being expected to take in the older ones. His family avoided that tradition. They had become American after all.

"Your mom and dad found some things for me at a garage sale," Manda said. "They're bringing them later if you want to stay."

"I don't think I can," Ben said.

"Busy, busy, busy," Manda chanted.

The thought of everyone being together again made Ben tense. He didn't even like spending the night with his parents in their tiny condominium. They were sleeping in different rooms, something Siripon had insisted on when they moved in. She could stay on her own side of the place whenever she wanted to be left alone.

Ben opened Manda's refrigerator in search of water. Inside, he found only a jar of chili paste and a carton of coffee creamer. "Is the tap water safe to drink?" he asked.

Manda didn't hear him. She was reaching into one of the bags to rearrange some bottles that had toppled over. She had grown thicker. Her face was red, and she struggled to catch her breath after her exertion. Ben suddenly worried for her. "Make sure you take care of yourself," he said. "Find a grocery store where you can get vegetables. Go for walks."

"See? I knew you still loved me." And she went to him again, embraced him again, this time holding him longer.

But Ben didn't say anything in response. He wasn't prepared to make promises about visiting her regularly. The blame was still there. He had played out in his mind the scenarios of confronting her about what happened—the "exorcism," he had come to call it—but he had yet to say anything about it out loud. He couldn't imagine what would happen if she admitted to it, how they would navigate things afterward.

"This will make a nice home," he managed to say.

"Yes, I can finally arrange things the way I like them. I won't be under your mother's thumb anymore."

"That's a good way to look at it."

"What choice do I have?" She shook her head and returned to her bundles. From a tote bag, she produced a framed photograph that used to sit on her nightstand. It was a picture of the two of them in the garden, taken by a party guest who had wanted to show off a new camera. Manda was crouched beside a row of herbs with a spade in her hand. Ben was beside her in diapers; he dragged a plastic sack to catch the weeds she pulled out. "Our anniversary is coming up," she said. "In just a week, I will have been your aunt for twenty-one years."

"Twenty-one years," Ben said. They had lived together nearly all of that time, a boy and an aunt who had tried to erase part of his life, part of him. She hadn't succeeded. Ben didn't feel as if those things were gone. But he would need time to find them, to trace himself back to who he was before. He was angry, but he couldn't easily let go of the fact that Manda was a second mother to him. Even though nobody used those words, that was who she was.

They unpacked for a couple of hours. Ben moved things into cupboards and onto shelves. He hung up her clothes in the closets. He matched her shoes and socks. Manda had taken the photograph to the windowsill and positioned it in the light. Unable to ignore his curiosity, Ben stooped over to inspect it. He had been happy as a child. He had been carefree. The whole family had been so ignorant of what was to come. All the unavoidable complications of life were racing toward them, and they had not known to brace themselves.

"I need to leave soon. I need to take care of some things before I go back up north," he said. The place was hot, and he was still thirsty.

"Did you come down alone this time?" Manda asked. "Or is your friend here with you—what is his name?"

"Collin." Ben's voice grew tender.

"Whatever his name is. Ask him if you can stay longer."

Ben contemplated dialing Collin's number. He had no intention of delaying his departure, but hearing Collin's voice would comfort him, nonetheless. Lately, the two of them had begun to talk about becoming domestic partners. It was too soon—they knew this. Still, Ben could feel the tantalizing possibility of it.

He often wondered what Manda thought of Collin. She was too observant not to realize that there was something more than friendship between them. Or maybe she clung to the idea that the ceremony had worked. She had never been in love, as far as he knew. He hadn't ever heard about any other men in her life. The only person outside of the family that she had been close to was Aunt Seamstress, but he didn't know what had become of her. There were other details he couldn't figure out, gaps he had filled with monotony, as if her life—anyone's life—was suspended when he forgot to pay attention to it.

"I need to get going," Ben said.

"Wait just a moment. Just help me with this one last favor," Manda said. And while he waited, she patiently searched through her bags, not saying anything more. A long while passed before she produced a bundle of government bonds. She showed him that each slip had his name on it too. Had his aunt chased the American Dream when she first arrived in Los Angeles? That ambition must have been there at some point, at least in the beginning. "Take a few with you," she said. "Make sure you're able to cash them on your own in case something should happen to me. I don't have much, mind you, but it will all go to you when I'm gone."

"Aunt Manda, don't talk about dying."

"Death doesn't scare me anymore, ja. Ghosts don't scare me. Ha! Did you ever think I would say that?"

Ben remembered how often she had brought them up when he was a child. The dead had felt like silent watchers looming beyond the windows.

"Are you afraid of ghosts?" she asked suddenly.

"I've never seen one," he said.

"I suspect they're all around us. If they want to come and visit me, there probably isn't any way to stop them."

Manda had always lived halfway in the spiritual world. She didn't see a boundary between what was visible and what was not. Ben wasn't sure what he thought. He sometimes wondered if any part of the exorcism had been real. He wondered if the paper girl had any connection to him, if she was ever anything more than paper. He put on his shoes and stepped into the hall. He hoped he could say goodbye to her there, but she took his hand, followed him down to the lobby.

"Remember to cash the bonds. Let the bank know they're also in your name. I've only loved two things in my life: my garden and my child. Now I only have my child."

Ben stepped out onto the concrete path. He walked without turning back, but he could tell that she was still watching him.

"You won't forget me, will you? Not like your mother," Manda called out. "I've always looked after you. I've always made sure nothing bad happened to you."

Something in Ben flickered. He turned back, anxious to confront her. "Is that what you think?" There was a harshness in his voice that he couldn't control.

"What is it? Did I say something wrong?" Manda asked.

"I remember," Ben said. "I remember everything."

She didn't understand; she was waiting for him to say more. He started again, stitching together words in a language that was slipping away from him.

"I remember that night. I remember the monk you brought over. I remember what he did to me." Stopped there, a short distance away from his aunt, he felt as if they had come to a narrow ridge, and around them, the rest of the world had fallen away. "I was scared," he said. "You made me so scared for a long time."

"No, no. There was no monk." She shook her head. She lifted her hands halfway up, but then they stopped, not quite up and not quite down. She looked as if she were standing before something immense, something that awed her.

"And afterwards, you didn't do anything to help me," Ben said.

"You're imagining things." Her eyes closed. He knew that he and Manda had traveled back in time together. He lay on the floor of the shrine room, and she sat over him. They saw each other through the pattern of the cloth.

"You shouldn't have done it," he said. "There was nothing wrong with me." The words were out, and the thing he feared had not come to pass. Nothing had fallen apart. No one had been destroyed. Ben felt as if he was reclaiming himself. He was no longer the hopeless teenager he once was, the one who had been willing to give everything up. Maybe, sometime in the last year, or possibly in the last hour, he had grown, he had inherited his life.

"I know," Manda said. Standing in front of the building, she looked so small. She began to say that there was more to it, that there was a student in her past, someone whose name Ben didn't catch, but she struggled to organize her thoughts. Finally, flustered, she stopped trying. "I'm sorry," she said. "I beg you to forgive me." The tone of her voice had changed. It was defenseless, surrendered, a sound like the trickling of water. Ever since his memories had returned, Ben had been waiting for her apology, but now that it had come, he understood it was not enough, not for either of them. An apology was not an ending. It was only a way to let things begin. "Someday, maybe I can explain myself," she said. "For now, just know that I did it because I love you. You believe me, na? You believe that I love you? Now, hug me. Tell me you love me back. That's all I need in this life, and in the next one I will do better." She opened her arms and waited.

Acknowledgments

Thank you to Troy Nethercott for the partnership, love, and understanding that make my writing life possible. To Peanut for keeping me company and never judging. To Ian Bonaparte at Janklow & Nesbit for believing in my work—sometimes more than I do—and for offering wise counsel. To Oma Beharry at One World for ushering this book to publication and for expanding the dimensions of the story beyond what I could have seen on my own.

Thank you to One World and Penguin Random House, including Chris Jackson, Nicole Counts, Avideh Bashirrad, Elizabeth Méndez Berry, Andrea Pura, Milena Brown, Tiffani Ren, Andy Lefkowitz, Rebecca Berlant, Samuel Wetzler, Susan Turner, Evan Camfield, Greg Mollica, Jocelynn Pedro, Claire Fennell, Katryce Campbell, Ericka Serrano, and Wade Lucas, along with Na Kim, Marinda J. Valenti, Rebecca Maines, Taylor McGowan, David Goehring, and everyone who contributed to this book.

Thank you to Denton Loving for being an unwavering advocate, listener, and tireless reader. To Justin Torres (without whom this book would not exist), David Gates, Jill McCorkle, Claire Vaye Watkins, Alice Mattison, and Andrea Walker for guidance and insights on early drafts. To Fred Wells, Dianne Newman, Sabeeha Merchant, Mary Yukari Waters, Merrill Joan Gerber, Carol Phelan, Sally Abood, and Samantha Dunn for teaching me to think and write. To Craig Cotter, Billy Glidden, and Max Frazier for invaluable critique of the manuscript. To Ruemruk Malasarn, Marytza Rubio, Anna Gazmarian, Scott G.F. Bailey, Shari

Poindexter, Kelly March, Libby Flores, Jennifer Torres, Mark Wallace, and Elise Lasko for discussions and encouragement. To the Bennington Writing Seminars, including fellow workshop students and wonderful cohort members who joined me on the journey. To the Queens University of Charlotte Book Development Program, PEN America, and the Writing Downtown Residency. To Jennice Prajimnork, Jordan Mathisen, and the Pasadena Fire Department for technical expertise.

Flavors of Empire: Food and the Making of Thai America by Mark Padoongpatt, *The Making of Asian America* by Erika Lee, and the Monterey Park Historical Museum served as highly informative references, and any factual errors are my own.

An excerpt of this book was previously published in *The Lascaux Review*.

About the Author

Davin Malasarn was born and raised in Southern California. After completing his PhD in biology at the California Institute of Technology, he earned his MFA in creative writing from Bennington College and completed the Queens University of Charlotte Book Development Program. He was a PEN America Emerging Voices Fellow, a Plympton Writing Downtown Fellow, and a Bennington Alumni Fellow. He cofounded the Granum Foundation, a nonprofit dedicated to supporting writers, and hosts the *Artist's Statement* podcast.

davinmalasarn.com | Instagram: @writing_and_donuts